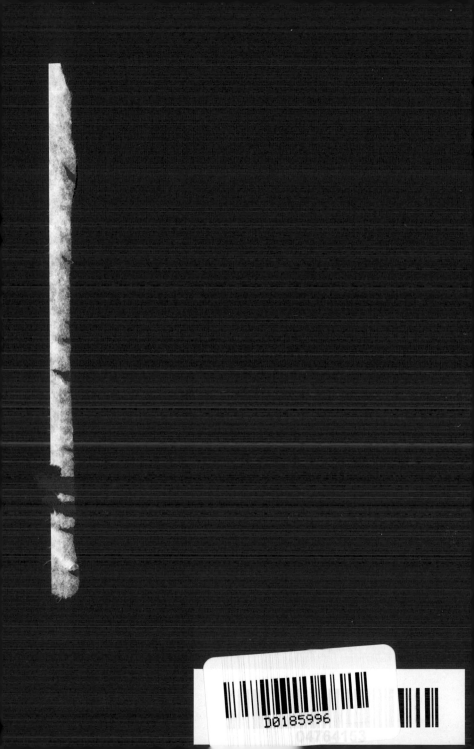

Mo said she was quirky

By the same author in Penguin Books

You Have to be Careful in the Land of the Free

Where I Was

Kieron Smith, boy

If it is your life

Mo said she was quirky

JAMES KELMAN

HAMISH HAMILTON
an imprint of
PENGUIN BOOKS

HAMISH HAMILTON

Published by the Penguin Group
Penguin Books Ltd, 80 Strand, London WC2R ORL, England
Penguin Group (USA) Inc., 375 Hudson Street, New York, New York 10014, USA
Penguin Group (Canada), 90 Eglinton Avenue East, Suite 700, Toronto, Ontario, Canada M4P 2Y3
(a division of Pearson Penguin Canada Inc.)
Penguin Ireland, 25 St Stephen's Green, Dublin 2, Ireland (a division of Penguin Books Ltd)
Penguin Group (Australia), 250 Camberwell Road, Camberwell, Victoria 3124, Australia
(a division of Pearson Australia Group Pty Ltd)
Penguin Books India Pvt Ltd, 11 Community Centre,
Panchsheel Park, New Delhi – 110 017, India
Penguin Group (NZ), 67 Apollo Drive, Rosedale, Auckland 0632, New Zealand
(a division of Pearson New Zealand Ltd)
Penguin Books (South Africa) (Pty) Ltd, Block D, Rosebank Office Park,
181 Jan Smuts Avenue, Parktown North, Gauteng 2193, South Africa

Penguin Books Ltd, Registered Offices: 80 Strand, London WC2R ORL, England

www.penguin.com

First published 2012
001

Copyright © James Kelman, 2012

The moral right of the author has been asserted

Set in 12/14.75 pt Dante MT Std
Typeset by Jouve (UK), Milton Keynes
Printed in Great Britain by Clays Ltd, St Ives plc

A CIP catalogue record for this book is available from the British Library

ISBN: 978-0-241-14456-5

www.greenpenguin.co.uk

ALWAYS LEARNING   **PEARSON**

for
Carly and Dylan

It happened on her way home from the casino one morning, Helen noticed the two men through the side passenger window. A pair of homeless guys. One was tall and skinny, the other smaller, heavier built and walking with a limp, quite a bad limp. They approached the traffic lights and were going to cross the road in front of her taxi, right in front of its nose. The lights were red but set to change. Surely the men knew that? The tall man was having to walk slowly to stay abreast of the other, almost having to stop. He was full bearded and wearing a woollen cap. Although he was taking small steps Helen could imagine him striding out, his stride would be long and it would be hard keeping up with him. There was something else about him, to do with his shape and the way he walked, just something.

Would they make it across in time? Only if they hurried. They wouldnt hurry, not them. You could tell just by looking. They went at their own pace and that was that.

Helen looked away, then looked back. Her workmates Caroline and Jill were beside her in the back seat but hadnt noticed the drama. The lights would change and the taxi would move. What would they do? Nothing, just keep walking. Oh God, Helen hated this kind of thing. Why did she even notice? Typical. She always had to. Other people didnt.

Only it was so tense, too tense.

Caroline and Jill were chatting about something else

together, Caroline's husband, the never-ending saga. They hadnt noticed any of it. But the taxi driver had. This was Danny, one of the regulars; Helen saw his eyes in the rear-view mirror, no doubt wondering the same as her; would the men make it across before the lights changed to green as surely they must, they must. Why was it taking so long? Another car pulled in on the outside lane.

Helen was holding her breath. She didnt realise this until suddenly she breathed in and it made a sound. The tension was just – my God, but they walked so slowly. Alkies, muttered Danny, but they didnt look drunk to her.

They reached the kerb. The small man's limp really was bad, even painful. Perhaps he had been in an accident. Then the tall skinny one, there was something about him too the way his elbows crooked, his hands in his side coat pockets. It was him Helen was watching. He was not in the slightest drunk. She recognised something, whatever it was; a kind of deliberate quality, in how he moved, slow but not slow; slow in his movements but not in his thoughts, seeing everything, even himself.

Helen settled back further in the seat. She didnt want him seeing her. Why didnt the lights change? This was the longest ever.

At the moment the amber joined the red the two men stepped out from the pavement onto the road. The exact moment. This was when they did it. It was so weird. At this time of the morning too, with everything so quiet, so peaceful. Helen could hardly believe it and was glad of the shadows there in the back. She didnt like being in taxis with poor people seeing her, as though she was rich, she wasnt. It was silly but sometimes she felt it. They were directly in front of the taxi. It lurched forwards a tiny fraction. Danny must have raised his foot on the accelerator pedal for one split moment only but it was enough for the lurch and the tall skinny guy turned his head and stared in at him and at Helen and the other two women. He was not that old either. Only how he looked, wild, wild-looking, wild as in – not dangerous. People might have thought it, almost like crazy, they would think that too, he was not, only mannerisms, how some people

Brian, it was Brian, her brother Brian.

How could it be but it was, it was his movements and his shape my God Brian, it was Brian. The car in the outside lane had rolled forwards then halted. The lights were green. The taxi quivered but couldnt move. How far had the pair travelled? Hardly at all; they didnt care. So aggressive! Brian was not aggressive. It was his physical shape but not his behaviour; the way he was staring in at them, so intimidating, and forcing them to wait. And Danny was waiting my God, he hated that. Patience, patience. Whoever heard of a patient taxi-driver? He rushed everywhere, giving people rows. Not this time. Helen saw his head lowered, not drawing attention to himself. Usually he was tough or acted like it. Helen had seen him before with other drivers, he never backed down. He would take them all on, that was how he acted. This was different. These two homeless guys made it different, they were going at their own pace and everybody else could wait.

Now the taxi was moving. Helen opened her eyes, seeing out the window. Danny shifted from second gear up to third, the engine roaring and rushing on, venting his anger and annoyance. Jill exchanged looks with her. The car in the outside lane must have been behind them, so too the homeless guys. Caroline had the phone in her hand and was smiling. I wanted to take their picture, she said, but I was too scared! Did you see his face? the one with the scraggy beard, the tall one?

Helen looked at her. Caroline gave an exaggerated shiver. Imagine meeting him on a dark night!

She spoke in a whisper. Why did she whisper? What was the

point of whispering? So silly, just so silly, and not nice either, as though there was something horrible, it was prejudice pure and simple.

Are you alright? asked Jill, leaning to Helen, nudging her arm.

Yes, said Helen but she wasnt alright at all. Just weird, that was how she felt. Caroline chattered on about his height and how he was so so thin and his beard and all of it, like as if something was wrong with being tall and with a beard, or being thin.

Why people are thin my God what kind of world was it, for having no food, they get made to blame, if you dont have enough to eat and end up thin it becomes your fault. It wasnt fair. Scraggy. That was a beard, so if you didnt comb it or shave it, if it was a beard, whatever men did – how could they if they were homeless and didnt have any scissors or razors? how could you blame them? Wild and scraggy, it wasnt fair talking like that and like he was dangerous. Not if it was Brian, he was not dangerous, never. Now Caroline was wanting to text her husband, even although he was asleep in bed. Why? What did she want to say? She didnt know anything. There wasnt anything to know. Except how he looked. Jill too. I thought he was creepy, she said.

It wasnt like Jill to say that. People were prejudiced. And Danny heard her and was listening. Helen saw his eyes reflected in the rear mirror. The word 'creepy' could be said about a lot of men. She didnt much like Danny. He acted as if he was there to protect them. But was he? No. Would he? No. Danny was there to drive his taxi and that was that, just get on with the job and make his money, that was him. He shouted back over his shoulder: What you think about them then eh, dirty filthy buggers! Dont give a rat's toss! Go where they want, walk where they want. They do what they want, whatever they want! I would run over the fucking top of them.

4

Oh watch your language you! called Caroline, but with a smile.

Danny waited a moment before replying. It's alright for you lot, working inside your casino, I'm out here on the street. Guys like me got to deal with them animals!

They are human beings, said Jill.

He wasnt listening. It reminded Helen of somebody, her ex-husband of course, the same mentality. Men like them didnt listen, they talked. Not so much talked as boasted, how good they were and all what they did and how they got the better of everybody else. That was Danny to a tee. He had his 'message' for comfort, wedged down the side of the driver's seat. He called it 'the message' but it was a weapon. If anybody tried it on with him, he had 'the message' and they would get 'the message'. Whoever it was, just let them try it and he would bash them. He had shown them it. A solid big shifting-spanner. If ever *they* messed with him, he would break their skull. Even without the weapon he would take them on. Although why anybody would want to mess with a taxi driver was beyond him. They had to be thick if they did because you mess with one you mess with them all. Other taxi drivers would be there in a moment. Every driver within a stone's throw, they would rush to back up a mate in trouble: that was how they operated. One for all and all for one.

That was what he said, and looked fierce while saying it. It might have been male boasting but that didnt mean it was false. Only this time was different, the two homeless guys made it different. What was it about them? Something.

Helen didnt see Danny as a coward. Neither was her ex. But they were not like the toughest, the real dangerous ones. When you worked in casinos you saw them. They had that certain quality. It didnt matter the nationality, it was them as indi-viduals, a thing they had that was dangerous, like a twisted mentality. Other men left them alone, just like now with the homeless guys. Except if it was bravado, if they had had too much to drink and were beyond the sensible stage. Then they tried to speak or joke with these dangerous ones, like they were on an equal footing. It was childish. The dangerous ones smiled or else ignored them but eventually they didnt; it might only be a stare but it was enough to call their bluff like in poker at the late stage, when somebody gets asked the question: You raising or what? What you doing? It is up to the bluffers what they do but whatever it is it will be a real thing with a real consequence. Bluffing doesnt come into it. If they arent ready for that then stop the stupidity, just shut up, go away.

Danny had kept his head down. It was the best thing too because what if he hadnt? The way the tall skinny one was staring at him. You didnt know what would happen. Some could be calmed. Some couldnt. That is part of the threat. What if they lose it altogether. These dangerous ones are telling you that, this is what they mean. Better stop it now, better leave me alone. Some men made you shiver. Nobody knew what they might do, and who to. Females or males, it didnt matter. They were capable of anything and would do it to anybody. Even children, poor innocent children, if they got in the way. Only look at them the wrong way, and if they lost their temper. If they had a knife, or just the violence, jumping and kicking, kicking people's heads. That violence was everywhere. So if that was Danny's worry, it might have been, and quite right too, why take chances. Except he didnt phone for help, why not? If these other drivers would have come to his rescue, why didnt he? Two homeless guys, surely that wasnt a worry? And if it was Brian, Brian was not dangerous, he wasnt.

So weird. Imagine she told Caroline and Jill. What would they say? Nothing. There wasnt anything really. Stop the car! Go and see him! But would they say that? No, they wanted home, home. Anyway, they would think she was mistaken.

How could it be Brian? He wasnt even in London. But he was in England, the last she heard, he was working in Liverpool. Mum must have told her.

They hadnt seen each other for twelve years. Gran's funeral. He had come home for that. Not for Dad's, he didnt come home for Dad's. He came home for his grandmother but not for his father.

Sad. It was another world. She shifted on the seat to see through the rear window. The taxi had left the riverside several streets ago, passed down a slope and beneath a railway bridge, turning and passing the place where the old mortuary building stood, near where they held the car-boot sale on Sundays. Her and Mo came regularly. Mo was her boyfriend. She and her six-year-old daughter lived with him. Her street was the first drop-off point, thank God. She would be there in ten minutes, in thirty lying beside him. The very thought! But it was true, Mo was like normality. If only she could close her eyes and count to ten, then open them again and there she was beside him. She sat back on the seat. Jill was looking at her. Helen smiled.

An hour later and she was home but still sitting in the kitchen, still wearing her coat and shoes. She held a photograph in her hand. Others lay on her lap, and a few on the floor. She brought them out as soon as she got home. It didnt depress her seeing them but neither did it cheer her up. Family was family. No matter what. People said that and it was true. Blood is thicker than water. If it was Brian it was Brian. It was so unlikely. But if it was. She smiled for some reason, a weary smile, ironic also. Families dont finish. You run away but they catch you up. Families are ghosts. Presences. What if he had recognised her?

She drew the coat about her shoulders, feeling a bit shivery. She should have gone to bed. Of course she should have, she had been working all night, she was tired and cold. A gas-boiler system gave the heating and hot water but made such a noisy clanking sound she never switched it on first thing in the morning in case it wakened the entire household. Mo said it needed an overhaul. Probably it did but he was wondering if he and a mate could do it themselves, and they couldnt. People had to be qualified for that job. Gas can be dangerous.

Anyway, tenants shouldnt have to overhaul the heating system, even if they know how, it was the landlord's job. Mo took matters on that he should have left alone. It wasnt his business.

She glanced at the photograph in her hand: one of her mother seated with a baby in her lap. The baby was Sophie. You couldnt tell the important thing which was Mum's lack of interest. That was something for a child to know about her own grandmother. Eventually she would. Children come to know these things. It was sad. Who was the loser? Not Sophie. If Mum wanted to be foolish that was her.

Imagine a child and she didnt go to you. A mother to daughter was something but a grandmother? What could a little child have done to deserve that? Nothing at all. It was not possible. It could only come from the grandmother. The truth revealed was the relationship between the grandmother and her own daughter. That was so glaring. How Mum was with Sophie was how she had been with Helen. She never had been close to Helen, never.

It was sad and didnt have to be. That made it sadder. It would have been so easy for it not to be the case. Sophie could be standing next to Mum and taken her hand the way children do, just reached up and taken her grandmother's hand, and Mum would – what? what would Mum do? She would look at the hand: a tiny hand in her own; her granddaughter's hand. She would wonder at that, why children are so trusting. She would think to let go the hand because that would be her inclination but wouldnt be able to because that tiny hand, the child's hand

Children take things for granted, and why shouldnt they? In the nursery back in Glasgow parents had been encouraged to stay with the children for periods of the day. Helen stayed occasionally and saw how a child looks at you to see if you are friendly. They look at you. If you arent friendly they see it in you, even the smaller ones like if you try to lift them and they arent yours. People do that, they lift up a child and the child doesnt want to be lifted. She does but she doesnt. Not by somebody strange. If it was Sophie: Leave me leave me leave me! Mum Mum Mum, and kicking and kicking and the person would have to put her down and just smile, pretending it was okay. It happened once when Mo was with her, in that same nursery and Sophie started screaming at a man who lifted her. He was one of the fathers. Sophie fell and he picked her up. He didnt see Mo or if he did he didnt think he was the parent. Mo was Asian so how could he be? That would have been the man's thinking. It was accidental. The man had acted instinctively, and Sophie too. The teacher said she was 'over-reacting' which made it sound like Sophie's fault and that was total nonsense. Sophie screamed and thank God she screamed. It was right that she screamed, she was defending herself. Girls have to; just dont lay a finger on me, dont dare lay a finger on me, and if anybody did, God help them. Screaming was so important. Men could laugh but it was. It was men had to learn. Some did and some didnt.

'Over-reacting'. It was so wrong to say that. And another woman saying it made it worse. The child was *reacting*. So would anybody if a stranger came along and grabbed you. Why did he? Oh because she had fallen. Excuse me? Helen didnt accept that argument. She didnt care if it happened in other cultures, if people went around lifting people up. Or if it was the olden days, oh they do it in the olden days. This was not the olden days. What right does a man have to come along and lift up a little girl? He doesnt have any right, not for that, that is just like a violation, almost it is.

Helen glanced at the clock on the mantelpiece, lifted the cup to swallow what was left of the tea but it was cold and she replaced the cup. It was nice seeing the photographs of herself and Brian. They *were* close. And there were other photographs. Mum must have had them, and of the older generations.

She yawned again, she should have been in bed. But she wouldnt sleep, not now, thinking about everything, she wouldnt be able to, she knew she wouldnt, just worrying about things all the time over and over, worry worry worry, then when daylight came, oh well. Helen made to rise but forgetting the photographs on her lap and they landed on the floor. It was another cup of tea, she had been going to boil the water. Stupid, but that was her.

She left the photographs on the floor. Her eyes were closed. An image in mind, sort of memory. Whatever, it had gone. These images, what else to call them, you expect to see the person and you dont.

An image isnt a person, it only makes you think of the person. Although if it is yourself, if you are the person, you as a child. The supposed-to-be happy time, when life is supposed to be good. People said that, they didnt mean it. Boredom and lies and just what it was, dishonesty. Childhood was not something to look back on and wish things were the same nowadays. Not for Helen anyway. God knows how Sophie would come out of it all.

Those lives were mostly gone now, the older generation. Helen's own grandmother would have been eighty-three had she been alive. She was Mum's mother. Dad's died when she was young. Helen had never known her.

Life goes on but people dont, individuals.

Helen's hand went to her forehead; she massaged there, thinking of something, whatever. Oh but it was true enough, divorce, what people say about it. So horrible an experience. Mo said he understood but he didnt. How could he? How could anybody, if they hadnt gone through it themself. Although he had been there for her. That was true, of course he had. And never would she forget it, if she hadnt met Mo, if he hadnt been in Glasgow, and it was only a fluke he had been, helping people at a restaurant, cousins of the ones he worked for in London. Typical Mo. He called it 'troubleshooting' and made a joke about being the sheriff in a cowboy movie. But it was true, he was there to sort out the problems. At weekends it was past three in the morning when he finished. He and a couple of workmates used Helen's casino as a place to wind down. They spent an hour drinking tea and chatting by the bar, talking over things, how the evening had gone and whatever else. Casino staff knew them and occasionally used their restaurant. Helen was one of a group that booked in for their Christmas dinner. During it the guys who came to the casino sat with them, including Mo. She hadnt looked at him. He was smaller than her, and like younger, or seemed to be. Then he was sitting behind her, then talking to her directly. She just liked him. That was the truth. How he spoke, just like an ordinary Londoner. But he was an ordinary Londoner. Helen had lived and worked in London before getting married, it was nice talking about that, she didnt get the opportunity much. And he wasnt younger he was older – by one month! A month is a month; a month is older. That was him talking. God he was a cheery bugger, and the way he was chatting her – and he was!

He was chatting her. It was just so silly, and nice, so so nice and just – normality, after what she had been through, it was like boy meets girl.

He had seen her at the tables, had she not noticed? No. Surely she had noticed? No! She hadnt! Not even one time? She hadnt noticed any of them sitting at the bar and sipping their tea. It was not her job to notice, not when she was dealing cards.

He didnt believe her. Then he did. It was an honest smile too. She saw that it was. He was being straight with her, this wee London guy, Asian guy, making her laugh, and watching her, closely. If she was racist? Anyway, she was watching him, and he knew she was. I got two wooden legs. Stupid, but it made her laugh. She covered her mouth but couldnt stop herself giggling, it was a giggle, so silly. She stopped it. Only it *was* funny. 'Giggling'. When had she last 'giggled'?

Mo and his smiles, Mo and his laughs. If he hadnt been there for her. If he hadnt. There was nobody else. Not her family. Nobody.

Things make you strong.

The actual divorce experience itself, people wouldnt believe how dreadful it was. Not the stress my God the stress it puts you under. The children too, some dont recover, become damaged emotionally, psychological scars, the whole thing a nightmare. Only they never wake from it. No matter how bad the nightmare is in the ordinary world you wake up from it but they dont.

The photographs on the floor. She didnt want to pick them up. Ones facing up and ones facing down. It wasnt her choice. Things land at random. If her mother's photograph was face down. She didnt want to see it if it was. As if it was her fault! It wasnt. Silly thinking such a thing.

She made her way through to the bedroom. It was a good-size room and must have been a lounge originally. They used it as a bedroom and a place to store things. There was plenty light coming in through the curtains. Mo's huddled shape in the double bed, she listened to his breathing. Sophie slept in the walk-in cupboard. The door was kept ajar when she was in bed otherwise it would have gone from cosy to claustrophobic. There was no window in the cupboard. Cupboards dont have windows, even the walk-in variety, so no fresh air. When Sophie was in bed the door had to be left properly open. So things were awkward; it meant the room was out of bounds. The kitchen was where they lived. They needed a new place, whenever that might happen. Probably never. They didnt do the lottery.

Helen sat by the entrance with the chair angled that she might reach into Sophie without shifting position. An empty glass stood by the wall. Not quite empty; inside was a drop of water. Mo must have left it there. He would have checked how she was when he came home, then last thing before getting into bed; perhaps sat with her if she had been awake, if the movement had disturbed her. She could have been awake; sometimes she was. She still liked to come into bed with Helen, even when Mo was there. She had suffered bad dreams for a while. It still happened though not so much but on Helen's night off the girl used it as an excuse to wangle her way in beside them, unless it was a form of jealousy. Mo said that. And jealousy could happen; parents and children, it did, jealousy and envy, spite, everything.

Turning the cupboard into a 'bedroom' had been Mo's brilliant idea. But it was good. Really, and made a huge huge difference. He bought an old bed from a so-called furniture store down near the market. It was secondhand junk they sold and the bed wasnt just old it was like prehistoric, with a nailed-down metal frame. It was so so heavy. Two of his mates helped with the lifting and manoeuvring. They managed to squeeze it into the cupboard by taking off the end frames, and the legs too, sawing bits off and nailing bits on as supports, then putting bricks underneath the sides. Obviously the mattress didnt fit.

Obviously. Helen hunted about and found long settee-style cushions made of foam-rubber. These had been designed for a caravan but could be fitted together, and would do meantime. What the landlord didnt know wouldnt hurt him.

Although landlords have a habit of finding things out. Surely he would have had no complaints? If changes werent structural and no damage occurred. What could he say?

Oh but he would find something. They always do. Any excuse to keep the deposit. The cupboard shelves, he would have had something to say about them. They were high above Sophie's bed and couldnt be reached without stepladders but he definitely would see them. How could he miss them?

Mo built them before the bed went in. You had to twist about to get up because you couldnt set the ladders inside the cupboard, you climbed up then twisted and reached across; and the stepladders were old and shoogly; greasy and oily into the bargain; horrible old things. Everybody in the house used them and they were just horrible.

In this place everything was old. Nothing worked. Especially if she was using it. What worked for Helen? Nothing. It didnt matter what.

It was true.

No it wasnt. It was not true at all, and she was stupid and foolish for thinking such a thing and she had to stop it stop it, stop thinking negative thoughts all the time, things were good. They were.

But what would the landlord do if he saw the shelves? Surely it was structural if you interfered with the walls? And you werent supposed to do anything structural.

That was Mo. He interfered. He did. Walls came under fittings, you werent to touch fittings, it was interfering and you werent to interfere. He went in and did things, and that was the shelves, building them and so high. And he kept heavy stuff up there; old computers and bits and pieces; cables and connections, leads and other stuff, all fankled together. He hunted the secondhand shops and came home with junk. Ancient junk. Why did he do it? There was nothing in them. Spare parts, it was stupid. Two old video machines under the bed my God why did he keep them? outmoded junk. What a waste of space. Spare parts for what? The IT industry didnt work like that. She knew enough to know junk when she saw it, and that was junk. It was all relics. The technology changed every couple of years. Less. It had to. That was how the industry worked, that was profit and loss, people had to be buying and people had to be selling. And like the ones that made the things, them too, the people doing the actual jobs, poor people in foreign countries, whatever they did for a measly pittance of a wage and catching all the cancers. Mo wanted to talk about them and that was good but he didnt make the other connection. A man he knew worked down town selling the stuff, why didnt he ask him? That old junk was not going to be useful and come in handy; it would sit up there gathering dust. Why clog up your home? What was the use of that? eBay, nobody was going to buy these things on eBay. Even if they did, a pound here and a pound there. And these big hi-fi speakers on the top shelf. What were they for? They were completely obsolete. Things became obsolete because they had to be so people were forced to update. Everybody knew that. Mo was clever but he could be thick. He had blank spots. All men did, it was like a gender issue. They did things that were silly. They didnt see the consequences. Mo said the shelves were strong but they had to be strong because what happened if they fell down? so that was not an answer. Even the walls themselves: what if they fell down, because of all the shelves and all the heavy objects piled on top of them? This wasnt Glasgow where you got big thick sandstone lasting a hundred years. The buildings here were flimsy, their wee thin bricks, the big bad wolf could have blown it down. She got sick of talking about it. He wore her down. Not everything was a joke. When you looked up to the ceiling and saw the stuff all piled high, then down below and it was Sophie's bed! My God!

Oh but the walls would never collapse. It was just her worrying.

Even the nails, see the nails.

Mo showed her them. They were big strong nails. They were too. Helen could see they were.

Nothing would happen. He called her 'girl'. Dont worry about it girl. What did he mean by that? As if 'girl' because she was a 'girl' and a girl was a child like not an adult and not to be taken seriously. It was annoying. They said 'girl' in London but so what? Mo wasnt even a real Londoner he was Middlesex my God he said it often enough, 'Middlesex', like being proud of Middlesex. Danny the driver said 'girl' too. She didnt like it from him either. 'Girl', it was not like an adult.

What did it matter? She closed her eyes, although thoughts of her ex, his image; she was too tired to shudder. Why could she not be rid of him forever? It wasnt fair that his image could still be there and come into her brain, not after such a long time. Why could she not wipe it out? If the brain was a computer. People say that, as though things can be deleted and then *erased*, but the brain is not a computer, things cannot be *erased*, not like that.

Even now her main worry – laughable, so laughable – that she might turn a corner and bump into him. She knew he was in Glasgow and there was no reason to worry but she did. So it was like why? He would never come to London. Except perhaps it was a new job, and he came down for it, if she was with Mo, and Sophie too, Mo walking with them and it was hand in hand and they turned a corner and there he was. But he would never do it, he would never leave Glasgow and there was no reason ever to worry, never more, he could do what he liked. She could too. She could. It was up to her; if she wanted to do something she could do it.

Oh God.

Mo was nothing at all like her ex. Nonsense even thinking it. Only he could be silly. She liked it about him but also she didnt like it.

But the walls wouldnt fall down. She accepted that. She did. Mo knew what he was doing. She didnt have to nag him, if you could call it nagging. That was what he called it though with a smile on his face to make it a joke; but it was still nagging. That was what he thought about Helen safeguarding and protecting her child, he called it nagging. But if one hair on her little girl's head was ever hurt by one single thing relating to these damn shelves, one thing, that was all, then that was that.

She was not going to lose her temper about it. Only if anything happened, if anything ever happened.

But that was why she worried and why she nagged him so that it wouldnt happen and it wouldnt be too late and it didnt matter if he sighed or how much he sighed. She was not a silly child. He got exasperated. It was his word, *exasperated*. She exasperated him. She felt like slapping him never mind exasperated, he exasperated her. Then when he laughed. She hated that. It was like – why did he do it? As if she was thick, she wasnt thick. Why did he make her feel that way? It was a thing about Mo and why Helen compared him with her ex. Of course she did, it was natural. He had mates from the restaurant. One came to the house and Helen saw him smiling at something Mo said. Helen knew it was about her, whatever Mo said. Else why whisper? Mo had whispered. He did it so Helen couldnt hear. What other reason was there? So she was the one excluded, so it was about her.

Why else would he have whispered? It was like speaking in

Urdu. His mate did that until Mo corrected him because with Helen there, it was just bad manners. So was whispering if it excluded people. Especially matters between a man and a woman, these are private things, it could be anything, sex or whatever, if it was about her he was speaking, that was horrible, like behind her back and in the same room too, it was horrible, so so horrible, any man that could do that. Helen just could not ever, ever, never ever. She would never stand for it, how could she she never ever

That was a trust. He would have broken the trust. She had trusted him and he had broken the trust. That is how it would be. There was no excuse. She had trusted him, even with her own daughter. My God, if ever Sophie suffered. That was the one thing, if ever one thing happened, one little tiny thing.

It was beyond talking about except it had to be because with people in the house; there had to be people in the house. But who were they? That was the trouble with lodging houses with people all coming and going. Strangers: you were surrounded by them.

Of course some strangers were necessary. You had to bring people into your home. Childminders. They had Azizah and thank God. She was a lovely girl and they were so so lucky to get her. Who else could they have relied upon for weekend working? All Azizah did was read. She barely spoke at all. Perhaps she did when Helen wasnt there. Mo said she did, it was only shyness. She couldnt look Helen in the eye never mind say hullo. The scarlet woman! Teenage girls have an imagination. Helen didnt care. Yes she did, but not much. Sophie liked her and that was the difference. Even if she didnt, childminders dont last forever, sooner or later it would be somebody else. And who might it be, you never knew, horror stories abounded. She was right to worry. Of course she was. It was impossible not to. But what choice did she have? None. That was divorce, that was being a parent. It was always difficult and you were always taking a chance.

She had worked in casinos for years so was well used to it; at the same time, she got weary. There was nothing wrong in admitting it. Nightshift was difficult with young children, the constant organising, everything, it got you down. She was lucky with Mo. Mo was good. He wouldnt hurt a fly. And so gentle with Sophie. More than her ex. He threw her up in the air! My God! Why did men do that? He put her to the highest chute in the park. No wonder she was nervous. Two years of age my God she was entitled to be. He knew better. He always knew better. That was him, Mr Know-Better. Because he was a man? What did that mean? a man? Did it mean something special? Not as far as she was concerned. Mo wasnt like that, not even close. If ever he was she would tell him. He was one good thing that had happened to her, amongst many others. She acted like they didnt but they did. Even if they did they didnt. If it was her they were happening to it meant they were not good. Because good things didnt happen to her. If they did they would come to an end; sooner or later they would. Anything good came to an end. That was her and that was life, her life anyway.

Her daughter's head had moved on the pillow. The dampness was evident, her thick head of hair and the furry toy too close to her face, La Divina, Helen reached to ease it away, careful not to screech the chair legs. She kept her hand near to Sophie's forehead but without touching. Even so there was movement, the tiniest wisp, but more than a pulse beat. Sophie's brain must have picked up a signal. Mother and daughter, it was so so sensitive, so sensitive between them.

She would be up for school soon enough, poor wee soul. She had to be strong. Children had to be, nowadays, and resilient, just to survive. But they began strong. Mo said that. Their bodies were strong when they left the womb. Gradually they weakened, until late in life they died. That was humanity's story. From birth on the spirit was strong but then it got knocked out you. The best part of life is birth, from there on it is downhill, downhill all the way!

What a terrible way of looking at the world. Helen wondered if it was his religion, then saw he was laughing. He had made it all up. He was always doing it, always laughing at her. Thank goodness, she loved it about him, she needed it so much, seeing life like he did, he was just so so cheery and so so – just cheery, it was so necessary.

It was lovely the way he had transformed the cupboard. It was a bedroom; it really was – perhaps not a proper one but

But it was a proper one! Helen knew that now. She hadnt at first, unlike Sophie who had believed from the beginning. That wonderful story about the doll who lived in a cupboard: so it *was* a bedroom.

But it was wonderful. It made you want to curl up and just, just listen, close your eyes, or open them. It was so so – just unbelievable. Who could believe it? The book had been put there for Sophie. If miracles did happen. It was for them to find and they did. The doll who lived in the cupboard had been written for Sophie. Mo said it. There was nothing surer than that. It was the exact same cupboard. So amazing, exciting. Even the doll, it didnt look like La Divina but it was her best first cousin, you could see that. Mo held the book-page next to the doll to show the resemblance. When the story was read to her Sophie's eyes were huge as she looked round the interior walls. Whatever she was seeing, she was seeing something. Such an imagination. Oh but she got it from Helen. Her imagination my God it was notorious. Dad used to joke about it!

Poor girl if that was what she had. Helen felt sorry for her. It wasnt sweet and wasnt cute. Mundane thoughts were better.

Boys had those. Girls were different. Boys thought what they thought but girls didnt, girls had their own world. They loved stories and loved reading books. Sophie too. Helen was so glad and would encourage it all the way. Real books and not just computers. Real books to help with her studying. So she would get away from it all, the horrible stuff, just get out of it all and get away and just – if she got a worthwhile job and just away from the hopeless world, all the horrible and dark side and all

Helen had an urge to touch Sophie: she resisted. When the girl was asleep like this you had to stop yourself. What had she wanted to do? She didnt know, perhaps hold her. No, only touch her, only that. Helen wanted to laugh, and seeing her brow; there was a strength there, strength of purpose.

Her breathing was irregular but not to worry about – a particle catching in her throat. It made the breathing catarrhal, a little, but it was fine and nothing at all, really, not to worry about, just being silly, that was Helen all over.

The pillow and the side of her head damp with sweat. Of course it was normal. Boys were even worse apparently. Mo certainly was. He burned, it was like feverish. But Sophie burned too, and the side of her head, the temple, my God, it was so so thin and would be damaged

Oh so easily damaged. Easily.

You saw children throwing stones, girls as well as boys, and if they hit the side of the head, where the scalp was so thin, it would cause an injury, a dreadful one, and if it was by the ear. Children could be rough.

She was sound asleep. She was, she couldnt be more asleep.

Touch wood she was okay now but she had had such a hard time settling in at school. People said boys were the shy ones. It was hard for them, harder than it was for girls, supposedly, but Helen didnt believe it. Girls were every bit as shy, perhaps shyer. And it wasnt harder for boys. Definitely not. And girls could be horrible too. If it was bullying especially, if they had to fight. And worse with the Glasgow accent. London children would just look at her and think she was funny, they would laugh at her and perhaps might fight her. You could imagine it, because she was a stranger and with the different voice.

Sophie didnt like fighting. Some girls did. Some fought all the time, they hit boys too. And they could torture. Girls could torture. Helen remembered it from her own day. Perhaps worse than boys. Did boys even do it? Perhaps they didnt. Girls did, oh my God they did, they were so so good at it too.

Why did people have to hurt each other? Why did they not accept things, and accept each other. Helen was not clever and knew she was not but that was what she believed. Anyway, you didnt have to be clever to believe that, not if it was the truth. And it was the truth, people did hurt each other.

Helen shivered. She could have been into bed in one minute; into the warmth. Why didnt she? She didnt want to. She did but she didnt. Her head was too full, she would be tossing and turning. And she had a headache too. Of course that was normal.

But if everybody was different their thoughts too would be different and all their points of view, everything. You couldnt have everyone different but their thoughts all the same. That was just stupid. Why did people want everybody to be the same? Or act like they did. Usually it was men. But not all the time. You heard women politicians and they were tough as old boots, you saw their faces; they were worse than men, they would tell somebody to push the button for the whole human race, they would give the order. They could be mothers. Of course they could. It was hatred, people hated; why did people hate? They did, they hated.

She eased La Divina out from beneath the girl's head. It was just a little furry creature but she had had it since she was a baby. Mo teased her about it. Helen wished he would stop. But maybe it was for the best. It was a new life now and the sooner Sophie got rid of the old stuff the better. But it didnt apply to dolls. There was nothing wrong in dolls. If she could break with the old associations. That was what counted. Mo was good with Sophie, she could have been his own daughter. Helen was so lucky with Mo, but perhaps she wasnt.

That was an odd idea. What did it mean?

Nothing. Odd ideas were – odd! And she got them. But she was odd. She was; just hopeless, hopeless. She knew it about herself. If she wasnt hopeless she would never have got involved with him in the first place, her ex, never. And marriage would have been out the question. Marriage! My God imagine marrying him! But she did; it was never a strong point, sense. People thought she was sensible. She wasnt. They thought she was and she wasnt. She had to be thick to have married him. At the same time he was Sophie's father. So if not for him.

She lifted the empty glass and rose from the chair, the floorboards squeaking, treading so very carefully when she passed the end of the bed, although Mo would have slept through thunder. She clicked open the door into the hallway, and closed it so very gently.

That draught under the front door, my God, you could actually feel the chill. Her feet were always cold.

The light was still on in the kitchen. She had forgotten to switch it off. Oh well, she switched it off now, stepped across between the fallen photographs and settled into the chair. She was tired, sitting with the coat shielding her. It was weary. Weary and tired, that was her. Tiredness. Where did it come from? From living. Exhaustion. She was too weary to smile, she had been working all night dealing cards, dealing cards and taking money, putting up with it all, everything. And now here she was, not sound asleep and she should have been, snug,

warm, just warm, the heat from Mo he was so so, so warm, so
warm, in beside him and away from everything, and his body,
she loved his body; she did, why did she, men and women,

all these things and in her mind too all just going round and
round. Her head lolled, her eyes open; only the tiredness, but
not wanting to go to bed, she didnt want to.

Morning light but shadows lingered. Shadows of our lives. A
shadow of our life. What our lives are. Those shadows, into
those shadows. Brian at the traffic lights, that look in his eye, it
was wild. Why was he staring at her? It was horrible. He didnt
know her. If he had it would have been different, he wouldnt
have seemed so murderous and dangerous. Because that is
how he was to the others; that was how he appeared: murderous and dangerous. Not to her. Of course not, not at all.
Because she knew who he was and if he had known it was her,
if he had he would have looked at her differently.

He would have, because of who she was and who he was –
her big brother. He was her big brother my God and it wouldnt
matter about anything else; all what had happened, whatever
had happened was away in the past. If anything had happened.
She didnt even know if anything had happened. It was all past
now, everything, she was his wee sister, she was only little, she
had been; if anything had ever happened, she was only little.
Nothing had happened anyway, what had happened? nothing.

Other shadows now, and a darkness. Oh but darkness, what
is darkness, just darkness of mood, if her mood was dark.

These shadows. Shadows shadows, this is the past.

Memories are memories. Memories are not dark. It was
Helen herself and her imagination, too many books as a girl,

Mum always said it. Shadows and images, darkness. These were only memories, all crowding in, her and the family when she was very small; the ones from the beach where she was sitting up on Brian's shoulders. He took her down to the water. Other brothers would have skipped away and left her but he took her, walking over and over the sand, a far stretch of sand, across twirly little sandworms. She would not step on them although they were not real sandworms and would never hurt her. Brian said that. And nothing ever would hurt her if he was there. Helen knew that. But you could imagine worms, how they twirled round and were hiding there in the little piles my God and you could not walk to the water without stepping on them they were everywhere you looked and made you shudder and she hated touching them how boys could touch them oh my God and she could just look down at them, from high up on Brian's shoulders.

She couldnt have had a better brother. Did people not know? It was just so obvious. Dad knew that too. He must have. Why wouldnt he? Because he didnt like him. Poor Dad, his voice was a roar filling the whole house. Frightening and horrible. Helen hated it and wished she could stop it and just hide, she could just hide, if there were blankets, and just pulling them over her head, it was so so horrible.

If he didnt like his own son. My God. Surely not, but yes. It isnt strange to find in families a parent doesnt like a child. You had it in stories and films. It was an old subject; even in the bible. The parent tries but cannot bring himself to do it. It does happen. It is nobody's fault and just such a horrible shame, for everybody – not only the child. Dad would have felt it the worst. Poor Dad, fifty-four years of age. That is young for people dying. Cholesterol and blood pressure, or blood through the veins; to do with blood, something. Scotland was horrible for dying. She hadnt known it was so bad. Porridge and whisky, kilts and haggises. People laughed. It was a warped sense of humour. It happened in the casino. Anything about Scotland and they made a fool of it. Even Mo, and that was racist too, if he wanted to talk. Okay it was a laugh but just as well Mum didnt hear him. She was for Scotland and against anybody who said different. Scotland is a Protestant country. So if people came here they just had to put up with it. Or stay in their own place; why didnt they? Nobody asked them to come.

Mo said he liked Mum but how could he? If people dont like you how can you like them? She couldnt look in his direction except with lowered eyes. Nobody would have succeeded with her. Even Dad failed. Of course Brian.

Helen glanced at the photograph in her hand, she had lifted it from the floor, one of Mum and Dad but half turned so she couldnt see the actual surface, the image. She didnt want to see them. Not at this moment. The ones of Brian, she didnt have many. Mum had more, she liked him. Of course she did, her son. Mum loved Brian and it was nice to know. She had never loved Helen and she loved Brian so that was nice, nice to know, she loved somebody.

But that could never have been him at the traffic lights. It was just too coincidental. The entire population of London my God millions and millions of people. Brian went to England but a long long time ago: Doncaster or someplace; he liked Doncaster, then it was Liverpool. Although of course he could have left and come to London, of course he could. But if he had seen her he would have known her. Surely he would have known her?

Not through the windscreen and the side windows. She would have been a shape, only a shape.

Oh my God if he had recognised her he would have been so so glad, just so glad to see her. He would have been. He was her big brother. She didnt have anyone else. Other people had lots of relations. She didnt. Brian was the one and he went away, and poor old Dad. Nobody was left except Mum. If people want to complain, Helen could have, she could easily have complained. Yes life was unfair. If you expected life to be fair you were in for a shock. Dad was hardly turned fifty and it was a heart attack. What is a heart attack? Your heart stops, a heart seizure. It was a seizure. Blood and cholesterol. What does it mean? The doctor asked if he smoked my God it had nothing to do with smoking, Dad didnt smoke; he used to but it was years ago.

Why did they say these things? Oh but it was all the time, the same with Mo's uncle dying of cancer. People blame the wrong things. It happened to her dealing cards, if they kept getting bust or if she kept getting blackjack, so the bank kept winning, so it was like her fault. It wasnt her fault. They blamed her for bad cards. Total stupidity. And it wasnt her money, did they think it was her winning for goodness sake it was not her winning, it was the bank, and it was not her fault if they lost. Punters lost their wages so blame the dealer. All the time they did it, as if she was responsible for how the cards fell. What did they think, that she had stacked the deck? How could she do that? They saw the cards under their very nose, that was how they were shuffled, they just came out and it happened, and they cut the deck themself, it was them done it, so why blame her? What about fate, do they never think of fate? Or luck? Why not luck? People were lucky. Some were and some werent. That was life.

A slice of toast. She needed something.

Once Sophie had gone to school she would fall into bed, just fall in. Everything. It was everything. You got tired of it all. She had been about to say 'death'. Even death, being tired of death. Why was she thinking about death? It wasnt morbid, she wasnt morbid, not generally, although her thoughts, her imagination.

Her thoughts were the darkest, often they were, they could be. Not herself, if it was the smear, she always went and always would, and ordinary cancer, people dont pass it on to one another, not like a contagion, cancer is not a contagion, and people survive. Mo's uncle hadnt smoked one cigarette in his whole life. He was a religious man and a non-drinker too. Why did the medical people say that? Because it was lung cancer. Mo's family were angry and no wonder. Didnt they read the medical records? His uncle was a sportsman my God didnt they know he was a sportsman? They dont even read his files! Mo could hardly get the words out when he was telling her. Then too his family, his mum and dad up visiting most every day of the week and what a strain it put on them.

But at least they had had time together as a family. Not like when the person is just struck down. That is the horror. People have no time. Helen's father was dead before he hit the pavement. So said the doctors. He was walking along the road and collapsed, and was dead. Children in the street witnessed it happen. So horrible. Those children looking at him and he was dead, they saw him falling down, it was a dead body, they saw a dead body falling and it was her father, my God, nobody knowing, not getting the chance to see him and wish him cheerio. It sounded stupid; foolish and just crass. But that was it, to say cheerio or bid farewell, how do you say it? goodbye, if your father is dying and you know he is and he does too, farewell or cheerio Dad or what, what happens? just holding his hand. Helen would have held his hand, pressed his hand and just

so he would know she was there, just being there for him. That was his life! That is the parent's family, father or mother, it isnt just mothers. Dad had been so important for her. He had a right, he had a right, only to have the contact and know this at the end of his days, it isnt too much to ask, not to die like he did in the middle of the horrible street it was just so so unfair, for people believing in God, it was just silly and not only silly but not at all justice, who could ever believe in justice, poor Dad, he deserved something better than that. If there was no justice then there wasnt any so what was there?

He died the year before Sophie was born. Imagine how unfair, so so unfair. Dad would have loved a granddaughter. But it wasnt to be. Things dont work out. You plan things to happen and they dont. Whose fault is it? it is nobody's, whether God or whoever, life is life, if it is fate. Helen didnt believe in fate, not too much, and not too much about God either. Mo could do what he wanted but not for Helen and not for Sophie, it was not their culture; he didnt speak about it to her and she didnt want him to. Really, she didnt. He went to Mosque a lot, and that was him and it was fine, the pillars of faith.

It was all too big anyway. Sometimes Helen felt that, and she was nothing, she knew she was nothing. Except she wanted nothing, so that was something. She wasnt asking for stuff and wanting things all the time like fame and fortune it was just stupidity. If she had no right to have something she didnt want it. She didnt want anything like that and didnt care. She wanted her family, that was all.

Mo laughed at her. But it wasnt her fault. She was different to what he knew but what did that mean? He thought it was Scottishness but it wasnt Scottishness, it was nothing to do with Scottishness. What was Scottishness? She didnt know what it was and it didnt matter because it wasnt her.

Anyway, she wondered about him. There were things he didnt tell her. That was men. The man who talked, but not about everything. They had had very different life experiences. Even just male and female was different, never mind families. People fight to live. Some do and some dont. Mo's people did but what about hers? Would they fight? Did they?

Sad thoughts, sadness about the thoughts; the thoughts were not sad in themselves, the sadness was from thinking about them, their lives, their lives were just poor, poor lives, the casino too and the people she saw and encountered day in day out, night after night after night, frittering and superficial and some horrible, just horrible, horrible people and all their horrible attitudes, going out into the night, avoiding the shadows, the back alleys and side streets, they didnt want to know about them.

Brian *was* skinny. He was a skinny malinky; awkward and just lanky. He was lanky. She was not being disloyal saying that if it was the truth, and it was the truth.

There were questions you couldnt ask people.

She was peering down at the photographs on the floor. Families were ghosts coming back to haunt you. It was symbolic to see faces and bodies staring back up, but symbolic of what? They werent really staring. People in photographs dont stare. If it was a symbol for her what did it 'represent'? if symbols 'represent' something, what? Dad just looked silly in the one she was seeing, caught in a pose with the New Zealand cousins and bending in a funny way. Bats and balls, they had been playing a silly game. There was another of Mum and Dad standing someplace on a pier. It was quite old. Mum was smiling to the camera. She had a nice smile but you hardly ever saw it.

Mum had survived without Dad. Helen knew she would. It was not being unkind saying this about her. Life shouldnt stop because one person dies. Mum had friends and she got out and about and why shouldnt she? There was nothing disloyal in that. It was nice seeing Mum smile. Who had taken the photograph? Brian? She would have smiled for Brian. Not for Helen. Frowns and sad faces. Oh well, mothers and daughters, what could you do about it? nothing. Poor Brian. Poor everybody! Did you have to feel sorry for everybody? Yes! Helen especially! Imagine it had been a full cup of tea she knocked over! On top of the photographs, and soaked them. Dad would turn in his grave. A full cup of tea on top of the family photographs, imagine that, all ruined, that was them like forever, forever and ever.

It would have been too because she didnt have them on hard drive. She should have. Only she hadnt got round to it, but she would, and would be silly not to. She did value them. They only fell out her lap, she hadnt knocked them over, not like intentionally. It was an accident and accidents do happen. It isnt our fault for everything.

People blamed people all the time. Dad blamed Brian. He gave him rows. Why? Because he was clumsy, awkward, banging into things, and lanky, a big lanky long-legs. He just seemed so lanky. Other girls said it, look at big lanky, that was what they said, it was embarrassing, just silly. Dad was silly, saying these things. It was not Brian's fault. And sarcastic too, why was Dad so sarcastic? Sarcasm made people awkward and they get nervous. People are nervous, especially if they are young.

She left the photographs lying a moment, then reached for them. It wasnt nice leaving them on the floor. And it wasnt nice calling Dad silly. Helen said things and did things. She didnt think it through. She should have but didnt. The same as a child she did things and said things and then trouble because of it and Dad was so quick always quick just so quick to jump, poor Brian. Too quick. That was Dad. He was just too quick, and with Brian especially, it was not fair. But how could she be responsible? If she was a wee girl. That was all she was my God, why should she have felt guilty? there was no reason at all, it was complete stupidity, childish stupidity. It wasnt her fault if Dad gave Brian into trouble and didnt punish her, why should she be guilty? Not if she wasnt, if she didnt do anything. People arent guilty.

It was complete nonsense.

These old things going round inside her head.

No wonder. She was so tired.

People's lives depressed her. The subject alone. Even to think about. My God she even depressed herself. She couldnt stop it. And too she was on her own. She was. Mo was great but people are on their own, isolated, they get isolated. Although she had Sophie who was flesh and blood and a piece of herself. Helen felt that she was, just like so so close to her, she could feel the pain, and would feel the pain, when Sophie grew and experienced life, all the ups and downs, Helen would feel it too, she would be with her. Because it would be like herself it was happening to, she couldnt describe it properly, flesh of her flesh, people said that and it was true, Helen felt it so strongly, they were your own flesh and blood, children, they really were.

It was so true.

A slice of toast. Her stomach was empty. She didnt eat properly. Mo said it too. But it was nerves, it was only nerves. If people dont eat, they think it is a disorder, other people think it is, and it isnt because you want to eat but you cannot, you cannot.

It would have been good to talk to somebody. Not Mo. Mo was good but it needed somebody different, who knew her differently. Another woman especially. Ann Marie. Who else! Helen smiled. No wonder. Ann Marie made anybody smile. Even the way she talked, like in a movie. She was a cleaner at the last casino Helen worked at in Glasgow but had been a croupier when she was younger and told good stories about the old days: all the characters, the gangsters and crazy people. There were more of them back then. Ann Marie made anything funny. She was great at jokes. Helen was hopeless. Helen couldnt tell a joke to save her life. She tried to but she couldnt. Every time she did it went wrong. People never laughed. They never laughed! And she knew they wouldnt. Halfway through telling it, if she was telling a joke or a funny story, she saw the person's face and knew they wouldnt. Were they even listening? Perhaps they werent. Even Mo. He laughed but why did he? It wasnt because her jokes were funny. More like sad. She was sad, a sad case.

You had to make it funny. Others did. Even Jill could be funny; she didnt think she was but she really really was. It was the way she said things in her posh voice. She wasnt being snobbish. Yes she was serious but funny serious. Helen wasnt. Helen was always serious, serious serious, serious about everything, serious serious serious oh God why was she always so serious?

But she wasnt always. Not *always*. She wasnt. My God! Not as a girl. Never. She hadnt been. Even now. She loved to laugh. Ann Marie made her laugh. Mo too, he made her laugh all the time And Sophie, who was a born comedian the way she made faces and acted her parts, a born actress into the bargain, if ever she got the chance, she would be so good, if she worked at it, she had to; if she did she would make the grade. All she needed was a chance. People had to get a chance. That was society's fault how people were so stifled and everything so hopeless. People said it was the western world but it wasnt only the western world.

It wasnt.

People are no different from each other. Some think they are. Why do they? They think they are different and they arent. No one is. Mo or whoever. Brian too; he might have had problems but he wasnt unique. Not even her ex was unique my God even if he thought he was.

But Helen wasnt either, and never thought she was. He could never have accused her of that. You had to go out in the world and do things for yourself. Helen knew that from an early age, even if her ex didnt. Nothing came to you, you got it by yourself. And if you took a chance. People tried to and they got defeated, they lost and lost everything. Then they tried to hide it from those closest to them, putting on their brave face; that was the saddest thing about it. But what did they do when they went home and locked the door? If they had lost everything. What did they do when nobody else was there? Except if they had a partner, their wife or somebody. Oh my God, the things Helen had seen, and the violence, just at the tables and the way the man looked at the woman, and she wasnt doing anything! She wasnt. She was just there and there beside him and it was him losing everything, losing everything and she was there and knew it and no one else did and he was acting just so cool and laughing if somebody made a joke, but he had lost everything. Then getting up to leave, the woman not looking at anybody. Sometimes they just sat there and didnt move, they had forgotten to move away from the table and it was up to the dealer to attract their attention. It would have been embarrassing for some. They hardly noticed.

Oh well.

Helen had a cup of tea now, and sipped at it. Having Ann Marie there would have made a difference. Just somebody to talk to who *knew*. Ann Marie knew.

They kept in touch by phone. Once in a blue moon. It was Helen's fault. She left it to Ann Marie to make the phone call because she didnt want to bother her. But she should have bothered her. Ann Marie gave her rows about that. Although nightshift hours made it extra difficult. It would have been better to text. But even Ann Marie's voice made her smile, the way she spoke, not even like what she said, it didnt matter. Although she was wrong to say there were no characters left, as if they had all died off! Perhaps in Glasgow but not down here. There were real characters down here, and charmers, real smoothies. What about the mad doctor? Really he was a surgeon. But a true character. Not a smoothie but nice, but also a flirt, he was. Some flirts are funny and cheery and he was like that. He came from a rich family in India and gambled every night near enough. All his money went on blackjack and roulette. But he was a nice man and a good person. If he was high caste, he didnt have a down on people, not like you got from some who only looked at you if they wanted something and hardly even then, they thought you should know in advance – like a servant; that was what it was, they treated you like a servant. The mad doctor was not like that. He was generous to the dealers, the boys too, everybody; even when he didnt win he tipped them, that was his way, and he chatted to anybody, chatted all the time. He got tipsy on rum and lost fortunes. It was a special Indian blend they kept for him and once he started he didnt stop. I am a disappointment. My family have cast me asunder. I am doomed to walk in the wilderness.

Because he was a disappointment to them. They were wealthy people and upper class. Being a surgeon or something like a doctor was a disappointment to them. In Britain this was the best but not for them. They were high caste and very high up. They had a caste system in India and they were top people. He was not degenerate. Mo said he was but he wasnt. It was a horrible word and sounded like perversion, as if the surgeon was perverted and he was not at all perverted, it was not fair to say it.

Mo was biased against rich people; and biased against India too. He said he wasnt but he was. Caste and class; rich people and poor people and how the rich ones always take the best for themself and just go with whoever gives them it, just like soldiers and prostitutes. But it wasnt fair saying that, only if it was mercenary soldiers, and that didnt apply to them all. Mo was wrong. It was generalisations. That was why Muslim people got a bad name, you cant tar everybody with the same brush, even Americans, most soldiers were just poor people needing a job, the same with casinos. If he hated them too. He did hate them, and was on shaky ground as well he knew. Anyway, she didnt talk to him about work matters. Not unless she had to. The same with her ex who hated hearing about high stakes and big gamblers and said it was boring. Mo didnt say that although for him it might have been. But about other men was Mo jealous? Helen was not sure. Sometimes it seemed liked he was. But not like a jealousy, not a real one. If ever it was she would walk. She had had enough of that to last a lifetime. The very idea, it was so not ever ever going to happen again. Never. The slightest thing, and she was away. He was vicious. People wouldnt have believed her because they didnt see bruises. Women got bruised in other ways. Men can have cheery words and jokes. It fools some people. So let them be fooled. If they wanted to be fooled, let them.

Mo was nothing at all like him. Only he was silly and did things for fun, and also like a compliment, so Helen felt good about herself. It was nice being valued.

The mad doctor may have been a decent man but she was not about to run off with him. What nonsense it all was. If ever she ran off with anybody, she would know. Anyway, he was not her type. If she had a type, he was not it.

There was a serious side to this: you wouldnt look twice at certain men; it didnt matter if they were good-looking, so-called, it didnt matter. But he was not what you would expect of a surgeon. Surgeons were delicate, or supposed to be, that was their job, everything with pin-point accuracy. He was nothing like that. He was not at all athletic. You couldnt imagine him ever running, or if he played a game like tennis or squash, you just could not imagine it. Never an ordinary game like football, it would never be football. His body too! My God. Big and clumsy, that was him. Imagine his body! She couldnt, pure and simple.

It wasnt fair to say, but if she did have a type he was not it.

Not everybody liked him either. His chattering spoiled people's concentration. Some gamblers never spoke, only very basic words, so when he was doing it they looked away.

It was understandable. If people are losing they have to concentrate. They need to. The surgeon was like a nuisance. Some regulars thought that, and with his drinking. When the cards were dealt they didnt want distractions. And if he said the wrong thing. You never knew who was at the table. Once in Glasgow a man brought out a gun and just laughed, he pretended it was absent-mindedness but really he did it for a joke, laying it on the table edge as he searched for his cigarettes. He was about to go out for a smoke. Ann Marie was dealing the cards at that time. She made a witty comment about tissues: at least it wasnt a snottery tissue like how some people leave their snottery tissues on the baize. That was so disgusting, never mind pistol-guns. People had been barred from the casino for less than that but this guy wasnt. He was a regular and played for big money. That came first before everything. He apologised to the Inspector and the manager and apologised to Ann Marie as well, if he made her scared. Of course he made her scared! Imagine a pistol-gun. Ann Marie called them 'pistol-guns'. What was he doing with a pistol-gun? People laughed. Helen did too, when Ann Marie was telling her, because it was funny and you couldnt help it, but it was the laugh you do when you shiver. Some men made you shiver. You had to be careful. Helen was, or tried to be.

Jill came out with something daft about the surgeon, thinking he might be gay. He only *appears* to flirt, she said, he isnt serious. If you made a move he would run a mile.

Helen smiled when Jill said that. It was so unlike her. And very very silly. So if the guy was not serious with her, so then he was gay? Is that what she was saying? It was silly and not what you would expect from Jill.

Anyway, if he was, Helen would have known, and she was not a boaster saying that. Men looked at her and the surgeon was one. Their brains were someplace else. Men dont have brains. That was Ann Marie, 'it' thinks for them, 'it' meaning 'thing' as in penis. Their eyes were watching you when you glanced up from the cards and you saw them for that one split second before they looked away, unless they wanted you to see. Then if they went further and gave a wee signal, smiling longer or else whatever, men did it in a certain way and it was obvious, you knew it was happening, even when it was a surprise; people who should have known better, if they were in the public eye like on television or football players. Two were regulars. They were new in their football team, new in the country, and this was where they came, them and their French voices; it was French they spoke, just sexy and funny and the women talked about them. But they were only boys, they shouldnt have been spending their time in casinos. And if they were reported? People tell stories, they phone up the newspapers. Their football manager wouldnt have liked it.

Just being alive was a gamble. You opened a door and what was behind? You never knew. Everybody took risks. Helen too, she had done. Never again. Never. Never never. Oh my God the thought, the very thought! The one she went with made her shiver. Even thinking about him. It was true. Who made her feel like that? Nobody. Oh how he looked at her, he just had to, even away over, he would be standing away over and she would be dealing and perhaps somebody asking for a card and she happened to see him, just glancing across. Then he was gone; she looked and she didnt see him. She couldnt stop thinking about him, he just arrived and she saw him and then he was away and she couldnt think of anything else. That was *so* against the rules. You could act ordinary in the job but when it came to men and it took away your concentration, oh no, then their hands were in the till and you were out a job.

It was dangerous too. He was dangerous. Men that made you feel that way, some did and he was one.

There were rumours about him. Nothing bad; not that Helen ever heard and she would have heard because she listened for it. And never anything to her, not in the slightest, only how he made her feel, and the respect for her, that was what he had. He never acted badly towards her. So if it was sex my God that was her business. It was. He just made her feel good. That was him and the man he was. If he was different with men, well of course he was: men are different with men and so are women, different from women, different from each other; of course they are. It made life a puzzle. Men could be strange, they did unexpected things, foolish things, they took foolish risks. Why had he chosen her. Because it was true that he did, he did choose her.

It was her he chose. My God. Out of everybody.

He was a puzzle. Men were. But him, he really was. Being older too, that made it more so. Helen didnt like older men, and their bodies. No, she didnt. It was only him. What did he do to her? it was like he did something. He didnt attract her: he made it so that she could be attracted; then it was up to her, she could allow it or not, so it was her, so that is the risk and she took it.

And he parted from her.

He did! You would have thought the other way round, her leaving the man, but not Mr Adams, just disappearing like as if she had done something. She hadnt. It was him. He just went out her life. People do that. You want to know why, they dont tell you. Brian was the same. He was exactly the same. That was men, why do they do it? Even a brother.

Oh but she was glad it finished with Mr Adams because with her ex, it didnt bear thinking if he found out, he would have killed him. Or said he would. Fantasy-land. It was only her he would have killed. In comparison to Mr Adams he was a boy, not fit for the company. Vulgar and silly, silly and stupid, a vulgar and stupid young guy, that was her ex. It was hard to imagine him in the same room. Mr Adams only would have looked at him. If even he noticed him. That would have been nice to see: that would have put him in his place.

The arrogance of it. And what had he to be arrogant about? Just a stupid stupid, stupid and vulgar and just silly, and foolish, so so foolish.

But if ever he had found out. My God!

Helen could have told him. Imagine she had. To set against the arrogance, the pure arrogance, how somebody could be so arrogant, so stupid and so

and with so nothing to be arrogant about!

That would have been something to see, if she had told her ex. What might he have done? Nothing. There was nothing. He might have thought he could. Small chance. He would have had another think coming, if he so much as touched her, the slightest thing.

Yes she had gone with Mr Adams, so she had taken the risk. That was her and her own personal experience.

Even now he would have had that effect. If ever she was to see him my God, trembling hands if she was drinking tea, it was ridiculous, a grown woman.

Her life was so strange. Things happened. She didnt know anything about him. But she went with him and it was to a hotel. Of course he was married, she knew nothing about that. What did she know? She knew she was safe: that was what she knew. Knowledge was not a fault. Helen wanted it for Sophie. Mum hadnt wanted it for her. Why was that? Imagine not wanting knowledge for your daughter. Knowledge helped you survive. You needed it as a woman.

Helen closed her eyes.

If something bad had happened to him, she wouldnt have known. Who would have told her? Nobody. She sought news of him in the newspapers, watched television, listened to radio. She wasnt being silly. Mr Adams had that about him. He *was* somebody. She knew he was.

She should have been in bed. Why was she still sitting here? She wasnt fit to sleep. She didnt deserve it.

Daylight had come so if she was not asleep, well, she never would be, and no wonder, it was all just men, how many were there? not that many, she wasnt thinking about that, only how they looked, they always looked. It wasnt her fault. Why did Mum blame her? But she did. If a boy was at the door or shouted up at the window or what? whistled in the street. Mum blamed her. Why? It wasnt her fault. Men looked, they always looked. A mother should know the girl isnt to blame. Brian wasnt the only one who left home.

Oh poor Brian, poor Brian. That was Mum. Never poor Helen. But Helen stayed in touch and Brian didnt.

Mum should have looked at herself. Why didnt she? Her and Dad both, if they wanted to know the truth, but people dont.

Yes people took risks. Of course they did. Grannie used to say it about Dad how he picked on Brian, that was a risk because if he pushed him too far, the size he was. Brian didnt have to be scared of anybody, only hitting them too hard. That was what Grannie said, if ever Brian hit back, that was the time to worry. And she gave Mum a hard look because she was talking about Dad, if he kept picking on Brian all the time, why didnt he just stop it? It wasnt nice picking on people. Dad did pick on Brian. He goaded him. That was Grannie's word, *goaded*, he *goads* the boy.

41

Fathers with sons; there are stories in the bible. But girls too, they have to take risks because with boys, what if they talk? Boys talk. They tell each other if you do something if you are a girl, so then they all come to your door, it is horrible, even if it is your dad answers, they ask him, or if it is your brother, they dont care, they say it to him, oh is your sister coming out to play? *to play*, what does *to play* mean, and laughing to each other; so nasty, and unfair, them all smiling and thinking what they are thinking. Whose fault is that? How can the girl be blamed if she hasnt done anything? The girl gets blamed. It is so unfair.

They have to do it and they learn, that is how they learn, if it is the first boy. That is the real world. Why can parents not accept the real world, boys go for girls and girls have to let them, and if it is the wrong one; it cannot always be the right one. It would be impossible, so then they gain in understanding. Women get stoned to death, they get burned to death and buried alive and suffocated at birth. A girl is a woman, a baby girl too, she is a woman; a woman gets suffocated at birth, not a baby, they dont see a baby. That is the real world. People dont see the real world. That is up to them, if they want to hide the truth. They suffocate a baby because the baby is a woman, they stone her to death.

Knowing Mr Adams let her see about her ex what she didnt want in life. Him! It didnt affect their relationship because that was already finished. Only she hadnt told him. She knew and he didnt. How many times, lying there beside him in the dark and he was awake, and she could have said it to him, she could have. And she knew he was awake. Oh she knew alright because when he swallowed. People dont swallow, not if they are asleep. He was wondering if *she* was awake. She hardly breathed, she wouldnt have, not for him; never. Her mind could go any place. She was able to lie there and think it, whatever it was, whatever she wanted to think, and he was powerless because he could not stop her brains. He would if he could but he couldnt. Except if he nudged her. He did that, nudged her. Horrible. Even with strength. So it was like hitting her. Imagine that. That was what it was. If it was the hip it was real pain because it was his elbow doing it and that was like the bone, so you could be bruised, and it was only pretence, to waken her up, hitting her to waken her up.

He didnt know how lucky he was. If she had done what she could have done and told Mr Adams, but she didnt. Imagine she had! My God. He would have come and beat him up, or got men to do it. Although if he didnt recover: that was the worry. What if the men hurt him on the head or damaged his neck or his back or even his legs and like something happened so it was lasting damage? My God, what if it was a wheelchair? Sophie would have to push him around too. And she would when she was older and travelled up to Glasgow, because he would never come to London, never. Such a selfish bugger, just so selfish. Whyever did she get mixed up with him? That was Helen, that was so typical, so so typical; she was hopeless, really, she was.

Not in a hundred years, marrying him, imagine, if she had known anything.

The word 'respect'.

'Respect' was such a beautiful word. 'Respect', what it was. There were these men in her life. Sometimes she was sick of it, of men, just all men, and if she had another child oh if it could be a son and the way she would bring him up, it would be *respect*, to respect people, whether men or women, or children. Why not children! We should respect children too. Mo did it with Sophie. He made sure of that. Helen watched to see. How does the man treat the girl? just the littlest girl, if he watches her undress. He has to do it, so how does he do it? And the little girl just trusts him. It is not a risk. She doesnt know that it is because she doesnt know, she doesnt know anything. What does a girl know? Nothing. She doesnt know anything. How can you blame her? You cant. A girl cannot be blamed. That is so so wrong, just so so wrong. Of course she trusts him. She doesnt know and sits on the carpet and with her legs open or sits on him and it is on him, on his thighs and front; what does he do? because if he has to do something, if it is a man he is so sensitive there, even if it is a father, you just have to touch him. But what if it is a little girl?

No one in the entire world had known about Mr Adams, until Ann Marie. Helen told her. Imagine telling *her*! Typical. But why, why why why!

Because she had to. Otherwise explode, exploded, she would have exploded because who to tell if not Ann Marie it would have been him, her ex, that was who she was going to tell. The one person never to tell was the one she would. She thought she would, she was bursting to, really, she was, lying beside him and she was going to explode my God the words reaching up from her throat into her mouth and if she unzipped her lips out it would come: everything would come out; not in a confession; only how wonderful it was, she wanted to tell him because he didnt know and didnt know anything about how it could be if it was two people, he just had no knowledge at all, such an ignorant ignorant

But she needed to tell someone and told Ann Marie. Then others knew. They were smiling. They knew. Ann Marie told them. Imagine telling them. But she did.

So sad, so so sad, really. A friend is a friend but is not a friend, not a real friend. What is a real friend? That is like family, a real family. Mo had a real family. Helen didnt. Sophie was her family.

It was the last time she would confide in anybody. Who was

there? Not another living soul. She didnt have one proper friend. Imagine a sister, how that would be; just talking and being able to say things. Some said about mothers and daughters, but not hers. Even brothers; in stories you got them, sisters confided in brothers.

Oh but Ann Marie had had a tough life. It was true. Everybody had tough lives but Ann Marie really really did have, just how things had been for her, so very very difficult. But other people's lives were difficult too. Everybody's life. Ann Marie had a habit of going on and on about how tough it was. Other people were the same, like they were the only ones with troubles. Nobody knew the meaning of 'tough' except them. It was so so foolish. They knew nothing about people but dismissed them anyway, and said things that were nonsensical. If they could only think, why didnt they think? There were countless millions of people. How many of them had tough lives? Most of the world. What if it was Africa and Asia and these countries where they starved to death? People were killed in these countries. But oh no, they didnt want to hear about that, they didnt like political things and thought they knew better. If you said about other countries they just looked at you so it was you, you were the naïve one.

That was a fault people had. Older ones especially, they had to be the experienced person, as if they knew everything because they had seen hard times and their lives were tough.

Nobody knew everything; nobody had the right to say that. It was like a woman's story in a magazine Helen had been reading. This woman sent in her own personal diary and they published it. Her dad had Alzheimer's and her mum was an invalid, unable to leave the home without assistance. The daughter had to call in every day. Every single day. She visited her parents every single day of her life. A train and a bus on the return journey. She was married herself although she had no children. How could she have? There wasnt any time. It was just so tough. Helen wouldnt have coped. Every single day. The travelling alone was two and a half hours, then the time she spent looking after them, say an hour and a half, so four hours daily, four hours out your life, every day of the week. Imagine it. Every single day! My God. So she did have it tough. But was it the toughest? It didnt give her the right to act like she knew everything, although she could have but she didnt. Some people were humble but some were the opposite. It was interesting when you read about their lives. There were hidden parts for everybody.

It was true. You never knew about other people. Nobody told you everything. Why should they? Every night of the week Helen saw people in the casino: what about them? What were their stories? These old Chinese women. You couldnt imagine. Where she worked in Glasgow they spent more time there than their own home. People said that and it was not prejudice. Some didnt even gamble. They only came in for a cup of tea, and a chat with their friends, or else just sat there looking at nothing. The management didnt bother, even if their voices were loud and carried. If it was ordinary Glasgow people they would have been asked to quieten down but not the Chinese. Management wanted them because they were regulars, they were the 'bread and butter'. Some nights it was like their own casino. Then if they were all talking round your table. Ann Marie said that, if they compared notes in their own language like what happened when she was dealing years ago, you didnt know what they were saying yet it was your table, you were supposed to be in charge. So that was annoying. But if management didnt bother who else would? You had to be careful at the tables, you never knew who you were facing.

Her workmate Caroline said that to her once. What a cheek. Helen wouldnt have minded if it had been Ann Marie, but

Caroline? Helen had forgotten more about casinos than she ever knew. She seemed to think Helen had led a sheltered life. Oh you are so innocent. That was how she looked at her. It rankled. People think they know better. Caroline wasnt the only one. They were surprised Helen had a six-year-old daughter, they didnt think she was old enough. So she was supposed to take it as a compliment. Ha ha. So patronising. After what she had been through. How ironic, how very very ironic.

Really, they knew nothing about her. And if it was women talking about men, that was another ha ha.

In some ways she might have been naive. She would admit that. So if she was, everybody is, in some way. Helen didnt care. She really didnt. Why should she? It was all meaningless nonsense and she couldnt be bothered with it.

It was her turn to phone Ann Marie. She would eventually. It was nice to talk. Only not for important matters. But she could still enjoy her company. It was cheery. She had a boyfriend or as she called him, 'a manfriend'. Ann Marie's stories concerned men. She called them 'the great lost cause'. Men. What use were they? None at all – except hanging a hat.

That was Ann Marie's sense of humour. Only women were there when she said it and they didnt all get the joke. Helen knew immediately and spluttered on her coffee – literally, she did, the coffee went over her – it was just so funny, the tears would be streaming out your eyes. Ann Marie didnt care about men except for sex, that was what she meant, and most of them were hopeless even for that. It was true, my God, and smelly. Ann Marie was right. Why did they not wash? It was so obvious but they didnt do it; and these personal things, it was disgusting. And their breath, even Mr Adams. He was so clean except when it came to his teeth, and he brushed them regularly, but it didnt matter, the smell of his breath made her think of old people, and he wasnt old. Although forty-eight, and she was twenty-seven. It was old. But not too old and just so clean, he was. But then her ex, my God, her ex washed himself in the washhand basin, that was just so bad like his private parts, the very thought; and afterwards there were hairs stuck to the sides. Hairs! What would they have been? private ones, pubics. A washhand basin. People had to wash their faces. Disgusting wasnt the word. The word was *pig*. For him it was. That was one of them, 'pig', there were others. Mo was so much better. Perhaps it was the culture. Muslim men seemed cleaner, even the beardies. That was her, probably she was wrong, prejudice in reverse, she didnt care. She couldnt always think, not when she was tired tired tired, tired beyond anything, and could not sleep, if she went to bed now, she would not sleep, she knew she wouldnt; exhaustion, except her mind; minds were the strangest thing, they were.

She shivered, drew the coat about her shoulders, raising her knees, snuggling in on herself; better snuggling in with Mo, he was like feverish he was so warm; he was, you worried if he was catching the flu. She did anyway, but she worried about everything, anything and everything, everything and anything, the slightest shiver, life is full of shivers. She was comfy where she was, except the headache, which was only slight. They would be up soon for school; Sophie had to be there by eight thirty.

If it was Brian.

Life is so weird. Families especially, what families are. You looked at photographs but what did you see?

He just went away. What happened? Nobody said anything and you were not to talk about it. If there was a phone call Mum was to take it but not in front of Dad. Even his name, you were not to speak his name. What were you not to think about him, your own brother? Helen did. Of course she did, she was his sister; did that not count for anything? She would have spoken about him to Mum except Mum never spoke about anything. Not to Helen anyway. Oh well of course she did, but not much.

And she thought about Brian. It was obvious. She sat in her armchair with the television on and the magazine in her lap but she wasnt looking at them and wasnt thinking about them, only about Brian. And why shouldnt she my God he was her son!

Even after Dad died and it was only the two of them. So unfair; it really was. And selfish. Mum was Brian's mother but Helen was his sister. Why should she be excluded? She *was* excluded, Mum excluded her. Even the marriage; parents should be happy at their daughter's marriage. Oh God. Resentments were the worst. One day she would tell Mo. He just didnt understand it because with families, his was like a world of difference, a total world away.

Parents could be unfair. It was the one thing with Sophie, if ever Helen had another child, she would not treat her unfairly. That was so wrong, the very worst. Children knew. It doesnt matter if the injustice is to another, it is every bit as horrible. It was like that with Dad towards Brian, and it was horrible to see. Why did a parent do that? It so spoiled things. And Dad smiling to her as if she was on his side, and she wasnt; she wasnt on anybody's side; it just wasnt fair, and when she got older too

Brian was a good brother and she loved him. Her memories from childhood were fond. The photographs were there and there was nothing to say otherwise. He was so tall and she was so wee, he was the horse and he went galloping with her. She was up on his shoulders clinging on, oh clinging on because of how he galloped and the force threw her back and she had to hold on, hold on, gripping his forehead and him just laughing and galloping. My horsie; she shouted that.

Oh and she would not fall, she would never fall, he wouldnt let her.

There was nothing about his behaviour. If it ever crossed anybody's mind. If they ever thought anything. What could they think, it was just horrible, if it was his head or neck and her legs, just a little girl, that was all she was, if her legs were wrapped round him, that was nothing, it was just nothing, if ever people thought such a thing.

Unless Dad, if it was something with him but there was nothing with him. It was only the favouritism. She was her daddy's girl and Brian was a big boy. What was unusual about that? Would any dad be different? She was his girl; that was how he said it, You are my wee girl. And he called her 'jelly-belly'. Mum didnt like him saying it. Why not? 'Jellybelly'. What was wrong with it, 'jellybelly' like it was her fault, it wasnt her fault, how could it be, she didnt ask for it my God it was only fun, father to daughter. It wasnt rude, did Mum think it was rude?

There was a coldness in Mum. With Sophie too. There wasnt the sparkle when she phoned, not what you might expect from a grandmother. She hardly asked a question; what are you doing in school, have you got a best friend. Nothing like that. She was tough. Helen would never have been so tough, not on a child. Perhaps if it was a grandson Mum would have acted differently; she preferred boys, or seemed to.

Oh well, nothing could be done about that. Boys were supposed to get on with things and not bother. Perhaps that was it. If it was even true. Children are children. Sophie was quite girlish but why not if she was a girl? A girl was allowed to be a girl, my God, what do people want?

None of Helen's toys ever remained in Mum's house, not even as keepsakes. Although why else would they have been kept? For sentimental value? That was a joke, Mum and senti-mentality.

It was so unfair. What had she ever done? Nothing, except

wanting things to be nice. They were if people tried. People didnt try. Why didnt they? Helen could never understand that. Only if they tried, if people tried. Mum never tried.

It was so different for Mo with his cousins and uncles and aunties. Relations still wrote to his parents from Pakistan. They kept in touch with one another. Mo knew some of their names and could speak about them as if they were ordinary relations and they werent, he had never seen them. Even his father hadnt seen some of them. It was amazing and wonderful. And quite strange really. Helen had nothing like that, except the cousins in New Zealand and the pile of ones in Australia. She spoke to Mum about it but they were Dad's relations and Mum had lost their address, or didnt have it in the first place. It would have been nice to make the contact.

Helen wouldnt phone her about Brian. Not if it wasnt him: why raise her hopes? She should only be told if it was him for certain. It was so unlikely. All those years. Why had he not been in touch? You shouldnt act like that to your own family, your mother a widow. That was so selfish. If he did hold a grudge it was against Dad but Dad was dead. He knew Dad was dead. The police traced him and told him. He had the choice to go to the funeral; it was his decision not to. He came home for Grannie's. So it was a grudge. But not against the whole family, surely? That was so very foolish. And not normal. Helen was only twelve years old when he left home. It should have been *her* grudge to him! He never got in touch with her. Imagine that, his wee sister. Did he even know she was a mother! He couldnt have. Not unless Mum told him. He was Sophie's uncle for God sake surely that was something? That was like a miraculous thing, another human being. It *was* miraculous. Miraculous is miracle. A new human being in the world is a miracle. Surely a brother would want to know about that? His very own niece. Of course he would.

He had been a good brother to Helen and he would love Sophie. He would. It wasnt too much to say. This is the way brothers and sisters are. If ever they hate each other they love each other, they really do. Brian was quiet and went his own way but he would be tender. He had been. That was what Dad didnt understand. Dad was not tender, you wouldnt say it about him but you would about Brian.

Of course Helen would help him. Of course she would. Whatever his troubles were my God he was her brother, if times were hard for him; they knew about hard times, her and Mo. Perhaps Brian couldnt stay with them but they could help in other ways and they would, Helen would make sure of that.

Mo and Brian would get on well together. Mo was easygoing. Brian would like him and be so comfortable with him. Mo knew London like the back of his hand and would take him places.

If they had had more space; life would have been easier if they had – unless he slept on the kitchen floor. Because where else? Then Helen coming home in early morning and not able to sit, not able to have a cup of tea, and wee Sophie coming in in her underclothes. That would have been so awkward. Really, it would have been.

The flat was too small. That was the truth. Too easy to clutter, never mind Mo and the junk he brought home.

Although if it had been his family my God even a distant relative, a tenth cousin! There would be no question. People just appeared. That was Mo's childhood. You woke up in the morning and two uncles were in sleeping bags on the carpet. All for one one for all. It was a worthwhile attitude. Even if it wasnt family it was friends, arriving unannounced, no money and no place to go. It wouldnt have been one night for them. It would be for as long as it took. Of course it would. And if the person was in need, in genuine need, if he needed looking after, or just care, and attention.

Oh God.

Mum's flat in Glasgow would have been ideal. She had a spare room. It was a bedroom in the past but was now a workroom. She could move out the table and sewing machine. She used to have a folding bed sort of thing, a z-bed. Perhaps she still had it. Except Mum wasnt a hoarder; if things had no function she dumped them.

Mum would have changed the house for Brian. She would want to. She would be so glad to see him.

Although Helen could get a folding bed. She could. Mo would enjoy the hunt. Car-boot sales and secondhand shops, the old market they went to. Brian wouldnt have any money, not if he was living rough. An actual mattress was all they needed, and a sleeping bag or a duvet.

Oh God, why was he living rough! Unless he was ill and unable to fend for himself: people got trapped in vicious circles with government agencies, if you have no address they wont give you money, but you cant get an address until they give you money. It was appalling and obvious. Why did they not work it out? Surely they could work it out! People wandered around, ill, in need of care and attention and the government just oh my God why didnt people do something about it? if things were obvious, it was always obvious things, and everybody knew them, everybody, everybody knew yet nothing was done, it was horrible. Poor Brian.

Mo's family was straightforward, they seemed so. But only what she knew and what did she know? nothing. Did he tell her everything? Of course not. He didnt know himself. Nobody did. Nobody could. Because people didnt know everything. There were matters and events his parents and uncles and aunts wouldnt speak about, especially if the memories were

bad. If you went back two generations it became more complicated. It was the same with all families, unless you were rich,
there were things you didnt want to know and not if it was
Pakistan and India and these places where it was killings and all
that, people starving to death. Mo was going to go. His parents
hadnt been back for years but were saving to go again – one last
time, and Mo was going with them.

Helen wasnt. It was assumed she wasnt. She might have
liked to go, if it was only her, although not with Sophie. Even
the slightest risk. It would have been fine for herself but not a
little girl. If Mo had asked, but he hadnt. She still hadnt met his
parents. Oh well.

But the way it was portrayed, it could never have been as
bad as that: wars and bombs, suicides and assassinations and
the poverty and disease; religious fanatics everywhere all waving their fists at you; people just so angry, they were angry all
the time, why were they so angry? everybody was just so angry
it made you shudder seeing them and all millions of them; it
was America did it with their policies and how they didnt care
about people starving and dying but only their own wealth
and taking other people's resources, just stealing them really. It
was true. They stole everything and then were annoyed if you
told them to stop like how children behave. But Mo was prejudiced too because it was America so it had to be bad, him and
his mates, but if it was religion and men's attitudes my God
even walking down the street if it was over there, Pakistan or
wherever, what did he know about that? If you were a white
woman and just dressed ordinary then you were evil and no
better than a prostitute, men all looking at you and all their
hypocrisy, oh yes, they wanted you for sex and then called you
a prostitute, wanting to punish you and cover you up, it was so
shocking, they would put you in a sack, if you were a woman
my God if ever you did go there you would just be angry all the

54

time and if you went into the country and got lost, without any roads, not proper ones, or even in the city, a crowded street with market stalls and you could hardly move between people, all claustrophobic and you got separated. And if you were snatched. It happened. What if it was a little girl?

It would never have happened because Helen would never have taken her. That was the one thing. If Helen ever was to go it wouldnt be until Sophie had grown. Even then. Perhaps she would never take her at all.

Helen closed her eyes and rested back on the chair. She couldnt even sleep properly.

Then Mo's family too, what about them? Caught by a white woman. His mother said that, apparently. English woman was white woman. English woman with her own baby. They hadnt expected Mo to get *caught* by an English woman with her own baby which meant white woman with her own baby. 'Own baby'. Of course 'own baby'. Whose did they expect? It made you laugh if you didnt cry. Mo laughed. Helen didnt. She didnt cry either. It was just nothing. At one time it would have upset her. Now it didnt. Really, it didnt.

There was so much else. People's fights and feuds. It was silly nonsense. English woman. What did it matter? Scottish and English. Prejudice was everywhere. In casinos you met all nationalities under the sun but prejudice was there too, and hate, you saw hate. Then if you were white they expected you to be the same. You were prejudiced too. That was expected. They even winked at you when the person couldnt see. It was so so cowardly, and making you a coward too! Why bring you into it? If they want to be racist cowards they can be but why bring in other people? Just because you are white doesnt mean you are prejudiced. And the violence, always violence, wanting to hurt and kill. They were supposed to be Christians but didnt act like Christians.

That was the big joke for Mo because Christians, how do they act? meaning not good, meaning prejudiced; meaning that was the way they did act, in real life, them and the Jews, it was them that were prejudiced, even the Pope, if you heard what he said. Prejudice was everywhere and not under the surface. Every time you got on a bus; everywhere. But Mo's friends too. One time in the house she heard them about black people. She was in the company so what did it say about her? what they thought about her, to say it with her sitting there? It was so unforgivable. Helen couldnt believe her ears; a football match on television and the comments they made that were just like racist and horrible. Mo said it was a joke but it wasnt a joke, how could it be a joke it could not be a joke. If they were good men and went to the Mosque, what did it matter? and didnt smoke or drink, who cared about that? smoking or drinking, it was like eating fish, just silly, and then they abused people, other human beings. If that was Muslims and religion, my God, it was all just the same, Catholics and Protestants, it didnt stop the prejudice, they were all as bad, and her ex, just the same as him, hating people. She wanted away from it all, everything, from everything that was remotely like that, where you could bring up your children and be free from all of it; and the lies, she hated the lies; lies and falsity; pretending to be something they werent. That was people. It didnt matter where it came from, not if that was how they were and they hurt people; why did they hurt people? All the killings and murders and even babies, they didnt care if it was babies, and children, little boys and girls, you saw their smile, such innocence and like trust, trust, just believing what they would believe, little girls.

Oh God, where did her head go? Where did it not go. And Dad too, poor old Dad.

Why was she thinking of Dad? except if it was him and Brian, what went on with them. It was a mystery.

But she was glad Sophie was white. She had to say that because if she wasnt, if she was not white. It made things easier. She felt sorry for foreign people; immigrants and asylum seekers. Even before knowing Mo. At the same time it was an education. What if she hadnt met him? She was so lucky. He was different from the macho stuff, so different. He was gentle! He would hate her saying it but he was.

Oh why could she not sleep if she could only sleep! She couldnt. It didnt matter nights off and days off the only time she could sleep was when she wasnt supposed to, watching television or sitting down someplace, she did it in the cinema and in a restaurant too one time she nodded off and in company someone talking to her and trying to concentrate oh what was the woman saying what was she saying just trying to concentrate and losing it and her eyelids, drooping, drooping eyelids and you could not let them touch together and if they did they could not stay closed for long or you would be asleep and you could not it was so not polite and just not funny and she was trying so hard but only maybe a moment longer if she could only, her eyelids together and touching and that was her and she was oh then the voice breaking in Are you sleeping? Surely you arent sleeping!

And the person had been so annoyed my God instead of worrying if Helen was okay they took it personally, that they had been slighted; their conversation was so boring you fell asleep during it. Well perhaps it was. But no, it wasnt that and Helen had to say sorry. It was funny though. But bad manners, it was like bad manners. Dad wouldnt have minded her falling asleep, not like if she was tired and so so exhausted, he would have worried about her and how was she and how was her health, he would have worried about that, so if anything happened to her. Things did happen. It wasnt only foreign countries. The number of people who disappeared. What happened to them? Some were murdered and were found later. Some never were. Children too, they ran away from home and lived on the streets. Until they were old enough for a job, then they got a flat, if they could afford it, or shared in one, maybe rented a room, or a bed. People rented beds and shared them, one for nightshift one for dayshift, and it was the same bed. London was astronomical. People would be better elsewhere. They just preferred London, they could get by there and be safe, they felt safe, Mo said that, all different nationalities and colours, everything under the sun. But things did happen, horrible dreadful things.

Whatever time it was, she had to shift herself. But Mo wouldnt sleep in. She could rely on that. It didnt matter what else his alarm would go off and he would be out of bed. That was him thank God, above all else, that is what she wanted, somebody she could rely on, who would do what he said he would do; Mo was Mo and always that was him.

It was not cold. She pulled the coat to her chin.

Although it didnt matter. If she did sleep they would waken her. She wouldnt sleep, not now. But she had work to do anyway so that was good. Ironing and whatnot it was piling, it really was. Just so little space she needed space, space space space. And to make space she had to separate out the pile of clothes she had washed yesterday or the day before, whenever she had done it, the ironing and non-ironing pile, and put the next wash on and be ironing the ironing pile of Sophie's, it was all Sophie's, she had more clothes than Helen my God why shouldnt she, a little girl went through more and it was up to Mummy to see it right, Mummy Mummy, she was the one, she would do it, she could and she would; if she didnt sleep within ten minutes she was rising from this chair, even if she didnt sleep later, once they had left for school, she didnt always sleep, it didnt matter, she had too much to do. Even if she did fall asleep at the tables. But it would just be so funny if she did, and the customer was asking, Card please! And the dealer was snoring, oh my God that would just be so funny, the customer complaining to the Inspector: Oh I asked the dealer for a card and she was fast asleep!

Serve them right anyway with no homes to go to, in a casino at four o'clock in the morning gambling all their money and other people dont even have money, working six nights a week in restaurants and even that isnt enough. Mo needed another job during the day, three or four hours would do him. 10 a.m. until 2 p.m. was ideal. If he could, and he thought he could only he was resisting it because when would they see each other? He said they would never see each other.

So he had feelings for her!

Oh she knew he did. Only if he wasnt there she saw no one at all, not outside the casino. He had mates, he had family, she had nobody. Not in her home life, an actual conversation like with an adult, unless if she spoke to another mother at the school gate, when she was collecting Sophie. Mo had to be at the restaurant by 5 p.m. He was home by eleven thirty. This by special arrangement. He should have been there until one in the morning but the owners allowed it. He called them slave drivers but really they were friends and he did favours for them like when he worked up in Glasgow. A proper worker gets paid a wage, all I get is pocket money. Mo said that but he was kidding. It was through them also that they got Azizah. It was for her Mo had to be home by eleven thirty. She lived in the street round the corner so getting home was easy, but she was only fifteen years old and you couldnt be too careful.

Her parents had expected Mo to walk her home but how could he? Mo said he would be there and back in three minutes, but even three. A child in the home? Accidents everywhere. Anything could happen.

And what if it was to him it happened? People dont consider that. If he got knocked down crossing the street. Sophie wakes up and goes looking for him in the kitchen or like my God if she went downstairs and out. It was a nightmare. Gangs on the street. People got beat up, racists. Mo said not to worry about it but it was put upon her and she had to. She would have preferred not. But every time she stepped out the house. Mo laughed the first time she asked because every time you step out the house, if you include looks, that was the racism, every single time. Helen did include looks. Looks were horrible. Looks *pierced* your stomach. 'Pierced' was Mo's word. People stayed in their own place because of it. That was ghettoes, stay in your ghetto. Ghettoes sounded awful, that was Jews and Hitler. Stay in your own ghetto; so then you are safe. Mo told her. It was second nature to him. He remembered his mother cleaning beneath the front door because people shoved rubbish through the letterbox when she was wee, and excrement, and lighted newspapers to burn them alive, and people wouldnt care if it happened, little old ladies or boys and girls. Things happened and didnt get reported, only in the community, the community was strong. News travelled word of mouth. That was how you heard. It was a bit like neighbours, like how neighbours want to know your business, then everybody knows. But if you told the police it only got you in trouble; they asked *you* the questions so it was like you, you got the blame. Mo said that. They werent there to catch criminals, just control people, and that meant blacks and Asians or else asylum seekers, immigrants. But if these were crimes against people it was like criminals doing them so if they werent reported then they would get away with it, and keep doing the crimes. People had to stand up for things. That was what Helen thought and she told Mo, if you were too cynical, sometimes he was.

Even just talking to people. No wonder she worried. He was always talking to people, so if he met somebody and was chatting. Send him a message in the morning and he didnt come back till the afternoon. He couldnt have left Sophie for one minute never mind three. Azizah's grandfather came for her, he walked her home, when he could get away, because with him and Mo talking; Azizah had to drag him!

What was nice with Azizah was how Sophie liked her and became quite excited waiting for her to arrive. More excited than for her mother's departure! Oh well. But it was good she did.

Helen remembered being fifteen. People took advantage. They tried to anyway. Not everybody, Gary Thompson; he didnt try anything. Whatever happened to him? My God. Gary was just too young. Her first real boyfriend. He didnt try anything! He was so respectful, or he didnt know.

Some were too young and some were too old. And the in-between ones were the worst. They treated you like shit, they had no respect. You were not on any pedestal with them. The opposite. Did they even respect themselves? They start off okay then everything changes. People do change. Men especially. When had her ex changed? He didnt was the quick answer. He had all the arrogance going and was as selfish, so selfish, as selfish as anybody ever could be. My God, thinking about that, what she put up with, just so so – however could she have put up with it? She was at a 'low ebb', because she was at a *low ebb*. That was what Jill said. People put up with things at a low ebb. You have to get positive and then you dont put up with it, then you fight back. Yes, and that was what Helen did, and she managed it, and then Mo was there and like his support, she had that, and at the right time and that was so crucial, so so crucial. It didnt matter about her ex and the problems he had. Of course he had problems, everybody has problems. For her it was him. Not any longer.

Sophie still spoke about him, but not so often. She spoke about him to Mo. My dad this and my dad that. Mo only smiled, but it wasnt fair.

Children can be hurtful, even without knowing it, although sometimes they do, they do know it, they do things that are not good, like intentionally, a wee experiment. It made you shudder. Horror movies with children were the scariest. If you wanted to frighten people really and truly make children the evil-doers. They have the power; you know it as a child, you see the adult and you know you have it. Not all adults but some. You are the child but it is you with the power; you can make them do it, whatever it is, you get somebody a row, even like a smack; somebody gets smacked and it is you to blame. Nobody knows it, not even the one it happens to. Cats and cats' eyes, a cat's eyes looking at you. That is the knowing look, how a child looks at you.

Sophie would always want him. Mo said it, Your dad is your dad.

So that meant Helen too, she was stuck with him, her so-called 'ex'. Out of the blue it would come, and it would be him; one phone call. She could never escape, except if she emigrated, and that wasnt allowed, and would be unfair to Sophie. Even if he was a shit, none of it mattered for her. A special bond for daughters. Were mothers and sons the same? Yes! Mum and Brian!

Imagine a son. Helen couldnt. Except it would be beautiful. In what way she had no idea except that it would, and be beautiful. She didnt know how, she was tired and wanted to sleep. She needed to sleep, her body needed it. She was used to nightshift but she had to have it, she did. Shift workers need to rest. Doctors spoke about it. They didnt get enough sleep. Life becomes unbalanced, the social side of it. Shift workers were at the lower end; everything was geared to the 9 to 5s. Other folk had problems but not them. And then your children, how they had to go to school and school hours were school hours, and if you were trying to keep your head above water, trying to work, and your partner, and the hours you worked, it was a long shift, and also how you had to look, if you were a woman, it was just so time-consuming, everything, time time time, and if you had a family, what time did you have? None, none none none.

Oh God.

A fit of the yawns, all she did was yawn, even in work. That was nightshift. You would think she was used to it by now, and she was used to it, but still the difficulty. You werent supposed to yawn at the tables. That was frowned upon. In one casino the Inspector gave wee warnings about it. He was French and very irritable, things got to him and they shouldnt have, being an Inspector; Inspectors should be cool and laid back. Not him. He intimidated people, males especially, and him being gay, but he still intimidated them. If people thought he might not be tough because he was gay, oh well, they were wrong. But he wasnt kind either. If you thought somebody would be kind because they were gay; he wasnt. He didnt care about your domestic troubles. It was so irritating about him; you tried to explain something and he didnt listen, only sighed and looked away, shaking his head and seeing his watch, exaggerating his actions so you would stop talking. Oh the French are like that. People said this but not Helen, she liked their voices. It was his bad manners, and so lacking in respect. That is what bad manners are, disrespect. And if it was men to women. Men had these irritating habits and not listening to you was the worst. Why did they do it? They did not listen. Even Mo, if you were explaining about something, he came in and spoke, and what he said hardly related to what you were saying; it was so aggravating. Her ex didnt even pretend, he just looked at you so to shut you up, that was that, you werent to speak. Seen and not heard, that was him to women like they were all stupid, you were a stupid woman.

He denigrated people. Such arrogance.

And somebody else's problem. But still hers, he would always be hers. You saw it with Sophie. The phone call would come and she would go. He took her places and she enjoyed it. Helen would have known if she hadnt, the slightest thing and she would, slightest slightest thing my God she was only a child, what did she know? nothing, although she thought she did. That was girls. They thought they knew everything like at six years of age, it would be funny if it wasnt so dangerous. Girls might think it about men but it is wrong. Your life is not your own. You think it is and it isnt, not for girls. Nothing ever would be a surprise, not about men – males, because boys too. When they hold you down and open your legs and if it is not rape, or is it? yes, yes it is rape.

People had bits of you. Helen read a novel about a woman that was a journalist. She was just a young woman but quite famous in her own right because of her adventures. Some of it was fanciful but it was interesting too. Helen could recognise things and identify with her, especially how people clung to you. Oh but she was very different to Helen. Helen hadnt done anything with her life, not of interest to other people. Only ordinary stuff. Ordinary stuff weighed you down and like how you couldnt get moving, you couldnt, you were trapped and all of these adventures, whatever they were, whatever, what she was thinking, what was she thinking? Even the day, she didnt know the day. She didnt know anything. What did she know? She was a fool. Not at school she wasnt. Friends thought she was brainy. Her dad did, he said he did. Mum didnt. Did she? Perhaps she did. Her ex didnt but he was just absurd, so absurd, just like an absurd person. So different from Mo, one of those people who take; they take bits of you and just like what is it they want?

Everything. If you didnt have enough sleep. Who would give you that? She needed to sleep. Doze doze doze. She needed more than doze doze doze.

Even Sophie. It was her life now. It made you sad but relieved as well. Imagine living forever. My God.

All these people whose lives were alongside yours. They surrounded you. It was not suffocating. They existed alongside. You didnt know they were there and you didnt see them but there they were. They had their hopes and their dreams and good and bad all happening and they went away and led their own lives, perhaps in different cities, different countries; their lives were so faraway from your own and yet there were ripples. Look at Brian. It was just so amazing that he should have been there at that exact spot when she was in that exact taxi at that exact moment in time. If they had been one minute earlier at that junction: one minute! My God, it was so extraordinary.

And it was Caroline caused it. Imagine that, how another person, something just nonsensical. But it was. She wasted so much time in front of the mirror. Otherwise they would have saved five minutes. If it had only been Helen and Jill none of it would have happened. The taxi would have been long gone without Caroline, they wouldnt have been at the traffic lights, they wouldnt have been there, they wouldnt have seen them, it would just have been like nothing, nothing at all, none of it would have happened.

So amazing, so so amazing. Of all people. It couldnt have been otherwise. Nothing was predictable but it could never have been anyone else because life, like how amazing it is, it truly is, how some things are meant to be. The one man in the world, in the middle of millions. How could it be Brian? but it was, of course it was.

Although better if it had been Glasgow. Glasgow would have been easier. London was – what was London? Big. So big. So many places. People can hide; people hide in London. They hide. If Brian was wanting to hide. Why would he have wanted to hide?

Oh but she would have handled it better in Glasgow, it would have been so much easier, so very much my God and so so good to see him, just so good. London was awkward. Nothing was straightforward. If he was on the street living rough. Why was he?

All these years not communicating, it was inexcusable, his own father's funeral. Oh God. Her tummy. She was not going to cry. She might feel like it but she wasnt going to. What was sadder than that? The world. Nothing was sadder, it was just the saddest.

The photographs on the floor. And Dad there, how he was standing with the posture; that was his posture, and that was his smile. She reached to lift the photograph. She studied it. Of course she knew him although he looked different. He was her father, her own one. What was he? Now that he was dead, poor Dad.

Matters she hadnt thought about for so long. But that shouting, why did he shout? he always had to shout. Men shout, why do they shout?

When Mo spoke about his father it was true affection. That was the difference. He called him 'the old man'. Civil wars and assassinations, friends and family divided and lost. That was what they went through. Their lives had been so tough and their families before them when it was just as bad and even worse when it was all India, that was the worst of all, and it was like England's fault although when Mo said England he meant Britain, so it was Scotland's fault the same as England. English Imperial was British Imperial. Scotland was part of England. Foreigners thought it too. The only ones who didnt were Scottish. Dad used to go on about that, if he thought people were insulting Scotland he got annoyed. Helen didnt care, except in a small way. Others did and that was up to them, if they were proud of Scotland. Even Mo thought that and it was so patronising. He wasnt proud of England. Not Pakistan either. He didnt come from there so why should he have been proud of it? He liked Scotland. Scotch people are proud. He said that. But what did it mean? People arent whisky, if he thought Scotland was so good why didnt he go back? He could get nationalised. Helen would send him a postcard. She met some across the tables. They heard her accent and it was like they expected her to cheat for them, to deal them aces or bust the bank on their behalf. So stupid, then asking her personal questions like in front of everybody as if they shared something and other people didnt. She didnt want to share anything, not with them. Where are you from and what team do you support, meaning religion, Rangers or Celtic. A joke but not a joke. A joke for other people. She preferred not meeting them.

She didnt care about any of it, only her family, and her family was Sophie. And Mo. Yes. Mo was part of it. Mum wasnt. Of course she was. But she wasnt. Helen was part of Mum's family but Mum was not part of hers. The same for Brian. Or not, perhaps not. Brian could be part of hers. Of course he could. He was her brother so he had the choice, if he wanted to be a good brother and a good uncle. It was up to him, if the bad feeling had gone. There was no reason to keep anything going, whatever it was. How long does it last? People's lives ruined. Their own most of all, the ones that keep it going, so they disappear, they are the ones to suffer.

Bitterness haunts people. Why let it? Life is unfair. Of course. Everybody knows that. Events are distorted. You saw it at the tables; poor people and rich people and out on the street you had beggars and prostitutes and ill people who should have been in hospitals but couldnt get in because there were no beds; people with severe mental problems having to walk the street, it was appalling. They should have been hospitalised and werent. It was an absolute scandal. But life was full of scandals.

People waited for things. In her life too. Waiting for tea. The kettle took so long to boil. It was old, it was old. She didnt care. In a way she did but not much. Who had money these days? only rich people. Helen's wage got them by. Mo didnt earn enough and worried about mortgages and getting into debt, however would they survive. Helen didnt. At one time she might have. Not now. It was only what it meant in the home. They didnt lack important things. It was what you were used to. If it worked it worked; the kettle worked, it just took a while. Mo was good at finding stuff but like some of it was junk, useless, from secondhand shops, horrible old smelly places. She didnt want that sort of stuff. If it was her *own* house never, never. He did things for the best but he was not in charge, not if it was like her own place really and truly.

How different their relationship was, thinking about her ex. And if it was dads, imagine dads; they were men you had about the house and brought you up; you had fun with dads, they showed you things and took you places. That was Mo. *He* was Sophie's dad. *He* was the one she would remember. Not the other one; he didnt deserve a daughter's love, because that is what it was, love; a child gave love to a parent, so if you deserved it and were worthy of it. You had to be. You could not break that trust. Never ever. Never.

My God she was so lucky; so so lucky.

But it was true. How had it happened? You say these things and think it silly and just foolish wishful thinking nonsense, but then if it isnt, if it really is happening. And it was. Helen's life *had* changed. Things had been so wrong. There was no way ahead. There didnt seem to be. That didnt mean there wasnt. It only seemed that way. To you it did but other people were there, were all around, and they did it in their own individual ways, and those affected you. Even although you were unaware. Mo thought about her, even when she wasnt there. Okay smelly old places like the very worst but if he brought home something for her? then it was for her he brought it, so he was thinking of her, even there in that horrible old place.

She was not going back to Glasgow. Never. Although if she hadnt been there she wouldnt have met Mo. So good things did happen there, and happened to her. She was just ordinary. There was good and bad. Both happened and happened to everybody and she was the same. Only she was silly, so silly. Sometimes she was.

She did like him. Only it was so awkward because with the situation, the three of them in the same room, because that is all it was, with a walk-in cupboard. It was 'magnificent'. That was his word because in Glasgow he had to share a room with four other men, all their noises and sounds and everything, snoring and the rest. So he said. You couldnt always believe him.

Oh but he was sanity Mo was sanity, he was just sanity, that was Mo. It wasnt love at first sight. For him it was, so he said, and he had chased her. Of course he had, a small Asian chap, how else would he have got her?

She wished he hadnt said that. It was him joking. He always joked; a joke for everything.

Men were different. People said that and it was true. And you could never be true friends, not for everything. Everything meant everything. Mo was good but there were things he didnt see. That was strange, how he didnt. Men didnt, they didnt see things. It was something to remember.

Even how he didnt see one of his workmates who was looking at Helen. She caught the guy doing it. And he was happy she had because he was making it known. This older man, a little smile on his face, wondering what his own chances were. If you want a man here I am. That was him. He thought she was 'easy'. English woman white woman, the usual, but so offensive, so very offensive. The oglers, Muslim men any men, they dont even know they are doing it, like in the casino, you cannot hide in the casino, not if you are a dealer; you are there at the table and if they look they look, if they want to look, they just look, and you cant do anything. What did they think she was a naïve wee girl? Ha ha to that.

On holiday to Spain when Sophie was two years old, her and her ex that last time together, girls sunbathing topless at the hotel pool, just stretching out. Mainly English or German or from Holland, not Scottish. Helen and her ex were friendly with one couple like from Reading in England, at the poolside and chatting together, and her boobs my God, the other girl being topless like that, it was funny, and trying not to see them. And her ex: I didnt even notice them! That was him, liar, I didnt notice them it was just so natural, going on and on about how it was so good and so natural to see women like that, just relaxing how nature intended and not worrying about men being there because it is all so so natural if people only relaxed, why dont people relax? liar.

The usual, criticism. Why did she have to be different? Why did she have to cover up? But she didnt cover up. He didnt understand. He didnt know to understand. What did it matter about boobs? He didnt know about anything. It was only him showing off. It was men wanted it. The women all do what

70

they are told, and their bodies, look, look at them. There is my girlfriend there and her tits, look, she doesnt care, she is just so relaxed about her body, and me too, if she is there and guys look at her, what do I care because she is mine and nobody else's; lay a finger on her and you are dead. And uninhibited too, that is her in bed, and I just stick it in and she will do anything if I want her to she will do it. For me only, if I tell her. I dont care if you look because it is me, she does it for me, it is just me; me me me, the men all smiling together oh so mature, these men who really are boys, little boys and all their egos, the women belong to them, all naked and helpless.

It made her shudder, and angry too.

But it was how they acted, wanting their women to be naked. Because that is them helpless. What can they do? nothing, they are helpless, they are naked, just there and nothing, the men all smiling, oh it is the women, they are just stupid, and the men talking about something else, football, because *they* arent naked and showing *their* little things in front of everybody, oh no, they are too scared. Helen could laugh at that. Women would laugh. They would. And the men would hate that, they would lose their temper, being laughed at, and women would laugh at them. Helen would, she just would snigger. It was something to snigger about. Men. What else, nothing.

She could get so angry. She wished she didnt; if she could stop it, she couldnt. It welled inside her and would explode. Did women explode: women didnt explode. If one touched her, and they did, touching her, imagine touching her, cheek of them, she would kill them if she had a knife, touching her, who did they think, who they were, who were they, and rapes, just rapes, my God, and just little girls, that was men. And abusers. It was ones her age. Men who were boys. But if it was men that were adults. She could hate them all.

71

And if they were looking, if they really were looking and it was you in front of them and her ex there seeing. What would he do? If he could cope with that, he couldnt. If it was her ex, if he saw Helen and she was naked in front of other men and all were looking at her, they all were just seeing her there, just lying, and she was naked. What would he do?

Oh my God. It was just so funny.

But not stretching. If you stretched. The girl on holiday never stretched and her shoulders tightly together – Brenda, she could not relax. That was a plain name, Brenda, she didnt think of a Brenda. Did she ever relax? stretching. Helen could stretch. She could. Who else could? Not everybody. She didnt think so. If women spoke together she didnt hear one saying it, stretching. Helen could smile about that. Oh I stretched in front of him. Who else would say it?

Stretching means relaxed, and your whole body. Lying flat on top of the bed, naked, and stretching. It could be done and she had done it and like a man there and watching, she had closed her eyes. She could close her eyes. He was there and she didnt hardly know him. Oh she did. But she didnt. Yet she had done it, and he was there, she had closed her eyes, and was stretching out her body, oh my God people take chances. But she hadnt. She knew enough about him.

He was not controlling her. He didnt have that power. He could have had women to control, but was not controlling her.

Oh but he enjoyed seeing her and if he touched her, Mr Adams only touched her, stroking. She hadnt told Ann Marie that bit so like nobody knew, and never would, nobody, because he would never have spoken about her. He was an adult man and not a boy. Boys would tell each other, that was boys, then coming to your door and asking whoever, your mum, even your mum, oh Helen, is she coming out to play? My God, that was boys, Helen heard them at the door but wouldnt answer.

Men had no idea. They only *saw* you like a body, like imagine shagging her, oh my, sticking it in, it didnt matter anything else. If ever her ex had found out my God he would have killed Mo. He saw her as worrying all the time, worrying over nothing. What you worrying about? there is nothing to worry about. He thought he knew but he didnt. Although she *was* a worrier what woman wasnt? What mother wasnt? Mo had no idea the risks they were taking just chatting together. That was why London, thank God, never having to think of him.

And so false! Of all people. He would have been falling over himself to see that girl. That was the way he was. It was so false, so false. He always looked. He wouldnt have cared less if Helen had seen him, it was only for the other guy's benefit that he even pretended, because he was so cool, so so cool, if other men were there. That was her ex at the poolside, him and that girl's boyfriend, talking and not looking. Oh yes, so mature, so so mature like how they could just chat together drinking their beer and smoking a cigarette, with everything so normal except it wasnt because his girlfriend lying there and with her bare boobs, my God, wasnt he just so cool and mature! A chronic show-off, that was him, like an addiction. Because really he was drooling. It was so funny to see, drinking his beer and talking to that guy and he never ever looked. Of all people. Ha ha, liar.

You had to face things in this life. You could try hiding but sooner or later. If you didnt you still had it to face. That was something Helen had learned. Nobody taught her. Things dont go away, if they are there they are there and always will be there until you do something about it. Because if you dont. It haunts you if you dont.

There was nothing wrong with her memory. If anything the opposite. Details were too clear. Although you had to stop dwelling on details. It made things go wrong. Mo said that and he was right. It led to the bad side of life, as if it was all she could see and it wasnt, it really wasnt. She just had to put it behind her except to put it behind her meant putting it from her mind, Brian and the other one, the one with the limp, she didnt like him.

Anyway, it was Brian's decision. He went away and never came back. What were people supposed to do? go and look for you? That was fantasy. If you thought they would. You make your bed and sleep in it. That is what happens in this life. People are not going to come running. Did he think they were! He was never practical. Practical. Helen had forgotten that one like when Mum made excuses for him to Dad, Oh the boy isnt 'practical'. If he had made a mistake or done something silly and Dad was giving him a row. Oh Dad, he just isnt 'practical'.

Mum protected him. She didnt protect Helen. That was funny. Not protecting your daughter. She protected Brian but not her; protected the male but not the female. It was not usual. And if there is an imbalance in the affections, parents correct this, they try to. If one child is likeable and the other isnt. Dad favoured her. He did. Of course he did. But it wasnt her fault. If anybody thought it was. Brian thought Mum was wonderful: she was not wonderful. That was one thing she wasnt. Of course Helen had done things. Yes and would never deny it. Everybody does things. It has a name: 'being young'. Nobody is interested. Nobody cares. Why should they? It is just people's lives. Nobody can keep track. Everything goes on with everybody and everybody doing everything. That is life and it is all around. She didnt have one of those extended families with all cousins together. She didnt have that and didnt want it. She had what she had and was content, and the future too, saving for that.

And once they had they would see how things were, if they

could find a place of their own, but if not, even just if they were okay and surviving.

People want to survive, they cling on. Some by doing nothing, they go numb and their whole body freezes, they lie there and it is like a lizard and its body, a body and not a body, a suit of armour; a *hide*, it shields you and they cant get you. Going numb. People go numb beneath the threat of violence. Violence is everywhere and in all walks of life, not only the 'working class'. It sounded different how Jill said it, 'working class'. They were talking one night during the break. Somebody had made a silly statement and Jill spoke up. Others looked at her. It was because she had the posh voice. But if she was posh here she was on her own. She didnt have any man and she had the same job as them. She was escaping too. People escape.

The kitchen door had opened. Sophie was there. She was in her nightdress, standing almost without movement, staring into her mother's eyes, hand to her forehead as though testing her temperature. A moment passed. Helen smiled. You are so cheeky!

Sophie continued staring. Helen touched her hand. Dont worry.

Well why are you sitting here? I've been standing for ages and you didnt wake up, why are you not in bed? I've been looking at you!

Oh you have have you! I should tickle you.

But I was only waiting for you to wake up.

I was not sleeping.

Yes you were.

Helen smiled. I should tickle you all the same! That is so so cheeky!

I didnt mean to wake you.

I'm just tired honey. Do you know what I feel like? I've been trampled by an elephant. I'm not kidding.

Yes you are.

It was a big fat elephant with massive tusks!

No it wasnt.

It was, it really was.

You're just a fibber!

Huh! Oh – what a thing to say about your mum! Helen squeezed her arm and Sophie laughed.

Oh Mummy will you take me to school? You never do!

Pardon!

But you never!

I do when I'm not working!

Oh you're always working.

I'm not, no I'm not.

It's only Mo takes me.

I thought you liked going with Mo!

I want you. Will you? Please?

Oh love I cant, I have to go to bed! I'm just so horrible and sweaty.

Sophie was watching her. Helen widened her eyelids to appear menacing. Sophie smiled cautiously. Now Helen waved her hands in a circular fashion near to Sophie's eyes as though to hypnotise her, and she adopted the voice of a robot: Whyy did you wayyyken meee uhhhp?

Sophie laughed, jumping back the way.

Ssh, dont thump, said Helen, and resumed the robotic inflection: Ye-es youou diiid wayyyken meee uhhhp.

Oh but Mummy I didnt mean to. Sophie had stopped laughing and was almost scared. I didnt, she said, I really didnt! Oh Mum, I really didnt.

Helen took her by the hand. I'm joking.

I dont like it when you are.

But it's only for fun.

I dont like it.

Helen sat back down on the kitchen chair. It's not that bad, she said, dont take it so seriously.

I didnt mean to wake you up.

I know you didnt.

Honest Mum.

I know! Helen clapped her on the shoulder. Dont be so worried all the time! You are a wee worrier!

No I'm not!

Yes you are!

Sophie laughed, tried to squeeze in beside Helen on the chair but there wasnt the space, so moved to lie against her, slouching. She put her arms round Helen's neck, cuddling her cheek to cheek then forehead to forehead. Helen's eyes were closed. Oh thank you young lady, she said.

Why are you still wearing your coat?

Never you mind.

Why are you not in bed?

I am too tired.

No you arent.

I am. You're making it worse.

What's all them? said Sophie, pointing at the photographs. Most had been tidied and stacked together. She lifted one, of Helen's mother and father. Sophie studied it: Is it my grannie?

Your grandpa too.

My grandpa?

You know he's your grandpa. Helen yawned. I've told you before.

Is he not feeling well?

You're just being funny, said Helen.

I'm not.

Yes you are.

Sophie laid down the photograph and turned in the direction

of the door. If you're so sleepy you should go to bed, she said, if you are; if you are you should.

You, my girl, are cheeky.

Well Mum you always yawn.

Helen smiled. So did Azizah read you a story?

No.

No?

She just read her own book.

Aw.

She said sorry because she forgot.

That was nice of her.

Sophie didnt respond.

Helen glanced to the door. Where's Mr Noisy?

The girl still didnt respond, distracted by the photographs, or so pretending. More likely she was ignoring Helen. This was becoming a habit. She did it even more to Mo. It wasnt nice. Some adults would have been hurt. Among younger children it was acceptable but Sophie was too old. Helen remembered the way she and other kids had played together at nursery; 'together' was the wrong word, they were only in the same room. They were each on their own, playing their own individual games. That was the way they were. They didnt have any community spirit at all. They didnt. They werent born with any. Rather the reverse, they were selfish, they told tales about each other. It was true. Children were deceitful, they didnt care about each other. People liked to think otherwise but that was the reality. They were only interested in themselves, in getting their own way, twisting adults round their little fingers. Sophie was guilty of that, just like everybody else. If she had a little friend and Helen asked about her, Sophie acted as though she didnt know who she was or what Helen was even talking about. It was quite sad really, in a way. They called childhood a happy time but was it? Perhaps for some. Not so much for others.

Now she was about to lift the photographs, all the photo-graphs, all at the same time, pushing and pulling them for God sake Sophie! Sophie stop that!

Sophie looked at her.

Helen glared at her. Stop that, stop being so silly.

I'm not being silly.

You are.

I'm not. Sophie continued with the photographs but more carefully.

Helen reached to place her hand on the girl's wrist. Dont do it like that, she said, you'll bend them.

It was only to see this one, said Sophie.

Helen sighed. The girl was pointing to one with Helen and Brian, the same one Helen had been looking at earlier.

It wasnt strange; not really. Helen had been roughly the same age as the girl when it was taken. That's my big brother, she said.

Your big brother?

Yes! Helen chuckled.

Oh Mummy!

Do you like him?

Yes, said Sophie.

I showed it to you before.

No you didnt.

I did. You just dont remember.

Sophie grinned. You're holding hands, he's your boyfriend.

Cheeky.

You are! Sophie gripped the photograph, holding it more closely to her eyes.

Careful, said Helen.

But I just want to see.

Well you wont if you hold it too near.

You're holding hands.

Of course, he's my big brother.

Helen and Sophie continued to study the photograph. Helen *was* holding Brian's hand but he was holding hers too, you could see it, he was as self-conscious as ever but at the same time he looked pleased. They both did; it was in their smile that they were pleased with each other, and so pleased to be holding hands. This is what was nice.

Yet they never would have done it had they not been forced. Boys dont like holding hands and look for any excuse not to. Although fourteen years of age, Brian was fourteen years of age when this one was taken so he was not a child.

But girls dont like it either. They wont hold hands with boys at all unless they have to. But if they have to. If they have to they enjoy it, if the boys dont laugh, if they dont make a fool of you. If they dont. But some boys enjoy it, if they are forced to do it, they do it then, and they enjoy it, even if they pretend not to. Girls are the same.

My God she looked so happy in the photograph! Brian too. At least he seemed to be. Who took it? Dad? You wouldnt have expected it to be. But it must have been. Because who else? Mum didnt take photographs. Dad must have taken it.

Why do people not take photographs? Mum pretended she didnt know how to. It was nonsense. Mum was sharp, the sharpest; sharper than Dad. Why do women not do things? Because they arent allowed, it isnt encouraged; the same with her ex who did everything. He didnt want her to do anything. She used to like it and think he was a gentleman but he was just a control freak. Perhaps that was Dad. Although Mum was strong, very, she was. Helen was not; not with her ex. Although she was with Dad. Mum said that anyway, twisted him round her wee finger. Mum said that was how Helen *had* him, twisted round her finger. Not a nice thing to say about a child. They arent adults and shouldnt be treated as such. If Mum was critical then it should have been to a child she was critical but not like the child was an adult.

Sophie was speaking. Helen didnt answer. Sophie waited, then said: Is this you?

Pardon? Helen squinted at the photograph. It was the same one. What was she talking about? Of course it's me, she said, as well you know.

I thought it was another girl.

Oh did you!

Mummy I'm honest, that's honest. It is! Sophie pointed again: Who is he?

But you know who he is he's your Uncle Brian, he's my big brother.

Sophie frowned, slightly baffled. My Uncle Brian?

Yes, your uncle, my brother.

My God!

You've not to say my God.

But he's your big brother?

Of course. So he is your uncle. Your Uncle Brian is my brother Brian. My brother is your uncle.

Sophie was watching her.

He is your uncle because you are my wee girl and I'm your mum.

Sophie frowned. I wish I had a big brother.

But I told you before who he was.

But Mum what is his name?

Helen looked at her. I've just told you his name for goodness sake his name is Brian!

Could he be my big brother?

What a question. But she seemed in earnest. He is your Uncle Brian, said Helen, wagging her right forefinger. And he is my brother Brian. He cannot be your brother because he is mine, so dont be so smart, you cant have him as a brother if he is mine!

Sophie grinned. They each took a corner edge of the photograph, peering closely, but Sophie gripped her edge tightly; almost clinging onto it and making it bend yet again for goodness sake Sophie!

She let go the photograph at once, lifted another from the pile. Helen stared at her but the girl didnt react. So that was it again. And she wouldnt apologise either. She never did. Not unless forced. It was aggravating. You felt like smacking her and how could you? you couldnt, it was horrible. The very fact it crossed your mind was horrible. One of the nursery women used to smack the children's wrists. The parents turned a blind eye or like pretended there was nothing wrong. It was mainly boys she did it to. If it had happened to Sophie Helen would have complained.

Of course he was the biggest child of all. He never apologised, not for anything. If Sophie had inherited her father's way of acting, that would have been the absolute worst. Surely bad behaviour was not genetic? It had to be learned from other people; not passed between the generations. My God, it was so unfair if it was. Imagine a child having to go through life under that burden. It made you wonder about childish behaviour in adults, if it was genetic. Her ex in one corner, her mum in the other. Everybody else having to put up with it.

Helen looked again at the photograph of herself and Brian. It *was* quite special. She hadnt realised that before. It was really quite in a way *wonderful*. It was! A record of childhood. Yes they were pleased, with themselves, pleased with each other. It was not smug. It was because really they so liked each other. They did and it was there how they held hands together. A brother and sister. Brian's love for her. You could see it. Just like how Helen the girl trusted him, my God she did, it was so true: he *was* her big brother. It was in that sense of trust, how you trust someone in your own family, a male, you trust him, she trusted him.

That wasnt Brian at the traffic lights, with the big beard and all dirty looking. Brian was never dirty looking he was lovely, a lovely boy. He was. It was not silly saying so, a beautiful lovely brother. People would think it silly but it wasnt. She didnt care anyway what they thought. Why should she? People say what they like and think what they like, and always will. It didnt matter about her or anybody else, they said what they wanted to say and thought whatever they wanted. Nobody would stop them from that. That was life; real life; not fantasy. Helen sighed. Sophie was tugging at her coat. Oh Mum see this one! Mum, see this one?

What?

Who is this?

No.

Sophie continued the tugging.

Sophie!

But who is it?

I dont know because I'm not looking. Helen held onto the other, and the question who took it? who took the photograph? Dad. Twenty-five years ago. It must have been, my God – Sophie, stop pulling my sleeve!

But Mummy!

No.

Oh but

No, there's no time, you have to get ready. Come on. Oh my God look at the clock, you should have your clothes on by now! Hurry up! Hurry up hurry up! Helen sprang from the chair and chased the girl across the floor, spanking her on the bottom when in striking distance, the pair of them laughed their way out the kitchen.

★

Mo was in the bathroom, side on to the door. The space was so cramped there was hardly room for a washhand basin never mind the shower but there it was and so snug the way the man had fitted it; such a pleasure. Less than a month in the flat and Mo had arranged for a shower unit to be fitted. She didnt think he would have been able to get anybody but he had; and he did wee bits to help the man. He was good at do-it-yourself, even if she laughed at him and was critical too, he was good at it.

Mo was watching her in the mirror, warily.

Honestly, she said, you are such a genius, and I'm not being sarcastic.

Mo squinted at her, then looked a question to Sophie who didnt respond. Mo shuffled back the way to get a better look at Helen. And where are you going? All dressed up like that, you are going somewhere, where? that is the question.

I fell asleep.

Mo called to Sophie. Too tired to go to bed, that's her.

I sat down in the chair and dozed, said Helen.

A hard night at the cards eh! Mo studied her then kissed her on the nose. You take it easy girl, you look knackered.

So do you.

You look very knackered.

Helen smiled.

Go to bed.

I shall do.

Take off your coat first.

Nag nag.

You're a nag to me! called Sophie.

Oh I'm not, not like Mr Noisy, he nags me all the time.

Hey, you were snoring when I looked in!

I dont remember you looking in.

Of course not, you were snoring. Mo gestured to Sophie,

jerking his thumb at Helen. You mum is the only woman in the world who snores when she's awake.

Dont say that about my mum. It's not fair to say it.

Helen said, Oh Sophie, he didnt mean it.

Well it's not very fair.

He's only pretending.

You were not snoring.

Yes she was, said Mo. She is the biggest snorer in the whole house.

No she isnt, shouted Sophie and she turned from him.

Mo and Helen exchanged looks, Mo smiling and Helen sighing. He doesnt mean it, she said.

Mo was about to comment but Helen held her right fore-finger to her lips to shush him.

Well it's not fair to say, continued Sophie.

I bet you my mouth was open anyway.

It wasnt.

Mo grinned at Helen: You are such a paragon!

No she's not, said Sophie and strode out of the bathroom.

Oh huffy, called Helen.

I am not huffy, shouted Sophie.

Sorry, whispered Mo.

It's not your fault.

She thought I was insulting you.

You were!

Mo put his arm round her shoulders. Sophie had returned and was watching them. Girls are not boys! she said, then walked off again.

What does she mean? said Mo quietly. I dont know what she means.

Just what she says, girls are not boys. Helen stepped back from him.

It's like a crossword puzzle.

Helen held her forefinger to her lips again and indicated she was going after Sophie. She found her in the front room sitting on a chair between the double bed and the window. Helen waited a moment before saying, Oh come on love.

Sophie didnt look at her. After a moment she said, Why does he call me Soapy?

Dont be so huffy.

I'm not being huffy.

You have to get dressed.

I dont want to, I want to stay with you.

Get dressed.

Sophie stared out the window. Helen sighed. You know what my dad called me?

Jellybelly.

It's worse than Soapy.

Mum it isnt.

Yes it is.

No it isnt.

I dont want to go to school.

Oh for God sake Sophie come on, I dont have time for this.

I'm not wearing these leggings again.

What leggings again, I'm not saying anything about leggings again. Helen frowned when Sophie pointed behind to a pair draped on the handle of the walk-in cupboard door. I'm not telling you to wear them.

Well why did you?

Why did I what?

If you left them out?

I didnt leave them out!

Well why are they there?

I dont know why they're there, what do you mean?

They were just there, said Sophie. So if you put them.

I didnt put them, dont be silly.

86

I'm not being silly, if they were there.

Helen shut her eyes. She heard Sophie get up from the chair. She had gone to lift the leggings. Helen shook her head.

Sophie lifted and dropped them onto the floor then went to her small chest-of-drawers. She stood there without opening a drawer, glancing back to Helen. Helen pointed at the leggings: Pick them up.

But why were they there?

Pick them up.

But why were they?

Now you are being silly, that is just silly to say. Helen was glaring at her, then she sighed. Oh Sophie, you're not crying are you?

I hate you not being here. I hate it hate it. The girl had raised both hands to cover her eyes. Not enough to conceal the crying completely. It was almost comical, but it wasnt. Helen stepped to her, touched her on the left wrist and whispered: You're not crying are you?

Oh Mummy.

Dont cry.

I'm not.

But now she really was, and her face red with it, and her nose, poor wee thing. Helen took her in her arms and cuddled her.

One and a half minutes! called Mo from outside the room.

Sophie's crying was unabated, breaking her heart it was so real, just completely real. You could tell when she was acting. This wasnt it. Now you'll have to wash your face, whispered Helen.

Oh Mummy.

And get your clothes on you need to get your clothes on!

The crying continued. There was a box of tissues. Helen extracted two and dabbed round the girl's eyes, kissed her on the tip of the nose. Sophie was trying to laugh the wee soul, it was so tough for her, it just was so tough.

I dont want him coming in if I'm dressing.

He doesnt.

Well I dont want him to.

But he doesnt.

I dont want him to.

Yes but he doesnt.

Sophie had left the chair and was searching for clothes inside a drawer. Sometimes he does, she muttered.

No he doesnt, not unless he doesnt mean to, if he doesnt know.

Sophie ignored her, concentrating on the clothes inside the drawer, but she began dressing. Everything is all upside down, she said.

Helen watched her. Eventually Sophie glanced across. Helen said, I'm just watching you.

I dont like you to.

Well I'm going to Sophie, I'm your mother.

But I dont like you watching me, and if Azizah does it.

Azizah is there to help.

Sophie sighed.

One and a quarter minutes! called Mo.

Again Sophie sighed, but at least she was moving, spreading three blouses out on the side of the bed to compare. She did this methodically, yet in a self-conscious, defensive manner. Helen moved to the doorway. I'll get your breakfast, she said. What do you want? What do you want to eat?

Sophie didnt reply.

What do you want for breakfast, Sophie, what do you want?

Nothing.

Oh for goodness sake.

I dont want anything.

You'll have to eat something.

I dont want to.

It doesnt matter if you dont want to, you'll be hungry later on, so you've got to.

Yes but I dont want to.

I dont care.

Mum I dont want to.

Oh God.

Well if I dont want to?

I dont care if you dont want to.

Because I'm not hungry.

Yes but you havent eaten anything to not be hungry.

Sophie was fastening on her school skirt now, watching herself in the mirror but she paused while doing this. It is horrible, she said, it is just horrible.

I'll put crispies out for you.

I dont want crispies.

Weetabix . . .

I dont want Weetabix, I dont want anything Mum; if there's toast, can I have toast?

Just if you hurry!

Oh Mum.

Hurry up.

I cant.

Of course you can. Helen closed the door on her.

Mum!

She clicked it open, left it slightly ajar, and continued into the kitchen. Mo was at the table eating toast, sipping tea. Helen clasped her head with both hands and acted a scream: She's still dressing!

Hoh. She's been mooning about in her nightdress for the past half hour.

Females take longer.

89

Oh yeh?

We do that, havent you noticed?

There's a lot I havent noticed. Mo reached to her and held her hand. You are tired.

Mm.

Go to bed.

When you've taken her to school.

Helen went to the pantry, lifted out the packet of crispies, a bowl from the cupboard below, the milk from the fridge. Mo had noticed the photographs. I was looking at them earlier, said Helen.

Mo nodded. He watched her prepare the cereal. Cant she do her own? he said.

Be quiet.

She's past six.

Only just.

Only just is past.

Helen put her finger to her lips to stop him saying more. The kitchen door opened. Sophie walked to her chair, looked at the crispies in the bowl. I wanted Weetabix, she said.

Surprise surprise, murmured Mo.

Helen signalled him to be quiet, lifted a hairbrush as though threatening him. Mo mimicked panic, waving his hands above his head.

Sophie lifted her spoon, unaware this was happening. She studied the spoon. She began eating. While she did so Helen brushed her hair. Mo poured Helen a cup of tea and put a glass of orange juice out for the girl. She drank this swiftly, held out the empty glass.

Champion orange-juice drinker, said Mo.

You just talk all the time, she said.

It's because I'm a blabber.

Sophie craned forwards to allow Helen to brush the back of her head more easily.

I cant help myself, said Mo.

But if it is all the time?

I got to do it.

Yes but all the time?

All the time you dont eat your breakfast.

Not all the time.

I'm just listening to you two, said Helen.

Oh but Mum he doesnt have to do it all the time, not if it's talking.

You know Mr Noisy.

I'm not going to listen. Sophie stuck out her tongue at Mo.

I got to do it. It's like it's a disease, know what I mean?

No.

Helen finished brushing Sophie's hair, tapped her on the shoulder.

Maybe they'll send me to hospital! said Mo.

Helen had taken the loaf of bread from the cupboard, was inserting a slice of bread into the toaster although Sophie had forgotten about it and was getting up from the chair.

Maybe they'll do an operation on me tongue!

Big blabber, muttered Sophie.

Helen chuckled. Mo had raised his right hand in the air, forefinger extended. Look at you, she said, you're like a school-teacher scolding the class.

It is the whole truth and nothing but the truth. What am I? a big blabber! I should start a blabbers' anonymous. Guys with blabbing problems can all join up. Maybe they'll pay me a signing-on fee? I never thought of that!

Isn't he silly? said Helen.

Poo face!

Oh Sophie!

No, said Mo, poo-face blabber, that's even better! Poo-faced guys with blabbing problems, dribbling down my chin.

You're just silly, said Sophie.

I wont be silly once I'm a millionaire and everybody is all paying me money and I can go and buy old Totters Football Club.

The very very silliest. Helen said, A real Mr Silly.

I'm only one of the sillies. Silliness runs in my family you know, they came from a little village where everybody is silly. The name of the village is the very word for silly. My grand-father used to say, Oh we are all sillies, every last one of us, that's why we wound up in London, got on the wrong boat.

Helen chuckled. She saw Sophie looking at her and she winked.

No, it's true, me old gramps, him and me nan were heading for Toronto, Canada and what happened, yoicks and tally ho, London, England old chap. That's as true as I'm standing up.

Oh you fibber! Look Sophie, he's sitting down when he's saying it!

Sophie smiled, only for a moment, but a smile nevertheless. Mo made a startled face and clutched his throat, croaking: Hoh the smile, the young lady smiles, she smiles, my life is not in vain!

Sophie glanced at Helen with an expression on her face, a certain expression. It was nice seeing her smile, and that expression too, whatever it was. A mixture of amusement and wonder perhaps; puzzlement at the behaviour of adults, in particular the male of the species. The poor girl was glimpsing the future world; encounters with 'the male animal'. Helen called to her: Shoes Sophie!

Sophie sighed to the ceiling but her mood had shifted and off she went, almost cheerily. Mo could do that. He coped with her; it was so good that he did. Helen passed Mo the extra slice of toast. She wont eat it now.

Mo folded the slice into his mouth immediately.

Mr Hungry, she said but so quietly he either didnt hear or assumed it was not for his ears. He had the toast in his mouth so that it was half in half out when Sophie returned with her shoes in hand.

Helen had lifted her tea-cup and sat down for a moment; she signalled Sophie to hurry. Sophie sighed. Because she already was hurrying. Helen could see that she was and now she returned to the front room. In the huff or not? Helen was unsure. Mo winked, followed the girl from the kitchen.

But it was the two of them. If Mo coped with Sophie Sophie coped with him. First thing in the morning that was not easy. Mo and his jokes. Helen wouldnt have blamed her. Nothing against 'jokes' but there is a time and a place. People arent always capable of smiling, wearisome having to try. Perpetual smiles. Smile, smile, why dont you smile? That was it with some folk. Why do they do it? Not just men. Who wanted to smile all the time? Not all the time: cheer up, what's wrong with your face, give us a smile. So irritating. The same in work with some of the punters, like it was their job to make the dealers laugh, cracking jokes all the time and getting her to smile. Just shut up and play the cards. That was what she did, or tried to.

That was her with him too, her ex, what a pain it was being the audience, him and his stupid wee jokes. She even found him amusing, in the beginning. Talk about sad cases, that was her.

She did though. Imagine. What a confession! My God! Oh well. And it was childishness pure and simple, like in the class-room at school when a boy did it and you were supposed to look at how wonderful he was. It was him was the joke, a complete joke, showing off like a wee boy.

Mo was so different, he really was. He was funny for one thing. Genuinely funny. Sophie thought so too and she wasnt easy pleased.

At least she made the effort. Some children wouldnt. It showed she was learning. It should never be underestimated how difficult things had been for her. Mo said she was a woman already but she wasnt. Six years of age my God. Although he didnt mean it seriously, not literally; she was only a girl, and a little girl at that; a month ago she was like everywhere, legs everywhere, skirt round her neck, jumping up on Mo, and he had to *not* see. It was him that told her about that. And she listened. She did, she really did. The boys would laugh at her if she didnt sit properly. She had to sit properly and not jump up like that because they would see up her skirt. Boys did that. Thank God he told her. If she listened. She seemed to. It hadnt occurred to Helen until he said it. But of course they would laugh at her. Of course they would make her life a misery. Boys did that; they could do, they could be so so cruel. To them she was a girl, so fair game, girls and boys, a wee girl but a girl; she was. But that is all she was. Why would anyone ever think anything else, my God! Surely no one would ever ever, ever think anything else?

Or harm them. How could anyone ever harm a child? an innocent little child.

Mo would have made a wonderful teacher. He was so very patient. Patience was needed with children. Mo had it. Because he liked them. That was the difference. And Sophie could be difficult, there was no denying that. Things had been tough, very very tough. So no wonder about 'lacks enthusiasm'. What a horrible comment, 'lacks enthusiasm'. Sophie lacks enthusiasm. Her teacher said it. Does she talk at home?

Of course she talks at home.

But not all the time? no. What does that mean, all the time? You dont want a child talking all the time, not in the classroom. Surely? It was just a ridiculous question.

Talking was not a problem at all. Helen liked the teacher but she was too quick to judge. This was a new school and a new environment, completely new. Sophie was the only Scottish child in the class. Did it ever occur to them to wonder about that? She was on her own. It was significant for a girl, so so significant, and disappointing about Sophie's teacher because Helen liked her; she was a down-to-earth woman with a nice London accent; not snobby at all.

It was said about Helen too, people thought she was quiet; even *reserved*. Reserved! Caroline called her that. What a laugh. As though she was middle class! With her background! Ha ha to that. Really, it was just stupid. People didnt know; just what they made up out of their own brains. Helen had never been quiet. It was only England if she was. People didnt understand her at first but eventually they did because she spoke slowly and changed how she said things. They made fun of her anyway. Not nastily; stagey voices and jokes about kilts and being mean. Mo did it too at times. It wasnt meant to be nasty, and it wasnt. Do they all talk Scotch in Scotland? That was Mo's jokey question. He knew because he lived there but other English people might have wondered about it, even the teachers. Yes they did speak Scotch. It was not funny, even if some acted like it was.

Everything was so different. If Sophie was not talkative, well of course she wasnt. Who wouldnt have been? My God. It was so understandable. Even the school, Helen had been dreading it on Sophie's behalf. It had been such a relief to see this one and the children from all different backgrounds.

The girl had suffered during the past months. No question about that. The important thing was she had settled, thank God. She had settled. It seemed like she had. If she didnt they were not staying. Helen had discussed it with Mo. If the wee one didnt settle they would go home; they would pack their bags. Helen would make sure of that. She liked London but would leave immediately. Not to go home to Glasgow, not necessarily.

Helen had never been quiet. If people thought she was; never, and never as a girl. Dad called her the champion chatterbox, she was to get the gold medal. She didnt like him saying it but it was only Dad having fun. Helen did chatter. It was true. Sixteen to the dozen when she was little. Brian was the quiet one, he just looked, he looked and he said nothing. Dad didnt like that. He wanted people to talk.

Neither did Mum talk. Brian took after her. So Helen took after Dad.

Oh God, but it was true. Mum said it so it had to be. Imagine telling that to your daughter. So thoughtless, because of how Mum felt about Dad, did she even like him? No, not very much. Not that Helen ever saw, so thank you Mum, thank you very much.

It would have been funny if it wasnt so sad, sad if it wasnt so funny. Funny peculiar.

Mo was standing in the doorway, head cocked to the side. Hey, why you laughing? Come into the dressing room oh lady of the cards, your daughter needs assistance.

She rose and followed.

There were things Mo couldnt do and discussing clothes with Sophie was one of them. It would be the coat. Two weeks ago Helen bought her a new one but she didnt like it and created a fuss. It had a pattern down one side and some boy laughed. Sophie scrubbed her hand up and down the pattern in an effort to erase it. Helen was expecting another fuss but this morning it seemed not to bother her. Instead she chattered about a girl in her class and a funny funny joke that another boy did, one called Borden whom she had spoken about before – Borden? It sounded like Borden, if that was a name. Anyway, the joke wasnt against her, fingers crossed, and fingers crossed she no longer dreaded it all. Tantrums and tears. If all that had ended. With luck it had. Not so long ago she never would have allowed Mo to take her. It had to be Helen, and it didnt matter she needed a sleep. Even at the school gates my God, the girl wouldnt let go her hand. When she entered the school playground she lost the power of speech altogether. Yes it was a worry, of course it was a worry. So if the teachers couldnt get her to talk, no wonder, the wee soul.

She had been trying. Only she got herself into a state. The teachers could have let her stay with the other children. It would have calmed her. But there was no time no time, people had no time. Helen had to sleep with her phone next to the bed for emergencies. On a number of occasions she had been called to bring her home. A woman from the office was there and thought Sophie was having a fit, an actual *fit*. Sophie had reached a point beyond screaming. She was shaking, really. The woman called it 'spasms'. The child was having *spasms*! Spasms could cause brain damage in small children. Actual brain damage. Didnt Helen know that?

Of course Helen knew that, of course she knew it. Why do people say such stupid things? teachers especially. So like it was Helen's fault? Is that what she was saying? There must have been spasms in her own family the way she went on about it. It was just absurd. And obviously a criticism. As if Helen wasnt aware of the dangers. She didnt for one minute think spasms were *insignificant*. How patronising can you get? Because she was Scottish she didnt know how serious it was? Did she even have children of her own? People rushed to criticise.

If it wasnt one thing it was another. Sophie was a great wee girl, so let her be a wee girl. Helen had been worse when she was that age. The Queen of Sheba. That was what Dad called her, comical but not very nice. Dad's sense of humour. Better than jellybelly.

The outside door lay wide open. Sophie had her coat zipped and Mo was helping her pull up that heavy heavy backpack. Why did they have them so heavy? It weighed like a ton and must have slowed her down walking, six years of age for God sake she didnt need all that, surely.

She was waiting for a kiss. Helen gave her a big cuddle. Oh Sophie, she said.

Mummy are you tired? He said you were sleeping and I wasnt to go in.

I didnt say that! cried Mo.

Yes you did.

I did not.

You did!

Mo winked at Helen. He touched her upper arm. Helen smiled at him. Thanks, she said. She looked at the two of them. I feel like you're both watching me!

Well we are, said Sophie.

Because we like you, said Mo. Then he turned, reached his hand to Sophie. Hey Miss Goldilocks, you ready?

Dont call me that!

Mo sighed and made an apologetic gesture. Helen frowned at Sophie but in a humorous way. Sophie said: Okay Mummy, and she took Mo's hand. Away they went. On the first landing she turned to wave.

Helen listened to their footsteps down the stairs, closed the door eventually, walked to the front room window. The sky was the usual heavy clouds, even darker than usual, like a thunder storm, or lightning. Perhaps not, but it would still be clouds, it was always clouds, clouds clouds clouds. They said it was Glasgow but London was bad too, it could be.

Sophie and Mo appeared below, down the short flight of stairs onto the pavement. Immediately they turned and glanced upward to wave to her. Helen waved until they were out of sight, then was crying. She couldnt stop. It was so stupid, she just could not stop, tears flowing my God what was wrong with her she just could not stop. It was only to be seeing them hand in hand and the little girl just walking, and her shoes and coat, but even Mo, he wasnt small although he wasnt tall, and the two of them, it was so beautiful seeing them, and if anything happened, but it wouldnt. She was being silly. Buses and lorries and all traffic, it was normal, everything, except her and her worries and all worrying, constant, just so silly, but that was her, Mrs Silly, that is who she was. It was his place, he knew it inside out. One pub round the corner from his parents' home he tried never to pass, even in broad daylight, but that was miles away.

In the window of the house opposite a light was on. Helen imagined an elderly couple living there. A nice old couple who were always pleased to see Sophie if ever they saw her on the street or at the window. Their own children were long gone, and with families of their own. They had no grandchildren and when they died they might leave their fortune to Sophie. Why not? Or else a cats' home. Millionaires did that to annoy their families. No doubt they were a wizened and crabbit old pair of so and so's, who gobbled up children for breakfast like out of a fairytale – some of them were terrifying; wicked stepmothers and ogrish stepfathers. Why was it always them who were monsters? Why not the natural parents? In real life that is who it was.

Another cup of tea. Or bed? But would she sleep! It didnt matter 'would she', she had to. She was so very tired, beyond tired. Mo worried about her health. Why not? she worried about his! But it was nice all the same, somebody to worry. Helen worried about everything. And had to stop it. Because it was so stupid, stupid and foolish. Anything and everything. Dont be a worrier, you'll never leave the house. Mo said that. It was true.

But anybody with children, you always worried. They should be cherished. If children were cherished there would be far less pain and suffering in the world. How could people not cherish children? To not cherish a child. It was unthinkable

Sophie was safe with Mo. She knew that herself. Even the way she took his hand; the way they walked along the street together. Of course he wasnt her natural father but that was that and life moved on; here was Mo and he was so good with her and patient, and Sophie was responding. She was, it was beautiful to see.

Still sitting at the window, but she liked sitting at the window. One time she opened it and surprised a seagull perched on the ledge above. What a fright! A huge seagull flapping its wings and looking at her, annoyed – annoyed to see her! A big seagull! like in south London! My God. What rivers are there in south London? Do they even go on rivers?

Unless near a supermarket. That happened in Glasgow, flocks of seagulls congregated in the car-parks and roofs. There were stories about them swooping on people's heads. Frightening to think. Imagine a toddler. How would you fight them if it happened? perhaps with a brush or an umbrella except not with the telescopic sort because how could you hold it to hit? you couldnt, you couldnt hit with it. Seagulls are huge heavy beasts although not like an eagle. Eagles carry off a sheep never mind a child. You would have to hit the bird's head and do it hard; that would force it to open its beak. How else would you do it? Even pecking a child, they swoop down and peck into people's heads. That was in the news; was it true? It sounded far-fetched.

Women were the worriers. Men didnt bother, at least not so much. They chose not to. They let others do it for them. That was men.

When people are tired, everything goes everywhere, mingling

and merging, everywhere and anywhere, just scurrying about with no rhyme or reason. Her brains were always mince. She knew that. Empty vessels.

Anyway, Mo would be home soon, thank God, she would fall into bed, into sleep, before she hit the pillow,

only if her feet were cold, sometimes they were, in the morning especially, so then

But it was a safe district, although you could get too comfortable. That would be a mistake. In Glasgow you saw them coming. In London it caught you off-guard. Mo breathed easier up north. So he said. If she could believe him. She didnt believe him. For fresh air, yes, it was true about the parks; you could try different ones all around, and then get on a bus and go north of the river. There were so many places. People went farther afield. Helen wouldnt have been comfortable doing that. Visiting parks was one thing but travelling out the city was another. Taking a train down the coast to wherever; people did it but Helen would have found it difficult. They did get looks, even if Mo didnt notice. If he didnt, he said he didnt.

They were not to touch. Of course not, holding hands, of course they couldnt, how scandalous a thing, a man and a woman like shocking, so so shocking and surprising to see, so extraordinary horrible, horrible horrible, imagine, the very idea, a man and a woman touching; so they werent to do it.

One look from one person was enough. That was all it took. Even Sophie noticed. Parks were not a haven, if Mo said they were, they werent, not if you saw a pile of teenagers coming towards you; or like on a bus you were always watching, she preferred the tube, except you had to watch there too; the time of day, late evening, or mid-evening if it was quiet, or football supporters

From her chair she could see the street corner where Mo and Sophie walked, where Mo would return if he came by the direct route and didnt detour but he did detour, all the time, and without telling her. It was her fault for sitting there, if she didnt she wouldnt worry, she wouldnt be seeing the corner and wouldnt be thinking about what could happen.

But why should he tell her? a grown man. He could detour as much as he wanted. As long as he didnt take chances. She hated when he did. He once went to a bar where racists congregated; it was like a headquarters for one of these national front parties. Him and his mates went into it and ordered drinks. Why? Why would they do that? These stupid risks. Men did it all the time. You could tell because the guy himself, how he laid down the chips and these nervy looks or like staring at the wheel, staring at the cards or his own fingers. They stared at their own fingers. So the money wasnt theirs. Whose was it? They were gambling money and it wasnt theirs. So whose? His wife, his children, whose? laying it down on one spin of the wheel black or red, odds or even, twist or stay and please dont bust me oh dont bust me.

But Mo wasnt like that.

Helen's eyes closed a moment.

She would have to tell him about Brian. What would he say? That it didnt matter. That is what he would say. If he is your brother. Your brother is your brother. That is what Mo would say. Bring him home. No hesitation. Life was simple; for some people it was. Mo. Mo was not some people.

Only she worried, if he was gone the whole morning, depending on if he visited, where he visited. He called them his *ports of call* and put on a funny London accent. Me nasal whine voice. I got me ports of call. He's a port of call. People who worked in restaurants had different social lives, like with croupiers. One who worked beside Helen was from the Yemen or someplace, Lebanon, he went to the same café every day of the week; every single day, that was where he went. He was married too and had three wee boys. What did his wife think? A fine-looking man, you wondered about him, what all had happened in his life, his people dead, family members, people starving and no medicines either, how had he escaped? if his wife was from the same country or else if he had met her in London. Fate led you to places. He was not bitter, never bitter. That was a wonder. And his eyes too, there was an honesty and just how he was so gentle, he was, Helen noticed that about him. Every day of the week the same café. Imagine, the men all talking together in their own language about all what had happened since they were forced out their own country and how things might be if ever they could go home, if ever they could. But would they be able to? And now they had children, what about them? could their schooling be interrupted? Kids hated that. And where *was* home for them? if it was children, their home was here. And the wives too, if they had married here, so here was home, not the 'old country'; if they called it that. Perhaps they didnt. If it never was your country, so how could it be the 'old country'? not in the first place.

A cat was miaowing. It sounded like a baby. This one miaowed constantly. Its owner must have locked it in then went to work. Quite heartless really. There were a few animals in the neighbourhood. Mainly it was cats. Helen wasnt fond of cats. Sophie liked them but Sophie was a girl and girls liked all pets. And foxes! Not just foxes, in Glasgow you saw deer. Cafés sold venison and chips. It was said as a joke but you could imagine people killing them, baby deer. Teenage boys would do it for a laugh.

Oh well. She would fall into bed, to lie down and sleep for a month, that would have been nice, the Sleeping Beauty.

Mo had cold feet.

So then she would waken up, so she couldnt be a Sleeping Beauty.

A man and woman came round the corner. It should have been Mo. If he knew she was waiting, he knew she was waiting, just because she worried, she did worry but why did she? So foolish, like so so foolish. Foolish behaviour. Because she was foolish. Little Miss Foolish

and silly, so silly. Mo visited an old man who worked in a wee shop. He sat about or else shifted boxes and things. He looked like nothing but was a respected man in the community. If you saw him you wouldnt think anything. He wore an old-fashioned jacket, his shirt buttoned to the top without a tie. He had a white beard, straggly too and wore a certain hat with a pattern, not a turban, just like a round little tub. It didnt matter that he worked in a shop because a wise man is without power. In the Muslim religion people didnt have to be wealthy folk in great careers. The best man with the best intellect in the community might be a 'shit shoveller', he was the one who knew the old stories and all how things were, what was the right way and what was the wrong way. Mo said that. And what the old man said about Glasgow, like how he used to live there and it was *backward*, that was his word, 'backward', Glasgow was *backward*, meaning the local community, meaning Asian community. They suffered things they shouldnt, because they didnt want trouble. Things happened to them and they didnt report it to the police. The old man said that. If it was true. But you would believe him. Mo did. People punched a baby. Imagine that. The baby was in a pram. A man came along and punched it, a baby, like a man punching a baby. That must mean something. Unless if he was ill in the head. How could a man punch a baby? He must have been ill. That was Glasgow. But why not London? It could be real thugs and they attacked you. And if it was like knives, that was what Mo didnt consider, gangs used knives and bats, they smashed people with bats. They beat them up. Gangs did that. Thugs. They did it to children too. Nothing mattered to them.

Although he should have texted. Why didnt he? Because if she was in bed. He would have thought she was. She could have texted him. Except she was checking on him, he would think that, and she wasnt. Anyway her phone, she needed a top-up. But it was nothing to do with trust. She only worried. He was a flirt but that was all. It made Helen smile. Even the first time they met. Middlesexy; I was born in Middlesex; I am of the Middlesex breed. Male sex, same sex, trans sex. Any sex. You are a member of the female sex. I am Middlesexy.

But it was true, women liked him. He was a nice man. She was so so lucky. She felt that, strongly, she did, she did and she was, except foolish, foolish foolish Mrs Foolish that was her. She had expected him home by this time. So he must have stopped off.

But he was good at meeting people. Helen was hopeless. She hadnt always been hopeless. Oh God, God.

She hadnt though, she used to have friends. Nowadays she didnt get the chance. Anyway, who would look after Sophie?

Imagine a mother not babysitting. That was Mum. She would if asked but always had to be. Each and every time. She never offered, never ever offered. Imagine that, like never. Oh well. Self-reliance, Helen was good at that, she had to be with him, her ex. The complete opposite of Mo.

Thank God.

South London too. It was real life. So different to the West End, just so different. The casino wasnt reality. They didnt know what reality was.

Obviously he was talking to people and hearing the gossip. In his community everybody gossips, everybody bitches, everybody knows your business. If he wasnt home in five minutes she would go to bed.

She rose from the chair by the front room window. Her woollen socks and a hot-water bottle.

The door into Sophie's wee place. Oh well, she would make it later, the bed. In the kitchen she filled a kettle and put it to boil. Otherwise she would never sleep. Cold feet must have run in the family. What a trait. For some it is genius or musical instruments, hers had cold feet, it was ludicrous. Her entire family, if it wasnt so sad.

She listened to the water heat, elbow resting on the kitchen counter. Hot-water bottles were old-fashioned but they stood the test of time and she needed to sleep. Concentration. You worked on automatic pilot as a dealer but only to a point. If you made mistakes, too many.

She filled the rubber bottle and tiptoed through to bed, so so tired, and shivery, like just shivery and shivering beneath the duvet. Whyever did she wait so long? mad mad mad, that was her, mad, madness in the family. Snuggling into a small bundle, small as she could be, that was just making herself into it oh my God also because she was so so tired, oh she was, she was; exhausted, physically, and drained, so so unfair, just unfair, because she worked so damn hard, mental exhaustion too. If she was uncomfortable, from her side onto her back, her feet so cold, even in woolly socks my God she could not get warm, and dozing, she managed to doze then was not, and with Brian and the other one crossing the road – if it was Brian, and it was – and staring in at her, him with the limp, no, she didnt like him, it was a funny way to walk, just weird, why did he walk that way? it was strange but it was not her fault why they were staring at her, she had done nothing, she was just in the taxi and not doing a thing to anyone, nothing at all, she would not do anything to anybody, whyever they would think such a thing? they were wrong and should not have stared at her if Jill and Caroline were there too, it was so unfair, so so unfair, sitting beside her, unless if they were hiding, people hide, oh they hide, why do they hide

She had been sleeping and was awakened by draughts. He was causing draughts. He was under the sheet. She moved closer into him but where were his legs? They were off the bed, angled off; his legs drooped over the side. This was the draughts. She raised herself to see down at his feet; he had his socks on. His eyes were open. Why have you got your socks on? she said.

Mo chuckled.

And his tee-shirt and jogging trousers. He was wearing it all. His arm pushed under her head, the back of her neck; she raised her head to allow his arm below. What are you doing? she said.

Hey now you sound rough.

Mo had whispered and it was a lovely whisper. He was moving her head, onto his chest. *Lifting her head*. Oh God, breathing. Her left hand lay on his waist, her right between their thighs, his skin cool. What time is it? she said.

Never you mind.

Mo.

Quarter to two.

Oh God.

Dont worry.

Helen found the hot bottle, reached over the edge of the bed to lay it onto the floor. Mo clasped her left foot.

You got warm feet, can I have your socks?

He was laughing at her.

I dont know what you think, she said, like you can just come in here.

Heh heh.

Helen settled back beneath the sheets. I didnt think I slept.

You slept.

I did.

You can sleep some more too, you got plenty of time.

I should get up.

No you shouldnt. You should stay where you are.

You should have come in earlier.

Would you have let me!

Helen pretended a shiver and snuggled in more tightly. Mo said, You were so tired. I looked in three times but how could I waken you, it would have been cruel and I'm not a cruel man. That is one thing about me.

He reached to kiss her full on the lips. The kiss lingered; and a smacking sound when they parted. I'll be late, she said.

Late for what?

For school, to collect Sophie.

No you wont.

I will.

You're never late.

Sometimes I am.

Mo circled his arm round her shoulders. I'll go get her.

Helen said nothing. Mo was waiting for her. She was about to speak but didnt, then she did. She expects me to come.

Mo settled down further, holding her more firmly, her upper body to his chest.

She does.

His mouth was close to her ear and she felt the warmth of his breath. He whispered: Hey, you feels good m'dear.

He was touching and rubbing her body. She was so weary, she was, and his hand fully on her tummy a moment, then his fingers to her nipples; oh. If she had raised herself a little, meeting them.

What you call em fings anyway, boosums . . . bosuns . . .? When were they invented? is they a new fing? Hey, they're trapping me here, I cant hardly move. He was looking at her and she closed her eyes, only his talking and jokes. After a moment he said, Will I take off my clothes or what?

She moved from him and he got out of bed, undressing immediately, tugging off his socks, flinging them at the door. What's up? he said.

What? Helen paused, she had taken off her nightdress.

You smiled. You did. Yes you did girl you smiled. You smiled at *me*.

You're so enthusiastic, she said, her hands behind her head. She reached her right hand to the sheet and raised it to cover her breasts.

Mo gazed at her a moment longer. Yeh well it's still new to me, he said, that's why. I cant believe my luck. I mean that. It's like when you cook me a meal and burn the turnips.

Dont be so cheeky.

Helen watched him clamber into bed. He was self-conscious, turning side onto her so she might not see his penis. She did love him. She really did. You never seem to be cold, she said, it's all the talking you do, talking talking talking.

He moved closely into her, onto his back again, the same position as previously. His skin was like a draught, not cold but cool, and smoother, he had smooth skin.

No, he said, it's so unusual a thing it is like what they call it, a phenomenon; phenomenonon.

What?

So it's the first time over and over again, over and over and over and over.

Mo was whispering. Helen loved him whispering, two people together; she lowered her head onto his chest. Her arm and wrist lay between his thighs, then his thing, my God, already hard, she hadnt thought. He made a slight gulping sound. She moved her hand away. He didnt react. Sorry, she said.

What for?

I didnt realise.

What d'you expect?

He was twisting slightly, to kiss her, his body touching across her right nipple. I just want to kiss you. You feel so good. You do.

She didnt answer.

You feel so good.

So do you.

Do I?

He meant the question seriously. Helen stroked down his belly. Mo barely moved. She gripped his penis. Sometimes I cant feel my fingers touching.

He made the gulping sound again. She gripped tightly, and was listening to his breathing, how he wanted her so much, so much, and she could have lifted him up like it was a handle, my God it was, and he might only lie there, and it could be so hard, she knew it could; she knew it *would*, even without touching she knew, and he wouldnt move, he would not move, not until she did.

Why was that? She had to make it known. It was considerate of him. Her ex was the same. In that one way he was and she couldnt say differently. She herself had had to do it; she had to make it known. Her ex didnt until she said, and Mo too, she had *to make it known*, and it was like a secret brought from her, having to give in because like not having a choice. Her eyes were closed, hearing the breathing, him there and looking, hearing his breathing how that catch in the breathing and gulping sound seeing her, her body there and open, lying there, she was naked but for her pants, if he only would pull them down, he would be looking and seeing and his breath taken, her body had taken it from him, him seeing her, her beauty, it was true, the beauty of her body, she would be stretching, her eyes closed as though unaware, she did not know he was there, he was intruding into her space and she was as though unaware of his presence, knowing that he leaned to her and hearing his breathing now, excitement and even a warmth so his hand would come so gently and to the inside of her thigh, above her knee, ticklish a little and her own gulping, trying not to but it always had the effect, and how he did it, he only stroked her, he only stroked her, not anything more, and no one could say, not a word, never, not about him and not about her. That was what he did, he only stroked her and she could not move she could not move, only she would have, would have touched him if she could but she couldnt, she wasnt to touch him and was so wet, she knew she was, and she wanted him but he wouldnt; he never ever, never.

But Mo did. She raised her head and kissed him. She loved him. He turned side onto her and his right leg came over her; his right elbow lay by her side. She wished he would graze her nipples, this was a time and he didnt, she could have said; he didnt do it and this was a time, but now feeling his weight upon her, his pressing against her and her thighs parting, keeping her eyelids shut until then it entered, the head entering, it felt huge, sometimes it did, and the lobe of his ear by her mouth, she touched it with her lips, as though to nibble, she might have, and he pressed further into her, moving, and both their breathing now, and she waited, her hands resting on his waist, and this made her smile. He whispered, What?

She didnt answer but knew he was pleased, because he knew how she felt and how he wanted her. He said it again: What?

Helen shook her head. He only was who he was, that was Mo, and she loved him, truly she did, she felt that she did. Then when he had moved to orgasm and lowered his body onto her she wrapped her arms round him. She felt so sorry for him, he was so good and did his absolute best, for everybody. This was the kind of man he was. He didnt think it but he was. He thought he had failed in life but he hadnt failed, never ever, and if he had so had everybody, the most virtuous people, they all came through bad times, they too learned; they became good because they had been so imperfect, failings of youth and now were wise.

Mo too, he was the same, Helen knew that he was.

She heard his breathing, he was still inside her and she stroked his back. He didnt respond. She wondered if he would sleep. His weight onto her, it was a good feeling. If he only would relax completely. She could take his weight and wanted to, if he would, except he wouldnt, he wouldnt allow it. He took his weight on his elbows. If he only would be selfish, he was never selfish, always for other people; she wished he wasnt.

They lay without speaking, but his semen, she reached for the towel she kept by the side of the bed. He also used it to wipe himself, then she went to the bathroom.

Was he asleep when she returned?

Rain pattered against the window. She had been thinking about something. Whatever, it had gone now. But it wouldnt last forever and it would be sunshine.

So the casino was not ideal but it was fine for the present and better than most. She had no complaints. She was used to the wealth and wasted money. That was the job. So get used to it. Or get out.

Poor Mo. He was too good for a restaurant. He would have hated her saying it but it was true. Helen raised her head to see his face. His eyes were closed. But he was awake. He was talented and clever, and witty, he was. He could have been like an actor or somebody. In the entertainment world.

Not that he would be. What did it matter anyway, it was just silly, but it would be better if he didnt call her Soapy. Imagine he said it in front of her friends. That was what men didnt think about. Girls are not boys. Sophie was right about that.

Perhaps he was too good for like an actor or whatever. Perhaps he was too good for everything. What else would he do? He didnt like business. One of his friends was in business and he was making money. Oh well, perhaps his charm, the irresistible charm, he had his irresistible charm and everybody succumbed, except her. That was funny. Mo said it but it wasnt true. Only some days she was tired. She couldnt raise the curtain, if a curtain was there, it was like a curtain was there, drawn, thick and heavy, laden with dust, so so heavy and like, if anything was on the other side, what could there be? it was too dark, you were too tired. If positives were there, you knew they were, only you were tired, and it was dark. Things were dark, you saw them dark. Helen did

tired and dark

Something good happened today, what was it?

She had to think. Mo had whispered it to her. He would have been smiling. If she could see his face. She would have had to raise her head.

Helen got sick of smiling. Smiles were sewn on. Sometimes she wondered.

Positives and negatives, he talked about that, where there is darkness there is light. Something good happened today.

People can be smilers. She needed to smile. There were nice smiles. Natural honest smiles. She didnt have one. She didnt trust her smiles. They were not ordinary as from one person to another. It was why she needed him. She did need him. He made silly comments but they were true. Negatives became positives. He had that knack and it was so necessary. If she didnt find that in a person, if the other person wasnt positive, just down-in-the-dumps all the time, except how things happened in life. Not everybody was happy families. Experiences werent all good. A negative *was* a negative; it was only positive if it was positive. Everybody was different and it had to be remembered. People had their own personalities, each and every one. It applied to babies in the pram. Try to get one to do something. If she didnt want to. Boys too. They go off and do what they want. That was Brian. Off he went. A row with Dad and away. Was that responsible? Not to contact his own mother, even to contact her. That was boys. What an easy life they had in comparison.

Helen was not a brooder. Her ex called her that. Brood. Like a big hen. A woman was a big hen. A woman brooded and had a brood. A word for a woman but not a woman's word. It was like 'women's work', even to say it: women's work. Every week was every week. A brooder. Who did the ironing? Who did the washing who did everything

what did it matter, week in week out, Sophie not wearing the same clothes twice, what did it matter, everything having to be just so, none of it, it didnt matter, it was all like meaningless nonsense. She didnt want anything to do with it.

Mo and his criticisms about her worrying all the time. He didnt know, he really didnt. What world did he come from that people worrying was news?

Men didnt understand.

Mo's breathing, he was having a wee doze. That was nice, if she could too. This was the amusing part of it, how she had been asleep; she was, then he came home so now, of course, she wasnt. Oh well.

She would have loved a sister. Or a cousin with children and they could just maybe share, if one could babysit or else just meet up for a chat or it could even be Brian, if he was married and his wife was there and just like a friend, a good friend, and they could meet up, just shopping together or taking the children to the swing park or wherever, if there were not too many boys rushing around, it was off-putting for Sophie; she was at that stage. Mo tried to laugh her out it but she just looked at him. On her dignity at six years of age? Yes. It was so important. Women dont have many weapons but that was one of the best.

Less than twelve hours from now and she would be at the table so she needed to sleep, she did need it. She would though. She was tired. Oh so tired, so so tired, she was.

Every time her eyes closed she opened them. Anyway, she knew what a living death was. She had been married to one.

Her brains full to capacity; family family family, she was sick of it. Why does family rear its ugly head but it does, a lifetime, it is jail for a life sentence, families and ghosts

Mo's too, she hadnt even met them, why hadnt she met them?

Oh God if she could sleep. In one position then another, unable to settle, if she could settle, she couldnt settle, and she had to to sleep. You worked on automatic pilot as a dealer but only to a point and if your mind was someplace else like family problems. Everybody made mistakes. But not too many else you would be out on the street, and you couldnt blame them like for mistakes, mistakes are money.

She had been asleep, till he woke her up. He actually woke her up. So then *he* went to sleep and she stayed awake. Oh well. Perhaps a pill, nightshift workers took pills. Sex didnt knock *her* out.

The heat from his body. She wouldnt have needed the socks and hot bottle. If he had told her in advance, I'm coming back to bed

Only the waiting, how much of your life, waiting, and always for other people, their life is the important one, theirs and not yours.

That was Caroline, everybody waiting, she was the one,

they were due the taxi and waiting for her, she was the one preening, so if they hadnt waited, if she hadnt been so selfish because that is it, selfish.

You go home and you go home. Not like everything else, like the whole world and you are not able to, why cant you just go home? not like waiting and waiting

wee souls, all running around, you saw them in the school playground and Sophie was one, and she would be waiting, and if people are late, parents can be

if it is standby, a machine on standby, if she had no choice like brains functioning with or without like a purring, engines purring purring and we dont know the thing is on

What came first? Knowing they were there? Or seeing them?

There are enemies of children

What did God do there? It was just like bad luck

for Dad too, poor old Dad.

horrible horrible feeling. If it didnt happen in casinos, there was a privacy there. She felt that anyway. Others perhaps didnt, if they felt panicky, some would, and ogling ones looking at you and just staring,

wee souls

Hey . . . Helllenn, Helenn . . .

Mo the smiler. His breathing too, the regularity, you listen to someone's breathing. Breathing and voices, faces, distinguishing features, hear their breathing, people's breathing.

You are very welcome to sleep m'dear, most very welcome . . . Mo was already out the bed, halfway, about to lower his feet to the floor.

I was hardly asleep at all.

You were snoring.

No I wasnt.

He was about to turn from her but she raised her hand. I'm sorry, she said, but what does it matter about the neighbours?

That's six months now and I still havent met your family. You talk about your community and how about tradition and everything, the culture and everything, but to me it's like neighbours, that's 'the community', that's how it sounds to me. Oh heavens, what will the *neighbours* think? You tell one person and then everybody knows, the whole world. So it's like oh she's a white woman and got her own child. When your mother said 'English woman', that's what she meant, just like *white woman*.

She waited for him to say something but he didnt. I'm not bothered, she said, only it would be good to know like I dont care about meeting them, not if you dont want me to but if it's only the neighbours and worrying what they'll say. If that is all it is.

Again she waited. She adjusted her pillow and smiled: Now you wont talk to me.

Yeh I will, I will, but make it later.

She settled down on her back.

You took me by surprise. I want it the best way, he said, like when things are good love not now like now, I mean, everything's going on all the time, you know how it is. I want it to be right when it happens.

When what happens? Do you mean when I meet them? when *we* meet them, because Sophie will be there too.

Of course.

Things are never right Mo, not like that, because that isnt life. Not in families; there are too many people and too many lives, all different, and you cant wait for one because everybody else's goes on, it doesnt stop just because of you, because of one person. People think that but it's not true and like

Helen shut her eyes.

What is it?

Clenching her eyelids shut.

Hey love. Hey . . . We'll talk later, you need a sleep.

Mo's hand on her shoulder. He didnt smile when she looked at him. He would have wanted to but didnt, was not able to. She raised her hand to his face and smoothed his cheek, then pulled the sheet to her chin, turned onto her side. His hand touched her forehead. Thanks, she said. She heard him leave the room.

Anyway, she didnt care about it. Not really. And it was a bad time for his family because with Mo's uncle and the cancer, it was true, his mother and father were up and down to the hospital most days of the week, so her being critical, it wasnt fair. It wasnt. She shouldnt have said it. Silly. Worse than silly. She was worse than silly. What was worse than silly? She was. Everything was going on for his mother and father and him too. She shouldnt have raised the matter, better telling him about Brian. Brian was who she

She should have told him. She meant to, she thought she was going to; she started off to, to tell him.

She didnt need Mo's opinion. Because there was nothing else, only to find him, she had to find him, she knew she did. Brothers are brothers, that would have been Mo. You have to find him. If it is him it is him: he is your brother.

And a good brother. Only things had been tough for him, like they are for most people. One person cant do anything, something but not everything.

He had survived. He was not a weakling. However he managed, he did it, and was managing now, him and the other one, they were managing else they wouldnt have been there at the traffic lights, from wherever they had come, they had come from somewhere. Soup and bread. Shelters for the homeless. They would have been someplace.

Except if they had nowhere, people can have nowhere. So where do they go? Why one place and not another? If there is nothing there, so like no reason, if they have no reason, just walking about else sitting down. Or if they sold the Big Issue. But some arent allowed. They scare people too much. Nobody would buy the magazine, not if the ones selling it are scary-looking, *too* scary-looking, if it is like daylight, the police would move them on. They walk about and keep out the way until it is safe, using side streets, all the quiet places, the riverbank, and if there were benches to sit, him with the limp, he had to rest, then if it was raining, what if it was raining, and the toilet, where do people go?

Helen shifted her position and felt his side of the bed still warm. Had she been dozing? That was a while ago the outside door shut; how long? she couldnt remember. But it did shut, she heard it. Unless she *had* been dozing. That would have been good, and so needed, so so needed.

Over the grass and to the sand. She *had* been dreaming. Cutting grass. Sand grass is cutting grass. Grass-shoots out the sand, they cut your skin; draw one fast and you bled. That was Brian showing her how, cutting his own skin on purpose, making it bleed. Wee globules along the line, the red line. Blood. Was that a grown-up thing to do? A big brother? Of course not.

So much for Mum.

She wasnt in the dream except her presence, the idea of her and her arms outstretched like in a religious picture the woman with folded gowns and her hands out to you.

Helen could dream while dealing the cards. Times of the month and after sex. Men got relaxed, women the opposite. What is the opposite of relax?

Ha ha to men.

If Mum liked anybody it was males. You would have thought a granddaughter. No. How sad. Poor Mum. Because she was the loser, if she didnt know it. All wrapped up, a coat of chain-mail, not letting anybody near, keep your distance keep your distance. If that is what you call it, chainmail; chains male. Chains were male; males locked you up, they locked you into them, they did it with their chains, chaining you. The wife chained to a wall and then he bricked it up and she was suffocated there, unable to move until her dying day, her screams never heard. So horrible. Imagine her agony. The husband had gone mad. He always was. But that poor woman: what had she done? nothing at all, except being married to him, I divorce you I divorce you I divorce you. So why had she to die in such horrible agony like if it was him gone mad? Not her. That was so unfair. No wonder you got haunted houses. People said it about buildings, bricks and mortar, how a house could have a presence. Because the spirits were restless. You could have thought it about this house, considering the countless people who had passed through the doors. How many since it was built? All that suffering. People living and dying, diseases and degenerative conditions. People died in the olden days. If it was appendicitis, they died, the doctors didnt know to remove the appendix. That was so so sad. Yet with the tonsils, they took them out but didnt have to; it made no difference if the doctor took them out or left them in. People were ignorant. But happy too. Sad and happy, through all the years, all the different people. And scared! Children especially. In this one building how many children had been terrified out their wits? How many! It was a terrifying thought and there was an excruciating thing about it like how they locked them up too, forced into cupboards and cages, homemade cages.

Cages for children my God that was so evil. Who would do it to them? What animals! Men did it. Women helped. That was the worst. Whoever would terrify a child? It was the most sickening thing. Imagine terrifying a child. Who would do that? What kind of monster? bestial. They would have to be sick. Mentally ill. And not just ordinary mentally ill. Ordinary mentally ill people wouldnt act in that way toward children; it needed a special type of mental illness, like Nazis and torturers. The men who tortured people were mentally ill, even those not classified as such and in ordinary jobs. Soldiers and policemen were like that; priests, schoolteachers too, some of them, and they terrified people, then paedophiles. Horrors, torturers; what else was a paedophile? They were torturers of children, they were just vile, coming in the night and coming to children, hearing the handle of your door, just so so vile, and ill, if they were, or just torturers, are torturers ill

Oh but she was glad it wasnt Mo worked in the casino and her in the restaurant, being alone through the night. If she was she wouldnt cope; she wouldnt. The whole night long. Sophie would come into bed with her. She used to in Glasgow.

Then having to visit the loo my God you would think she was a child. She would have to leave the light on. She would. It was beyond silliness. She was such a foolish foolish female, just like so so foolish, she was, truly. Men didnt worry about such things. Unless if they didnt tell people. If they were scared too. If they were terrified! But Helen didnt believe it, not the ones she knew. They were strong; in their own ways they were, including Mo who seemed the weakest, but he wasnt, only for fighting, and she wasnt talking about fighting.

Anyway, Brian hadnt been a fighter and he wasnt small. The one at the traffic lights was angry-looking and dangerous and even like he wanted to fight. That wasnt Brian. Brian didnt fight and why should he have? It was nothing to be ashamed of. She remembered from childhood days and that time, she was with him, he was taking her someplace – where was he taking her? – they met boys and they were laughing at him. Brian could have thumped them so so easily and like if he had he would have hurt them. It was not nice. Helen was holding his hand, if they were laughing at her too, they didnt even know her and it was not fair how they could laugh at her, if they didnt know her. It should not have been her. Why were they laughing at her? What did it mean? Wee girls dont know. So much of what goes on, it passes over your head. Poor Brian. Boys had to stick up for themselves. They had to fight back. Helen would have. She would have slapped their faces. The cheek of them laughing at her. If she had been the boy. Dad said it too. Oh if it was your wee sister, she would have hit them back, she's the fighter in this house!

It was fun, Dad meant it as fun when she told them. Mum called it tittle-tattle. It wasnt tittle-tattle; that was a horrible thing to say. Helen was only telling her. She was her mother for God sake she had a right to tell her; and she should have listened. That was her duty. She was a mother and mothers had a duty. It wasnt tittle-tattle it was only a wee girl telling her about something exciting.

As if it was Helen's fault. It was not Helen's fault. These boys were laughing at Brian. So it was not her. It was only because she was there they laughed at her, because she was with him. It was horrible and cruel. Boys were torturers. She would have slapped them. Brian could have punched them. Boys can punch. Because if you have to. Children learn to take care of themself: girls most of all. That was what Mum didnt understand, because she favoured Brian, or she only liked boys, but it wasnt Helen's fault if she wasnt one. Dont blame the child. Why did Mum blame her? She seemed to, and it was not her fault. Girls shouldnt have to fight but people did things to you if you didnt. You couldnt hide anywhere; you couldnt find a place. People got you. They came and got you. Sophie had a picture book called *The Book of Secret Places*; it was a nice book but the title was a lie. There were no secret places. Sophie thought there were. What do you say to a child? They always find you.

School had been like that. And Marcelle Tierney.

Marcelle Tierney. Imagine thinking of her. She was just a bully. People thought she was marvellous but she wasnt. And taking the boys' side against her. Some girls did that, if boys were getting you, they just laughed, they joined the boys against you. You had to stick up for yourself. So if Brian didnt. Dad picked on him too. 'Picking on' was not bullying. Dad was not a bully. He *picked on* Brian. It was not the same as 'bullying'; and it was bullying Marcelle Tierney did to Helen which was worse than 'picking on' and especially she used the boys. That was what she did, it was horrible. The boys all liked her. They liked Helen too. They liked Marcelle because she was sporty but Helen was sporty. Everybody knew that. The worst was Ian Mathieson. It was just horrible and wouldnt have happened except for Marcelle and Marcelle was her friend – supposed to be, but friends dont act that way, not real friends, so she hadnt been a real friend, not like a real friend.

Silly nonsense, why was she thinking about it?

Anyway, she stuck up for herself, she had to. It wasnt always possible because how can it be? But for boys too. Imagine being a boy. Helen couldnt. Weak or strong, what would she have been? Weak. Or strong. She couldnt imagine.

It was survival. Children had to learn. People died or went mad.

Or not respecting you. Boys didnt. They could be animals. Not all animals, some were not like that. Sheep didnt hurt each other. Horses didnt, and cows; people worshipped cows. Human beings were worse. Only to respect another person, and they couldnt, they couldnt even do that. The human body is a 'hallowed temple' supposed to be but if it was not treated properly like only humiliated and made a thing to denigrate, if that was what happened, if they denigrated, girls too, they were the worst.

Helen dozed. Then was awake.

A blank period.

Not a doze. How long if it was? Half an hour. Half an hour is good. Even five minutes. Two. One and a half. Can people sleep for one and a half? Sleeping for one and a half minutes, not even the one with the limp, if that was a dream, but she didnt have any dream. Not unless it was longer. She hadnt checked the clock so it may only have been five, or ten, or even more although ten onto what she already had would have been good, and she was back to work at nine this evening. As soon as Azizah arrived she would be out the door, if Sophie allowed it. The crying fits had stopped thank God, thank God.

Nightshift didnt allow sleep. Perhaps if she lived in a castle or else the country, in a posh mansion with a hundred servants and finery and all furnishings, plush settees and beautiful soft cushions. But she needed bed, eyelids

A thickness too

But Brian

He wasnt a coward. He wasnt. They just were laughing. Why did they? It was horrible. He wasnt weak. Only with Dad, who was strong. Oh my God. Except with Mum. That was so strange. Take away Mum and he was the strongest. Who was stronger? Nobody. Nobody was stronger than Dad. Although not Helen, he didnt dominate her. He took her side in everything, even against Mum.

Although who did he dominate apart from Brian? That was a question too. But not a nice one. If it was Dad. Dad as a man. What like was he? If it was the company of men. That was a different question. If he was not strong, perhaps he wasnt. There was an arrogance in older men too, she saw them in the casino, ones who were loud and brash, showing off; that way they looked at you; you were just nothing to them, they rated you so low as a human being. They wouldnt think it was rape, you were so nothing, just like nothing. They didnt care about human beings. It was all twisted and perverted, it wasnt love, and not respect. And the women with them. Not them either. What were they for? What did they do? What did they care about? Zombies personified. You saw their eyes, they had no life, it was horrible and tragic. They took part in it, and it was so demeaning, and affected all women; little children too. What did these women think? Did they think of that? No, because these little girls were nothing to them with their expensive jewellery and piles and columns of chips, stacks of them. It was so so demeaning. Old-fashioned too. From an old-time Hollywood picture with all dumb blondes and gangsters. But these gangsters were not criminals in the ordinary sense, just men with loads of money. Mo's question was where did they get their money but what did it matter except they had it and waved it around and laughed if they lost. How did they *take* losing? Could they *take* it? That was the big question for them. One guy lost eighteen thousand pounds in twenty minutes and then said goodnight. So cool. He was like a hero. The dealers too, they spoke about him.

Perhaps Brian was weak but what did that mean? 'weak'. 'Weak' was not *weakness*. So if he had been 'weak', it wouldnt have been like a weakness, like it had always been there. How could it? He wouldnt have survived. Nobody would. Not if you were one person and all of them, all of them there, if it was only you, you were only one person. You wouldnt survive. Who could? Nobody. Girls were begging and prostituting. Young girls too, people touching you and all what, it didnt bear thinking about, and gang rapes and beatings, actual beatings, just beating women. What cowards! Men were cowards. To treat women in such a way, they were cowards and bullies and you had to stand up to them.

Oh God, but it was true.

The rain was heavy, it was. Had he even taken the umbrella? At least he carried one, unlike her ex who was too macho, so he got soaked, ha ha. Sophie carried a wee one in her school-bag which was just as well because she would not wear a hat. Put one on and she pulled it off. Even if it was raining. Some silliness to do with a girl in her class. Surely she didnt want her hair getting wet? Mo suggested pinning her hat to her coat collar. Imagine. So if the pin got loose and jammed there, the point sticking out beneath her chin, right at her neck. What if it did and she fell and the point sticking up oh God it was just so dangerous. It really was. You couldnt believe he would suggest such a thing. Trust a man, just so stupid. And like really thoughtless, it was.

She wouldnt sleep now.

Oh well, the television. The remote lay within reach. She pressed the power button, then the mute-setting on the volume-control. She didnt want people's voices, that was the last thing.

Before the screen image appeared she pulled the sheet and duvet up to her chin, closed her eyes. Eventually she looked at the screen then pressed the guide-setting for the listed programmes. The one about house-decor improvements was watchable. She quite liked being able to see things for when she got a house, if ever she did. She used to think so; perhaps she wouldnt. Mo called it window-shopping. That was what these programmes were, virtual walking down the virtual High Street. But what was wrong with that? At least it was something. If you didnt have any money it kept you going, even to see the things, and if you ever did get the money, if you got enough, you could go and buy something. Then too you got basic tips for do-it-yourself and that was good for painting and decorating. Helen liked all that and if they did get a place she wanted to do it herself. In his situation Mo should have appreciated that. When would he ever have money? He didnt even go in for the lottery.

Anyway, a cup of tea.

That was cheery. But it was true, she needed a cup desperately. If not disaster. Leastways a fainting fit. Helen smiled, but her eyes blinked shut. And a Nurofen.

She got out of bed and dressed.

At six years of age Helen had helped her mother. As far as she remembered. She thought she had; she used to pick things up and put them in drawers. Sophie didnt, she didnt pick up anything.

It was too early to collect her from school, so wherever Mo had gone it was someplace else. That happened after sex; he bounced about and had to do something, go and visit people. He used to play five-a-side football. Not now. She wished he would, it was just like *ordinary*. Other men slept, not Mo. But he had to be at the school for three ten on the dot, on the dot. As long as he remembered that. Helen would text him. Except she needed a top-up. Anyway, he would remember, he was good at remembering. Really, he was a responsible guy. If you forgot the doritos. Me doreeetos, I needs me doreeetos! Cheese and doritos, tomatos and doritos. Everything was like doritos. Doner doritos, everything. He took them in his cornflakes and made it fun. Sophie didnt know whether to laugh or not when she saw him, glancing to Helen for guidance. When Helen laughed Sophie nearly choked on her own, and when he poured in the milk and mixed it all in oh God it was like hysterical, just so so funny. He was such a fool! He truly was. A born comedian. He could have been on television, without any doubts.

The bag of doritos was on the kitchen-counter. Helen was nibbling another. They were full of fat and salt and sugar and all the 'gluegomerates' as he called them, I needs me gluegomerates.

She closed the bag and put it away in the cupboard, the salsa into the fridge, then filled the kettle.

Unleavened bread was good for diets but not so tasty, not for a sandwich; toast and cheese was what she felt like but was avoiding. Mo ate dried fruit in handfuls. She should have. It was a habit to acquire. One mouthful of chocolate. She was not going to because one is two; one is always two.

Life

It was a sigh. She did sigh. She sighed and didnt know she was sighing. Sophie's head would have turned, What's wrong Mummy? She always noticed; so so perceptive, the slightest sigh. Helen couldnt stop herself. Who could? You didnt know you were doing it until then you were, you heard yourself.

Green tea. There was an online site Helen visited which gave good information and green tea was one. It was will and commitment. You cant feed the horse if it doesnt take the food, you lead it to the well but if it doesnt drink. Good habits to acquire.

She would have a proper meal later, her and Sophie, after Mo had gone to work and before Azizah arrived. Although the ironing, she had a pile of ironing, oh God. In Glasgow they might have popped up to see Mum, even for half an hour. There were times she couldnt stay home, if you called this home, although it was. She just needed to get out. Her head was full. She needed to talk. There was nobody. Sad but true. Unless if she phoned Ann Marie. A proper phone call and just talk, and it didnt matter to Glasgow, just whatever, and not having to hide things. She wasnt hiding things. What things? Only her head, she needed to get out her head.

Jill too was somebody, she could be a friend. She already was a friend but a workfriend and there were boundaries with 'workfriends'. Helen discovered this a while ago. During the bad periods with the ex it was like who to turn to? Who was there? It was her own fault. She had moved away from friends, mentally, physically and felt like she was losing touch, just losing touch, if ever she would make another friend. A real friend: people had friends. Real friends, like who were there for you, if you were in trouble, even for advice, only to ask something, just a question, if they felt something rather than another thing, so you could just ask them, for advice, like what would they do my God if it was their brother and he was there and it truly was. She didnt even know if it was. It could be. Perhaps not.

My God, ridiculous, she was.

Only life was changing. Not just for her. Everywhere you looked, there was a hardness. People were tough. If ever it got too much at the casino she would leave. There was a link between it and the outside world; things that happened there. She didnt need Mo to tell her. If you saw the young men. She saw them all the time. What did tenderness even mean? They wouldnt know. None of them. Somebody like Brian, they would think nothing of him: he was just nothing; that is what they would think. Only the strong counted. They were admired and emulated. If anybody showed weakness they stamped on him. Hurt or be hurt. That was poker too, my God. Helen saw them in the tournaments, so cool with their sunglasses and cowboy hats and like the way they acted, filmstars or something. All watching one other. Pretending not to but they were. Such show-offs. I am the toughest look at me. Little boys. Some of the dealers joked with them. Some of them were the same. There was a foolishness about it all. It was like they had their own wee pretend world. Where did they get their money? It didnt matter. They saw nothing without it. Everything depended on having it. Without it there was nothing. They saw nothing. But that was society. It was forced on you and you had to live. It didnt matter if you thought something else you still had to live. There were men Mo knew were 'good', meaning *virtuous* but it was the same for them, they too had to live. How did they do it? People had to.

Mr Adams was not 'good'. Helen would never have said he was. Even he was crooked, he might have been. Although if it was business. Crooks and businessmen. But he was the strongest, not meaning physical – far from it. Although he might have been.

There was plenty she didnt know, not when it came down to it, about men, ones like him. You had to be careful. If you were not respectful, you met dealers who werent. It was risky, because who were you talking to? One like the mad doctor they patronised, even treating him with contempt. How come? Because he was a doctor? So like doctors were not to gamble? It was stupid. He was an actual surgeon anyway but he was a good guy and it wasnt fair. And they were taking risks too because how did they know about the person underneath? They only saw the surface. Stay or take a card. But the real actual person? They didnt do it to the Chinese; they were many and who was who? who was with who? you didnt know. There were ones never spoke to anybody, till then you saw them part of a group; the silent guy sitting at the edge, hardly even there, probably he was the toughest and the most dangerous. Too many stories. Criminals and gangsters, killers. One she knew was up on trial, a horror. He sat across from her. Gloating and horrible, that was him. The next thing was the newspaper photograph and she knew it was him, she knew it, although he wasnt smiling, that wasnt in the photograph. He wouldnt have cared. Another one the police took. He was playing the machines when they came for him. People would have expected him to run but he didnt. He just looked at them. What was that look? it was so – just something. Men could do it. Then the ones who vanished, just like disappeared. They were there every week until the time they werent, and you never saw them again. What was it? Had something happened? Had they changed their life? They had had enough of gambling, or were fighting against the addiction if that is what it was, if their partners had caught them lying, or their employer, they had been using somebody else's money so now it was like fraud, they were liars and cheats. So then the disgrace. People cannot cope, they run away. So understandable. It was shame, you were shamed, in front of your family and your community, your close friends, everybody. So then you escape, you disappear. Mo spoke about that because it happened to somebody close to him. For most people it is the same; at least once in their life, they do something that is just so so horrible, and hurtful for others, something that makes them so very very ashamed. It is a disgrace, they feel the disgrace. That is what Mo thought. Helen agreed with him, although with Mo, she could never imagine him doing anything. He said he had when he was young but it was hard to believe. People have different ideas. Disgrace for some is not for others.

Perhaps he did disgrace his family. People can think it. That doesnt mean it is true. Especially with families; families families.

People had mega disgraces, some had minor. For their family but not for others. Some families dont care. Some dont even know. Society sees it as a disgrace but they dont. Families can be sick, so can society.

This nonsense about tee-shirts and underwear, people ironed them, some did and some didnt, what did it matter? She had a pile of it waiting.

Unironed vests. There were families thought that a disgrace, girls especially. Sophie. But the same with gambling, if people dont know about it. Not all gambling is bad. What about lotteries? people do lotteries. Ministers and priests so they can rebuild their churches, so gambling isnt bad, not as such. The ones Jesus threw out the temple were gambling, some of them.

Helen knew about gambling. That was the one thing. Mo forgot how experienced she was. It was not like 'theory'. Mo knew in 'theory'. Helen knew from experience, and that was the difference. People lost everything gambling, their lives too. People kill themselves. And through their stupidity other people might die, the very ones closest to them. Helen heard stories. Everybody did. This was the reality if you worked in the gambling business. It wasnt only money people lost, it only starts that way. Mr Adams said that. Money leads to other matters, and sometimes quickly, before you know where you are, you have gambled and you have lost, and what comes next depends on other things. Rich people can have different competitions; they compete in different ways, for different things, things invisible to ordinary people. Lives depend upon it. And not their own, never their own.

Mr Adams said things that were different but so true, they always sounded true. Mo would have liked him. Helen really really believed that. She never told Mo about him but if she did, perhaps she could. When he said things, you felt like it was obvious and wondered why other people didnt seem to know. He didnt gamble much. Not that Helen knew about. Perhaps he did and she didnt find out. She didnt see him doing it, because him doing it was invisible; to her it was. *Invisible.* He only had sex with her on one occasion, like proper occasion. That was so strange because he could have had it on other occasions. He didnt want to. Helen wouldnt have said no. Really, it was up to him. He only wanted to have her there beside him, just seeing her, that was it, looking at her. Some men were like that. Supposed to be. She didnt know them! She had a 'beautiful body'! But she didnt. He said she did but it wasnt true. Her hips were too wide and her bum was so big, so big. It was always big. She never had slim hips; other girls did, they could be too slim; some were. Helen was slim from the waist up. But it didnt matter. Skinny ribs. You could see her ribs. Before she had Sophie she had no tummy at all. When she lay flat, it was like a bowl. Her ex said that. That was why he wanted her topless. Just show off your boobs. Nobody will see your ribs. That was him when they went to Majorca. You've got the biggest boobs. Who cares about your ribs. Nobody wants to see them. Your boobs are hanging down anyway so nobody will. If I was a woman I would show them off. What a fool he was. So stupid, so so stupid, and prejudiced, completely.

Anyway, it didnt matter. Prejudiced males were ten-a-penny. Never trust a word they say. That applied to most of them. Even Mo, sometimes it did. Imagine a break with other women. A long weekend. Just the company, having a laugh. There were clubs you could join and specialised holidays; only women went, they did painting and walks, sight-seeing, but proper sight-seeing, discovering about history and all different things; artefacts of archaeology. Women went together, all ages and all shapes and sizes and no one worrying about anything, what men said or anything about them, they just had no presence, *no presence*. When she first heard about the all-women holiday to the Greek islands it was the first name into her head. Lesbos. Just silliness. *Lesbos*. But it was a nice name. She liked it.

But he did make her shiver. It was an odd thing. An older guy. You would have expected her ex for that because of bodies. There was no comparison how his was better, more like 'attractive'. Mr Adams' body wasnt attractive at all. Not really, and she didnt think his – calling it penis, not how it looked, and it didnt go so hard, so she didnt – it wasnt so what you might think attractive. Helen didnt think so although she wasnt good on men. She didnt think she was. Jill was better. Helen liked Jill; it didnt matter she was posh. Caroline acted as if she and

Helen should stick together. Helen didnt care about that. Anyway, Jill wasnt really posh, it was just her voice, and it was only English, upper English or what, middle class. Women like Jill have posh voices but only because it is English middle class. Caroline's was English working class, so that and Scottish went together, so if they stuck together. Caroline thought they should. But not all Scottish was working class, some was posh, it just depended.

There was a drip at the kitchen sink, the tap there, it was so occasional it didnt seem like a drip at all but she found it aggravating. Then the effect it had on the heating system, if that knocking sort of clanking sound worsened. Mo spoke about fixing that but he couldnt, it was a specialised job. Why do men think they can do these things?

Oh God sinks, why was she thinking about sinks, she didnt want to think about sinks, damn sinks, bad enough with the ironing to do and she would have to do it.

It was true that she hadnt met his parents but he didnt have to worry, she was not bothered, not really, only about what she had, and she only wanted what she had. She wasnt looking for anything else, only for Sophie and things with her ex, if it all could be resolved properly about access matters and whatnot, everything, please God if it could be, that was all, nothing more, she was not being greedy or too wishful in her thinking, surely not, only if things would go as they were going. She didnt need to meet anybody, parents or like anybody. Really, she didnt care. A side of her was glad not to. Especially for Sophie. How she would cope with all the new people. It would be so like strange, a new family and a different family. But that was human beings; they were all different, all strange. Her and Mo. Who would have guessed about them? Nobody at all. Not like when it happened back in Glasgow, who could have guessed about that? Nobody.

It was also the sarcasm with men. So much of how they communicated was sarcasm-based. Not only did they do it to women, they did it to themselves. Mo didnt mean it but he was sharp, occasionally too sharp. Some of the comments he made, sometimes you wondered. He was a Londoner and used to speaking in certain ways but Glasgow was different; you had to be careful. Helen had worried about him there.

All the lives. People's lives. The ones you were glad to see the back of. It was good when they vanished. Away to annoy somebody else. You never knew who was at your table. And if they were looking at you. Creeps. They didnt care if you saw them. Some did and some didnt. Other ones only looked when you didnt. They didnt seem to be looking but they were and you knew they were, and it gave you the creeps how with their eyes on you and that was that, and how could you hide? you couldnt, unless a duvet cover from your chin down because even your neck, hanging down from your neck, the bumps would show, so it had to be from your chin, if it was hanging down to really hide them. Girls had their boobs taped to flatten them down. Fathers did that. Where did they do it? Some country. Then their feet, they taped the girls' feet so tightly the bones broke and that was them. What a thing. A horror. Feet. What was feet?

People were living in nightmares. You were *exposed*. That is how Helen felt. And if there were two of them staring at you, if they were together doing it, with their little smiles all the time, wanting you to see it. Men did that. They came to your table on purpose. Not just hers. But Helen could tell when they did, how they sat down and the little looks to each other. Then if they waited on till she finished her shift, not taking no for an answer, there they were on the pavement. My God! What did they think? That she would go with them! People are mad. Men are. Any woman in her right mind, none would ever, not in their right mind, never ever, not with any of them. Mr Adams was different. She chose him. He chose her but she chose him. He hadnt chosen anyone else. It was something to smile about. Why not? If it was true and it was. She was the one he chose. That is the true fact. Imagine Mum. If she had only known. The very idea. She wouldnt believe it, except it was the truth. Mum didnt rate her; not as a person. She made that plain often enough. Why deny it? Mum didnt rate her. Imagine that, a mother. So unfair, so very very unfair. A child is innocent. Why was Helen being blamed? What had she ever done? Children are innocent. Adults have a responsibility.

My God and it was even like she had extended it to Sophie. Okay if it was to Helen, her own daughter, then so be it, so be it, but not to the daughter's daughter, that horrible negativity, it was so unfair. The lack of interest, that is what it was, Mum turning her head. Helen saw her do it. Sophie was crying and Mum turned her head away, like just turned her head away. Turning away from a child.

Although Sophie's behaviour, sometimes, it was difficult; back then it was and no wonder, the wee soul. Complete turmoil. So no wonder she had the screaming fits, worse than tantrums. Poor Mo when it happened to him, people looking and seeing. It pierced him. Like a knife going in. Them all looking like he was a murderer or a paedophile. Him being Asian was so much the worse.

Then something from Mo the way he was looking, almost saying something but stopping himself, meaning molested. If anything had ever happened to Sophie. He wondered about it but not in so many words. Just come out and say it. Helen would have preferred if he had. Because never. Never never. Never never could that have happened and it was surprising Mo could ever think it, so so surprising, honestly astonishing, like how could he ever? That was 'piercing like a knife' but the knife was into Helen. Her own child my God. Nothing had happened to Sophie. Nothing ever would. Helen would die, she would die, nothing ever

Nothing ever could. If anything ever could, it would never. Nothing ever would.

Helen looked to the clock.

It seemed ages since he had gone to collect her. Occasionally they walked a different route home. Sophie liked to see things and Mo enjoyed pointing them out. The screaming stage had passed. He carried his ID anyway. In case somebody called the cops. Paki bastard. Going to sell her to the slave-trade you cunt, where's your ID then?

In me pocket.

And a photograph of the three of them together for further evidence, especially if he had to carry her in public, she hated him doing it. It was okay in the house if he did it for a laugh but not outside, going up the tube escalator or walking through a crowd or across a busy road. Mo joked about it but Sophie hated it. Put me down put me down! I dont want you to hold me! I dont want you to hold me!

He was not holding her he was carrying her. There is a difference. Sophie didnt understand that. At least it was better now than the early days in Glasgow. Leave me! Leave me! She wouldnt hold his hand without a fight, just being touched. Oh I dont like being touched! In this world you have to be touched. You learn that as a child. Although it can be an invasion, of course it can and was for Helen when she was a girl, people grabbing her and poking her. Why? Why did they think that was acceptable, poking your fingers into a child? They looked for an excuse to do it. Men were the worst, and so patronising, the way they did it, so actually just like patronising, like with dogs, stroking their muzzle. Pawing you. What a pretty little girl, stroking your head. Or taking you by the shoulder, What's

137

that love? grasping you, so you cant hardly move, What's that love? and you cant hardly breathe. Men did that. Imagine. If you asked them a question, the hand going round your shoulder, gripping, What's that love? suffocating. On television too you saw them doing it. Not to other men, oh no, they just did it to females. Helen didnt like it. Her own mother wasnt a toucher. Helen was so very glad of that, except the odd occasion, it would have been nice. A mother who doesnt touch. That was unusual, surely. There were times Helen had to touch Sophie, just pick her up and hold her, just hold her, she needed to do it – giving her a bath or she was in her nightdress my God what was wrong with that? just so she was alright. Nothing ever would happen to her, if anything ever did, if anything ever did she would die, Helen would die, she would, she would die, she would die, oh my God. Leave me leave me! Never.

Sophie wasnt spoiled. Helen didnt spoil her, she loved her. People who love dont *spoil*. What is *spoil*? People said it about children, Oh she is 'spoiled', but Sophie wasnt 'spoiled'; she was loved. It was the same for Helen when she was wee. Dad didnt spoil her he loved her. Mum said, Oh dont spoil the girl. But he didnt. It was unfair saying that. Dad only loved her. Love is different. If Mum couldnt recognise that. Helen felt sorry for her. A dad loves his daughter. So if her ex did want to take Sophie away for whatever, a long weekend or a holiday, if he did, if he did he did and he was entitled, it was up to him and he could come to London, just make the arrangements, it was up to him.

Parents love their children, and if they dont, well, if they dont they dont. Only dont let the children see it. If a child knows, surely that is the worst? An innocent little child.

No wonder she worried. People worried. No wonder they did because take your eye off a child for one solitary moment, just one.

Helen would die.

Mo knew better than to let her out his sight, so nothing would happen. Not with him. Because he wouldnt let it.

It was obvious. Who didnt know it. You had to keep your eye on children. Even that isnt enough. It isnt. Not if somebody is there, watching, waiting, with all the patience waiting and waiting for the moment to come and it does and they just they grab the child and steal it. Nobody means to let it happen but it does because the stealer is there to do it, the abductor and the child is gone, never to be seen again.

Families never recovered. Couples split, the relationship ended, divorce; because of what happened, people laying blame on themself and each other; if she hadnt done that and done that and if he hadnt gone there and come back from there, and who let go her hand, why did he let go her hand, for that one fraction of a second, and the wee girl jumped out and the motor hit her full on, in that one fraction of a second, when he lost concentration, he took his eye off her then when he turned back at that very very next moment she was gone, vanished, where on earth was she? and searching everywhere. But the girl had vanished, perhaps wundered off but no, she had been taken, a bad man took her and whisked her away and she would now be overseas, forever, in a country where you couldnt find out things, where nobody knew what you were talking about and the police didnt even care, they couldnt speak your language and didnt even try, they didnt care, nobody did.

Not even a proper ironing board but blankets and towels on the floor. She had to kneel on the floor to do it. Sore on the back but better than that old wobbly contraption thing Mo brought home from his travels. He called it an ironing board, it wasnt an ironing board, God knows what it was although it worked fine for his shirts because of the shoulders and sleeves but not for other things. His shirts had to be 'smart white'. That was a laugh. It was a constant battle. He hated the same shirt two nights in a row. Other men werent so finicky. He liked to be smart, fresh shirt, smart white, that was him. She helped him. She didnt have to, she just did; women were better at ironing. He spent hours, she did it in half the time. Oh well what did it matter. Anyway, she liked helping him.

Girls were ridiculous for clothes. Oh for a boy. The very idea of vests being ironed! No boy in his right mind

But surely Helen had ironed her own clothes? Not at six she hadnt. Even holding the iron, she couldnt have. Mum's old thing weighed a ton.

Sophie was fussy, so so fussy, too fussy. Mo made fun of her. Of course she didnt like it, but she was learning. Even how she smiled. That was unusual, really, and beautiful. She had fought so hard against him. Yet here he was winning her over. But had he? Yes. Sometimes.

Helen kept out it.

Sophie had been fourteen months when she started walking and even then, when she looked at you, it was as though she saw into you, and was asking, Who are you? Are you my mother? But these questions were within herself and the answers came from within herself. Are you my mother? Sophie asked the question and gave the answer, Yes, you are. It is you, you are my mother.

If it wasnt so silly she might have thought Sophie was special, her own daughter. This wee girl the size of nothing who had the power to defend herself against a full-grown man.

It was true, so resilient, really, and strong-willed. You wouldnt believe how strong-willed, and children needed to be. It was the survival instinct like in this day and age especially, the weak would not survive. People scrambled for scraps. And Sophie was a fighter thank God, such determination! There was a humorous side. Mo was inexperienced with children and didnt know about staring games. He tried to get Sophie to break the stare by laughing into her face and making funny faces. He failed. She focused on something faraway. Eventually her expression altered and she looked straight at him but a concentration was here and it could make you squirm. Squirm was a good word. Mo squirming, yes, he squirmed! He could never have broken her stare. He didnt have the power. It was Sophie broke the mood. She exercised the control. Mo adopted a gangster voice: Hey kid, why you staring at me? Wanna make something of it! You wanna fight me? Hey kid.

But still she stared at him and he was standing there – what? defeated. She had defeated him. So then he called her 'kid'. Why had he called her 'kid'? She was not a goat. Helen didnt like him calling her that. Why did he? Because she had won? A kid is an animal and children are not animals. Then he patted her, or tried to. It could be the most patronising thing one person ever did to another. That was a dog, not a child. Dogs are clapped, not people. People are people, even children. A kid is not a child, a kid is a baby goat.

Mo smiled when Helen said that but it was true.

Brian grabbed her and whizzed her off the floor. Helen would be walking by when he did it. Although it was fun she didnt always like it. And not the way he did it, if he jerked her too hard, her shoulders came back and it was sore and hurt her, hurt her chest. Not like Dad who did it smooth. Brian was just like so clumsy, so so clumsy. He just plucked her up; one moment you were walking. She didnt even see him till suddenly she was in the air and kicking, how could you not kick! of course she kicked. Because he shouldnt have done it without warning. It was only fun and it *was* fun but only if he warned her first, and he never. It wasnt a good thing to do, not to a little girl. It was inconsiderate. No wonder she kicked him! But it was not like she meant it my God how could a child be blamed for that? Nobody would. Not even Mum. Surely not. Brian was her pet. Skinny malinky long-legs. Dad called him that. Legs like kirby-grips. It was unfair, but that was Dad. But it was funny. Kirby-grips and legs. Big banana feet, went to the pictures and fell through the seat. If you were a child, you just imagined it and of course you laughed, skinny malinky long-legs. But Dad was Dad, an adult. So it wasnt funny. He shouldnt have done it. It was unfair, like for a son – or for any person, male or female, when you were growing and maturing.

What did people expect? A man grabs you up, are you supposed to surrender?

No but relax, relax, you never relax, when have you ever relaxed, you never fucking relax. That was her ex talking; his voice was still in her head. He liked to swear because he was the boss. That was him.

Helen put up with most things but swearing in front of children was difficult to take. Also if it was girls; so disrespectful. For women too. Guys swore round the blackjack table but what did that matter, you were only a dealer.

Respect was important. If men were respectful to women there would be no rapes and no humiliations, these horrible ones like the fourteen-year-old girl in France who was stripped by a crowd. She was wearing a hijab and they took it off, and they stripped her.

Men who could do that. Mature men, adults.

Just ugly brutality, cowards and bullies. What was worse? racism or sexism? But both at the same time. It was just like any excuse.

It was true what he said about relaxing. Helen did find it difficult, and always did. When Dad took her onto his knee she could only sit five seconds until needing down. She hated being trapped, struggled and struggled, she struggled and he still held her. But he shouldnt have held her. He held her too long. If the child wants down then put her down; dont hold onto her; not against her will. Why did Dad do that? That is what he did, bouncing her on his knee, making her still, having to be still, him forcing her to be still but she wouldnt be still, no, and why should she have been? never. Apparently she fought and struggled. No wonder. That wasnt fun. Would Dad have done it with Brian? He said he was beating the record. Five seconds is the record! It caused a bad fight with Mum. It was her told him to stop it, to put her down. She *ordered* him. She was the strong one. The strong silent type. That was supposed to be men; not in her house, Dad roared and Mum gave the orders

Oh God.

Anyway, some families were sick. What did it even mean? sick! Society began from there, the sickness. You only had to watch the news. What about hers where you had one member not speaking to the others, just cutting himself off? It was Dad's fault. He singled Brian out. Imagine he was alive and she brought home Mo. Nobody was good enough for her, not even the King of England, never mind 'the wee Paki' up the stair. That was how they spoke. They werent even being racist. They said that, oh it is not racist really, only 'ingrained'. Ingrained. The answer was children. If all children mixed together and had friends like from everywhere then if their parents met up and knew each other. Mo said that. Helen wasnt so sure, thinking of Glasgow and the Catholic Protestant thing. Mo knew nothing about it. You having a laugh? But it was something to laugh about. Oh it is only old-fashioned. People said that; that was how you felt it was so like backward, and they laughed, Helen didnt like how they laughed. Mo too. People could be patronising. Muslims wanted separate schools so why was that okay but not like for Catholics and Protestants? if they wanted their own education for their own religion. What difference would it be if it was them kept apart from other people? It would be the same if it was Muslims or if it was like Hindus and Sikhs or Jews, whoever it was. She didnt care if Mo disagreed, 'faith schools' or what you call them. Mo said they were good people but were they if they were going to be sectarian? How could they be? That was sectarian, that was communalism. What was communalism? If it was hurting, if people were being hurt, if they were being killed? Were they hilarious? Why were they not hilarious like if it was Catholics and Protestants? If that was funny what about the other stuff? Mo didnt think that was funny if it was like the Punjab or what he was talking about.

White woman with her own baby! That was the hilarious thing how Mum, if she found out about Mo's family not thinking she was good enough. Pakistanis! My God! The neighbours would laugh at that one. Not that Mum worried too much about neighbours. If anybody it was Dad. He was the petty one. But at least he would have been there for her. He would have been. Helen knew he would have been. He would have loved Sophie; just *having* a grandchild, Dad would have loved that, he would never have been off the phone, and asking questions, wanting to speak to the girl and just like my God a proper grandparent. No wonder Sophie showed no interest in talking to her. You cant blame the child for that, you have to look at the adult. Mum never asked questions, except the most basic. Why didnt she ask the wee soul a question? She never did, not a proper one. Her one and only granddaughter.

If it wasnt for Mo Helen wouldnt have bothered keeping in touch. He was cheery, or tried to be.

Although he could be too cheery. Mum didnt like 'cheeriness'. Helen didnt like it much either. Cheery men! Women werent 'cheery' in that way. It bordered on stupidity. With her ex it was forced. As though everything was fine when it wasnt,

it was awful; things were awful; lousy and horrible; just hopeless really and that voice going on and on, pretend cheeriness.
The way he did it was such a sham. Yes Mo was cheery but you
never felt he was acting. With him it was real. Because he was
good, a good man, so if he was cheery, it was an honest cheeriness. He respected people, and had a talent for them too.
Really, he did, like if Helen was late meeting him someplace he
would be hearing a stranger's life story by the time she arrived.
Even at the supermarket he got into conversations. It was nice
when it happened; an old person started talking and when Mo
replied that was him, just another London guy, it didnt matter
he had a different background, it was two London voices.
Helen liked that. It was so nice when it happened. He had the
London patter. They all had it, the ones Helen met, they tried
to patter her. So she wasnt always boring. Otherwise why
would they bother? They wouldnt bother otherwise.

Mo collected Sophie at ten past three and should have been
home by three thirty, at the latest. Helen could have done it
herself but him doing it was great: one less worry. When he
couldnt she had to be out of bed by half past one, and even
then it was a rush. Before Sophie started school was the very
worst; nurseries and childminders, that was the nightmare of
nightmares back in Glasgow, she was going mad, like truly, her
sanity, so that was a major thing how Mo had been so support-
ive. They had only just met. He was not like a bosom friend but
take away him and who was there? Because Mum, my God.
She could not rely on Mum. She made that plain enough. Dont
think of me, dont expect me. And that damn nursery and all
their officious damn officiousness, rows and tellings off, oh late
again, late again they hated you being late even two minutes,
just that officiousness and how mothers had to stay once a fort-
night to be with their child, to *be* with their child. What did that
mean? How presumptuous was that, it was just so incredibly

presumptuous. As if people didnt have jobs to go to. My God.
As if life wasnt complicated enough. What world did they
come from? People had to work, and it was five nights of every
week, it needed to be. Why did they not understand that?
People lived every day. Not just some. They didnt stop breathing and eating every so often, it was just so stupid. What did
people think? People didnt think. That was the problem. Thinking wasnt a strong point.

Without Mo she would have been stranded. She would
never have returned to London. It wouldnt even have occurred
to her because with Sophie and everything, if the nursery
scene was bad in Glasgow at least she knew about it there and
the travelling wasnt so bad. Then worrying about him all the
time, her ex, if he was going to interfere and he would have my
God he would have of course he would have.

She would never have managed. She didnt have the looks for
prostitution. Well of course she did. If you were young, you
only had to be young. She would never have considered it. She
didnt know how; even making enquiries, who would you have
asked? it was ridiculous, except in a roundabout way, but who
would have known? It was all guessing, and if you went up to
somebody and asked, what a laugh that would have been. The
'girls' came into the casino. Helen could have got talking to one,
or if she had gone into a casino herself, another casino, and just,
all she would do, just, if she just waited or sat down and what
would happen perhaps if a guy talked to her or what, she didnt
know. Except the problem then that people would know her in
these other casinos. You get to know people, and they know you.

Imagine walking the streets my God whoever could imagine. And the risks, imagine the risks. Helen saw girls on these
quiet streets, poor-looking and cold, behind buildings and in
back lanes and car-parks, so horrible and dangerous. Girls getting beaten up and raped and murdered, how many girls were

murdered every year? the figures were shocking; what were they? You saw these guys, horrible horrible guys, looking at you, just how they looked at you like sleazy, so so sleazy. Stripping you with their eyes, women said that, oh he strips you with his eyes. That was what they done, and to make you feel that way, you just turned your head and they were watching you and that was it, they wanted you to know, that is what they were doing. Sleazy and horrible. They wanted you to be a slave, you were just a woman, you meant so little to them, they looked down on you and didnt think you were anything, not a real human being, they didnt think you were, just a slave. That was him. You were a servant bringing up his child and for sex, that was what he wanted you for so he could penetrate you or if it was your mouth, that was penetration too, it was all just penetration, penetrating another human being; and you werent another human being, not to them. They only thought of men. They didnt think of women. That was the look, how they did it, sleazebags. That was a good word 'sleazebags'.

Helen watched for that look and if Mo was there too. Who is this little guy getting this white woman? she must like Asians, she must want it from Asians, smiling horrible smiles, if she wants it from anybody, perhaps she does so then they are looking. All she had to do was tell Mo, if ever one did. They were taking a risk because he had that in him too and he would do it; her ex would have found that out. Mo didnt care, big or small, he said he couldnt fight to save his life but it wasnt true it just wasnt true, she knew it wasnt, he had thick arms and could punch, she knew he could or else stick a knife in them, small men could do that. Dad always said it about tall skinny ones, forget about them it was the wee guys with the bad temper, they were the dangerous ones.

But that was the last thing, telling Mo, she would never take the risk because if she did.

She had learned not to react. People thought she was naive. They were the naive ones. If you worked in a casino you were used to men, being looked at and watched. You coped. You had to. Helen was young and men looked at her. She was a girl. Girls learned. As would Sophie. Helen would teach her. Mothers should teach daughters. Instead of criticising. Fathers could help. Real fathers. Not only biological ones, real fathers dont have to be 'biological', not if it is a natural feeling for children, and not like an enemy. There were enemies of children. Mo wasnt one and neither was her ex, she could never have charged him with that – oh God, a sharp pain in her tummy. Sometimes she experienced this. 'Anxiety' in the stomach. Caroline called it that. She might be dealing the cards then for no reason she got it. Anxiety.

She opened her eyes, seeing her slippers by the door. Fancy ones Mo had bought her. She liked the design. Her eyes had been closed. Why did she not raise her head? she didnt want to, she didnt want to see things. People dont have to see things, not if they dont want to. Just the ironing. What did it matter it was just so stupid and daft just day in day out clothes and worries. Ironing is just silly and foolish and the most foolish foolish

Helen left the kitchen. Through in the front room she opened the window to see out. In the old days women got a reputation for doing this. Nosey buggers. Around here it was like creepy-crawlies, that was the worry, if a driver saw you leaning out: he circled and came back again to see if you were still there and if so, if you were – what? Did you want a man? No thank you, nice of you to ask, she had one and one was plenty thank you very much.

Punctuality was not a strong point. He was good but not for time; he ignored it. Him and his chatting and meeting people. Who was he talking to now? Somebody anyway. Sophie would have to remind him on the way home, otherwise it was another port of call.

Men exaggerated about everything and he was no different. What was the opposite of expert? That was how she felt about men. Sometimes she thought she knew them, most times she didnt. And they lied. It was second nature. Helen hated lies and men did it the worst. Even the ones who didnt, they did too, they all did; white lies and black lies. Some guys tell them because they are lazy. Too lazy to tell the truth! A comedian on television talked about that and it was funny. Usually Helen didnt like comedians. Haw haw haw, ho ho ho, laughing all the time at horrible nonsense, stupid stupid silliness, showing off, that was them usually, you felt like putting your fingers in your ears.

It was a quiet street and that was good but you never saw children where were the children! At school. But they should have been home by now, nearly quarter to four my God so actually they were late. Of course he detoured, if he knew she was in bed, if he met a friend it was yap yap yap, he just talks all the time, Sophie making faces at him, pulling his sleeve. She was so right, just all the time talking, talk talk talk, even walking down the street on the mobile talking or texting people. When he came round the corner he would be texting.

In Glasgow too. For somebody who had never been to Glasgow, he knew more people than her. It was a knack he had. What about her friends? Why dont you introduce me to people? What people!

Her life had gone from top to bottom bottom to top, just screwy. How had it happened? It was just so *screwy*.

He had his own life and she was happy that he did. She didnt need to meet his family. Things might change but it didnt matter if it didnt. This was their relationship and it suited her, it suited her. Oh God.

He was her best friend. He even said it about the relationship, the first thing you should be is a friend. Friends come first. He called it a 'position'. That is my 'position'.

In Glasgow

there they were thank God, that was them coming from round the corner thank God oh thank God thank God. Hand in hand. Of course. Sophie had the schoolbag over one shoulder. Of course of course.

Helen closed the window quickly, returned to the kitchen, switched on the radio.

Sophie was supposed to wear the schoolbag over both shoulders but she didnt. It was pointless talking to her. Whether Mo tried or not it would have made no difference.

When they came in through the outside door Helen was kneeling by the ironing board iron in hand and she rose. Sophie called, Oh mummy I have things to show you.

All kinds of things! Mo chuckled.

Sophie was hopping on one foot while untying a shoestrap. Helen filled a kettle of water. We had an errand to go, said Mo, and to Sophie: Didnt we?

Yes.

It's a secret, said Mo and he winked at Helen while wagging his finger at Sophie: I thought you were bursting for the loo?

Sophie sighed, glaring at him.

You should have gone in the park!

She kicked off her other shoe and stepped sideways into the bathroom, snapping the door shut.

You went to the park? asked Helen.

No, we were passing but she wouldnt go in.

Sophie shouted from behind the door: I'm not doing the bathroom in the park it's all dirty!

Mo whispered very loudly at the bathroom door: But what if she explodes! We dont want exploding girls, who wants an exploding girl?

Sophie called: I'm not listening!

Helen returned to the ironing, rearranged the clothing. Mo followed her, wanting to talk but she wasnt wanting to listen, not just now, not when she was trying to work in this confined space. She held the iron and edged past him. Sophie was even worse, she stood far too close. It was how accidents happened. What if it was like boiling water in a pot, or if the kettle tipped over? Even the gasrings on top of the cooker were a hazard the way they had gaps. It wouldnt be the first time a pot wobbled and nearly fell. The design was bad. The ones who designed cookers had never cooked a meal in their life, not in a cramped space where people were knocking your elbows. It was all rich people, where you could just swan around and people might come in and have a chat, sit down at the table, a big table; probably there would be servants, and a cook doing the cooking or carry-outs from a high-class restaurant.

What did he want to talk about that was so important? It couldnt be that important, not that it couldnt wait five minutes. Everybody talked in the restaurant kitchen, according to him, they shouted at one another. Perhaps they did but what did that have to do with it? They were adults and like experienced kitchen-workers, that was their job. And he moved about he always moved about, why didnt he stand still? He was talking. People should stand still when they talk my God he never did – and the clothes there too, even if he lifted them because if he stood on them for God sake having to wash the damn things again and then – she always ended up – why couldnt he wait? could he not wait? surely he could wait?

Although he would be away to work soon. She knew that, so if he needed to talk, it had to be now, or soon. Only sometimes it wasnt important, not once he had said it. Chit-chat, that was all. Why couldnt it wait? He could wait. She had waited for him.

At least she wasnt cooking; that was the worst, no space at all, that so-called counter, having to keep it clear, everything stacked everywhere just because nowhere and nothing, no proper cupboards, no workplace my God this silly wire thing he brought home; the cutlery was supposed to like stand upright to dry off naturally but individual articles forever slipped through the gaps and landed in the sink and that sink, like gunge, always thick with it, and you had to wash them all again. It just created work. Why create work? That was labour-saving devices. He loved them but they were silly gadgets most of them.

He was talking again. Although it was cheery, Sophie was there and smiling at what he was saying and she put her arm round Helen. Helen said to her: Who does he remind you of? Does he remind you of anybody?

Mr Noisy.

Yes and Mr Nosey, rolled into one.

Mo laughed.

And Mr Grumpy, said Sophie.

Yes!

It aint me that's Mr Grumpy! called Mo. There's two Mr Grumpys in this house and they aint Misters let me tell you they are Misses.

Huh! said Helen.

Mo was beckoning to her: Guess what about?

Pardon?

Guess what I want to talk to you about?

I cant.

You have to.

Oh God.

Mo smiled.

You're going to work in an hour and here you are blethering!

Exactly, he said.

Blether blether blether.

Yes, he said.

Helen sighed. There was a chair positioned to the side of the counter gable. She rose from the floor, settled the iron upright on a space on the counter, switched on the kettle of water then plopped down onto the chair.

Sophie was watching her. Of course she was. Helen smiled and Sophie smiled in reply. That was a girl who worried; six years of age and already, already she was doing it.

It was *having* people, she *had* people, and had known loss, whatever the reality was her father was no longer the fixture and that was it, poor wee soul. No doubt she worried about Helen. Of course she would. Helen's arm was round her shoulder and she pulled Sophie to her. It was good having someone. Poor Brian if it *was* him. Imagine it was, down-and-out and on the street. A homeless person living rough. With psychological health problems. He should never have been on the street. That was so wrong. Britain was a horrible country. Everything being frittered and people in need. Brian should have been receiving care, he should have been in a nursing home. He was Helen's brother and she would have looked out for him, come to see him every day possible, as often as she could, help him get better. Mo would be good too. He was good with people, he liked them. And if you like people people like you. Oh my God.

Mo was smiling.

What? said Helen.

You're in fantasy-land!

No she isnt, said Sophie, leaning closely into her.

Yes she is, her head is in the clouds!

Dont be so cheeky, said Sophie.

She's miles away!

Oh I'm just thinking, said Helen.

What about? said Sophie.

Nothing for nosey folk! Helen smiled. But Sophie didnt. Sophie was staring, about to cry my God she was, blinking to stop the tears. Helen sighed. Oh Sophie, she said.

I'm not nosey. You said I was.

I didnt.

You did. I was nosey. You said it.

Oh but it was fun, it was fun; I dont think you're nosey at all.

I hate it when you say that.

Honestly, it was only fun.

You know your mum, said Mo, if there's a joke she'll make it.

Sophie looked at him. He poked his tongue out but she kept her face straight. A battle of wills. Helen shut her eyes. The water in the kettle had started boiling. She reached to switch it off. She thought to say something but didnt. They were both strong characters: stronger than Helen. At the same time it was comical, like how she had been herself, always on her dignity, on her *high horse*. Dad shouted that whenever Brian lifted her. Look at wee jellybelly, she's up on her high horse, and that was Brian. Dad always poked fun. He shouldnt have. It wasnt sarcasm but it wasnt nice. Insensitive. That was Dad, like a lot of men. They saw things differently so their jokes too, their jokes were just not funny. But why did he pick on his own son? All the time he did it and it wasnt nice. If he was doing his best. People do their best. Why did Dad do it? Mum didnt like him when he did. Helen saw that. She was a wee girl and she saw it. Mum didnt like Dad. Brian was only lifting her, putting her on his shoulders. What was wrong with that? That was a big brother, he was a great big brother. There wasnt a single piece of badness in him, there wasnt – him and his burnt toast, he loved burnt toast. So did she, although it was bad for your insides. Brian burnt it black then scraped off the worst portions, showing it to Helen making her jealous. Oh I love burnt toast, mmm. That was what he said, tormenting her. He did torment her so she did it back to him. Oh but it was playful. It was not in *spite*. There was no *spite*. There wasnt. They didnt blame each other. Why would they have if it was fun? It was fun. Nobody was at *fault*. She was a wee girl. There was no *fault*. Why *fault*? What *fault* was there? Only Dad. Dad was silly. He was. She saw that now. Grown-ups could be silly, their little jealousies and pettiness. It was the pettiness. Helen hated pettiness. She would far rather

what

too many things. That was life. Where was she in hers? She didnt know, just how her thoughts went with so much like all the time, so so – just on the go, so so much; here there and everywhere and worry worry, him too, her ex, Sophie hadnt said but she looked forward to seeing him; she didnt say because she didnt want to, saying it to Helen so if Helen took it the wrong way – Sophie was safeguarding her! That was what it was, that was this little girl, just so so perceptive about adults and all everything, just everything, an astute wee girl, worrying about her mum. She shouldnt have had to do that. Was that fair? Children shouldnt have to serve the parent.

It was twisted loyalties. He was her father. Your father is your father. It was difficult for him too with them in England. Helen could admit that. It wasnt his fault. He was her dad and your dad is your dad. It was Mo she felt sorry for. He could never be her father, if that was what he was trying, not her real father. If he was trying for that it was silly. All he could do was be nice and be thoughtful, try to be a friend, but not her father like her natural father, he couldnt be that, never. If he was trying that. But he wouldnt have been trying that. Mo was bright and intelligent. He was not stupid. A proper friend. One to one, as an adult to a young person, friendly in that fashion: be responsible and dont give a child everything she wants. Children want everything and cannot have it. Sophie was six years old and had to be controlled. All children do. They cannot do what they want like just anything because they would ruin themselves and what would happen? biscuits for breakfast and chocolate for tea, they would never grow, they would never develop. Adults have to take charge of their development, they have to take charge; a child is a child; a child is not responsible, not for everything. How can she be? It is unfair to expect it. Yes be friends but dont get led astray. That is so easy. Adults fall into the trap. Play their games but be careful too my God they are children, that is all they are, girls are not women, they are not women. Dont blame *them*.

But it would have been good to talk. Who to! There was nobody. Mo was the only one. Her friends in work were workmates. Perhaps if they met outside of work. That would have been nice, going for a coffee. If there was time, but it was difficult fitting things in. It had to be the day off. Although on some subjects you had to know the person. Who would you trust? Matters were private; you couldnt talk about everything, not to everybody. Not even Ann Marie, if she lived close by, although it would have been nice to chat. Anyway, it was Helen's fault; she should have phoned a while ago. Just to say hullo. Although Ann Marie would only talk herself. That was what she did. The conversation would begin with Helen then it would be her and her problems. Ann Marie's life was so taken up with the concerns of other people. Everything. Her parents every day of the week. My God it was so like just horrible, and *drastic*. Helen thought of it as *drastic*. It was your life but it wasnt, you had no control. You life was dominated by others.

It was not them doing it but their *lives*. Their lives dominated yours. Yours was important too but somehow

what happened to it? You were just like an audience. It wasnt their fault it was just their *lives*, how what had happened to them was being overtaken: their lives were being *overtaken*. And it was true, when you listened, my God, how could people's lives be like that? it was just like so so incredible what was happening to them, happening to their families. And they were happening right now like this very very minute these things were *happening*.

But in your life too things were happening. Your life was there and things were in it too, and that was important but who was it important to? Nobody apart from your own family. Nobody was interested. They were in a way but in another way they werent, they just switched the conversation, so you were left feeling what did it matter. You were the audience. They had celebrity lives and you were having to watch them talking about all what happened to them. It wasnt them dominating you, it was their *lives*; there was a difference. If it was only them it would be selfish. So you couldnt blame them, not the real person, only what was happening to them.

Only it would have been good to talk, you get left so you cant talk. That was how Helen felt. She couldnt talk and she didnt. She preferred that anyway. She didnt want to talk about her own life and what was going on. It would have driven her mad. People go mad. Their lives are so insane they became insane themselves, they have to. So they can cope. That was why celebrities were good. You heard what they had for dinner and how they liked cats better than dogs or if they were veggies or red-meat eaters and how they had to watch their calories because they wanted to become good dancers or practise their singing or take lessons to be a chef. Otherwise it was your own life and what happened in it. Your own world was so horrible and you wanted to shut it out. Their lives were so just – what were they? boring. That was what was good. It was all just stupid and silly, what they liked to eat, French or Italian and how their old grandmother always knew they would be rich and famous because that was their family, people always worked hard and were talented and went good holidays to where their family came from, wherever it was.

Oh well.

Tonight was another day. That was what nightshift workers said.

There were creaks in this house. Children were through the wall somewhere; forever thumping about. Helen didnt see them. Perhaps they were white. Most people were Asian or black but some were white. An old black woman came from the next house. Probably a grandmother and was looking after the children. Helen was envious. A mother to baby-sit. Although if Mum lived in London. Thank God she didnt.

Even to relax, it was good to relax. She couldnt have, if Mum was here she couldnt have. Because of whatever. This, that and the next thing.

So if it *was* Brian. If he had recognised her? If he had he would have been so so glad, so glad to see her. Why wouldnt he have been? Unless he was so far gone from the family he didnt want anything to do with anybody, including her, even especially her, if he had recognised her, he didnt want to see her, he didnt want to make the contact. The way he was looking in the taxi window. He was like staring straight at her. Really, he was. And his eyes were like quite frightening, my God they were, scary, that was what Caroline and Jill said, and Danny the driver too like what had he been? like so so wary, just so wary.

Perhaps he hated her. He couldnt hate her. Hate. Why would he hate, hate her? *Hate.*

A brother and sister; surely that *meant* something? He came home for Gran's funeral but not Dad's. So it was not like he disappeared off the face of the earth. Mum made the contact. Dad wouldnt have. So Mum knew how to reach him. But not when Dad died. It was the police traced him. So he was there for Gran's funeral but not for Dad's. Your own father. It was unforgivable. You couldnt have an excuse for that. It didnt matter the past and all what happened. That was over and done with. It was past tense. Get on with living, people have to. Somebody dies but the living go on, and they make a go of things. They have to. It isnt the whole world. Somebody dies everybody else lives. Bury the past. That is what people say. The past is past, it has passed. Brian and Mum were close. So were Helen and Dad. It happens in families; girl father, boy mother, it is so natural, a natural division, her and Dad, him and Mum; that is it, it is natural, it is not like lovers for goodness sake that isnt the relationship.

Life *always* goes on. So if Brian didnt care, neither did Helen. She didnt care either, so that was it too, if he didnt want to make contact with her, okay. It was a hard world out there. It wasnt only boys who had to stick up for themselves. If people try to hurt you you fight back. That was the world and that was what you did. If Brian didnt it was his fault. Boys laughed at Helen but it was not her it was him. Why didnt he fight them? He should have, boys look after girls.

What was Mo doing? He was through in the room, so he was doing something – getting ready to leave? Not yet surely. Nearly four o'clock, oh God, four o'clock, he was, it was time for him to leave.

Sophie glanced away from the television. Sophie said, Mummy are you saying something?

Helen smiled. How was school, you didnt tell me, was it good? Yes.

So what happened? Sophie, what happened? if it was good.

We went to the park.

You went to the park! Helen frowned. You went to the park?

Sophie looked at her.

I thought you didnt go to the park?

It was a film about animals.

What was the park?

Sophie said, The teacher was showing us.

The teacher was showing you the park?

It was a film and it was about animals, people go on motor cars, it's to a park and it's animals they have there. Sophie spoke while staring at the television. Jonathan pushed me. He was pushing me all the time. I told the teacher.

A name like Jonathan, he sounds nice, he sounds a nice boy.

Mum can we do a jigsaw?

Yes. But wait till Mo's gone.

Sophie sighed.

Because he's going to work soon Sophie, we can play after dinner. I'm making a nice dinner.

Oh but Mum.

Fish and potatoes. Fish is good for you. It's brain food, said Helen. Anyway, it isnt good if you tell the teacher on people.

Sophie glanced at her.

Even if a boy pushes you.

He always pushes me.

Because he likes you. Boys push girls because they like them.

Well it's sore, I dont like it.

Can you push him back?

Sophie didnt answer.

Did you say it to Mo about him pushing you? I think he'll say to push him back too.

The teacher said I'm not to.

Oh, well . . . Helen nodded. I dont think that's right. Not to push people. If the teacher said that, did she say that? Sophie, did she say that? If they hit you first and you hit them back, did she say you werent to do it?

Sophie stared at the television.

Helen watched her for a moment. Did *you* push somebody?

No.

Did you push Jonathan?

He pushed me.

Did you push him back? Well you can, if he pushes you.

He likes Evie. He said my coat was funny.

Helen sighed.

He said it was all like painted.

Painted? Well I dont know why he said that. It's a silly thing to say. Boys say silly things. Your coat isnt funny at all.

Mum can we not play the jigsaw?

No but you can play it yourself my girl because I'm starting the dinner.

Can Mo not do it?

No, he's going to work soon.

He's doing the computer.

Yes but he's soon going.

Sophie sighed. Helen watched her. It was the sigh. Children sighing. Of course Helen herself, she was a champion sigher, and it irritated people.

Never mind.

Whatever Sophie was thinking. What did a child think? Sometimes she tensed. Why did she tense like that? So many things. Jonathan had three girlfriends and Sophie wanted to be the fourth. Three girls and she was the fourth. That sounded familiar.

The jigsaw was two years old and Sophie could finish it blindfold. So why not a new one? she had new ones, why not one of them? Oh no, it had to be the old one. A psychologist would know. It certainly was not Sophie's father, and had nothing to do with any 'happier' time. Really, it didnt have that association. Helen would have known. It was her bought the damn thing and it wasnt even a birthday present, just one day they were out at a car-boot sale and she bought it back in Glasgow, that big one over in Royston that Mo discovered and loved all else in the entire whole world, so if that was the 'happy memory', Mo was there.

They went places here when they had the chance. Mo called it 'hunting'. We are going 'hunting' this morning. Sunday morning was best. Coming off the Saturday nightshift she had an hour's doze then it was the market and nice for Sophie that last time especially, seeing a wee girl from her school there with her parents. That was just so nice.

A car-boot sale was the most likely place for a folding bed, a proper one like Mum used to have, then if Brian, it would be there for emergencies, it would just be there, a proper one, if Brian. They had to be there for nine o'clock. So Mo said. Any later and why bother? By lunchtime people were packing up to go home. But it was true. But who cared if you were out for the day and it was family and you were just enjoying it all, and being out and just – life, it was life, life was good when it could be good, it was just so so good, really, and enjoyable. She would have to tell him about Brian.

Why?

But she would.

But why? If she told Mo she would have to find him because why hadnt she already? She could have got out the damn taxi. If it was him she could have. Her own brother my God. And she didnt get out the taxi, she didnt even do that. If she had she would have known, if she had got out the taxi and just like my God imagine not getting out the taxi? Why hadnt she? That was the one thing. Even if she hadnt known for sure, even if *she* hadnt *he* would have, even after all these years, his little sister, it would have been overwhelming.

She wouldnt have had to ask him. All she had to do was open the door and step out. He would have known her. But she didnt do that, she didnt get out the taxi. That was so shocking, so so – really, it was. Mo would have been surprised, only because like family, families for him. But they werent all like his. His was strong, Helen's wasnt.

That was the truth and only be honest. Helen felt that. She saw the time and reached to Sophie, clasping her shoulder. Sophie glanced at her. Helen didnt speak, she breathed deeply. Sophie smiled. Helen said, Is Mo on the computer?

Yes.

I'm going to see him.

Sophie got up from the chair.

You too?

Yes.

Oh well, girls together!

Sophie smiled. Helen pushed her ahead into the hallway and into the room. Mo looked up from his laptop. We're just being nosey, said Helen, arent we Sophie?

No.

Yes we are.

No we arent.

Helen laughed.

But we arent Mum, we arent being nosey.

Helen had her arm round the girl's shoulders and made a face at Mo. You see, we are not being nosey. But we did wonder why you were in here and not sitting beside us for the last five minutes before you go to work. Is *that* right Sophie?

Yes.

Yes. Helen nodded.

We're going to do the jigsaw, said Sophie quickly.

Oh yeah, so that's why you want me out of it!

Yes, said Sophie.

No! laughed Helen. Did nobody tell you you could do the computer on the kitchen table and not be out of everything and away from the company?

Mo smiled, lowering the lid of his laptop.

Seriously, you could.

I'll remember that.

Well you better!

Because what we want to ask, and this is true that we do, that we want to aahhsk, just as a special fayyyvour, we want to aahhsk when you intend taking me and Sophie to see a movie! Because we want to see a movie. Sure we do Sophie? and we want Mr Noisy to take us?

Yes! cried Sophie.

You want me to take you to a movie? I dont believe it!

Mo rose from his chair, glancing at his wristwatch. Except for his shoes and coat he was already dressed for leaving.

Dont be so cheeky. Isnt he so very cheeky Sophie?

Yes.

Helen paused a moment. But it's true that we dont go out very much.

I know.

We have to make time.

I been saying that for weeks!

I know you have.

Like I mean I really really want to go out.

Helen nodded. It was true that he did and she knew that he did. He had moved to lift something from the top of the dressing table; his wallet and keys. His phone lay next to his laptop and she passed it to him.

Ta, he said, reminds me about yours. You need it fixed dont you!

Well no actually I think I need a new one.

Oh right yeah . . .

Sophie had let go Helen's hand, she walked across to the window. Some of her dolls and things were here in boxes. She knelt on the floor to take them out. Helen watched her lining the first few along the window ledge. Mo turned to leave. Helen said, But it's true, we really dont go out much.

You're telling me, he said.

Oh Mo . . .

What?

Helen shook her head.

What is it? You okay?

Helen put her hand to her mouth, unable to answer. Mo stepped in front of Helen. He gripped her by the wrists, not forcibly; yet there was a pressure, however slight. He whispered: What's wrong love?

She shook her head with as little movement as possible, so that Sophie wouldnt notice. Sophie's concentration was to her toys. Mo relaxed his grip and dropped her hands, glanced at his wristwatch. Helen turned from him. She left the room. He followed her. Inside the kitchen entrance he put his arms round her. Helen what's wrong?

She couldnt speak.

Have I done something?

Only if he wouldnt hold her. Her eyes were watering and he saw it and his eyes closed because it upset him. It upset him to see her crying. She was crying. Silly tears. So stupid. So so stupid. Sophie could be there and worried. But where they stood Helen and Mo blocked the entrance. Sophie couldnt have opened the door without Helen knowing but still she whispered. I just wish you werent going, it's horrible.

Her eyes were closed. It was a serious wish. And for herself, how she wished she could stay home, every day. She so so wished it was only the two of them – and Sophie, the three of them – that their life could be as they wanted. She prayed for that, she did. She didnt know if she believed in God but it was more of a prayer than a wish, that they could experience something like a real freedom, a real one; and they could choose how life was to be instead of having it forced on them all the time not being able to do anything they wanted, even go someplace else, just go out together, why could they not just go out together? Why couldnt the three of them just go someplace? Not forever, even just a long long time, months, if they could have long long months together. She didnt want him to let her go and he didnt. Her head angled over his right shoulder; her left forefinger close to her mouth, and she bit on it.

Mo was worried. Okay . . .? he said.

Yes, she said but really she didnt know if she was. She didnt feel it. Sometimes she felt okay but not now she didnt, really, more like sad. Poor Mo.

What's wrong? he said.

She shook her head. Do you ever wonder if London isnt the answer? Perhaps it's only a stepping stone.

What's that?

Do you ever think we could go someplace else?

Mo frowned a moment, then smiled. I cant go no place. Where can I go? Apart from Glasgow!

Oh Mo.

I mean it. They wont take me.

Who wont?

All of them. Mo grinned. Me ethnicity is all wrong. Except the north of Scotland girl, right up the very top; in beside the penguins – what you call that place? oats, groats, porridge oats?

John O'Groats. Helen smiled. The two had separated now. Mo had his hands on the sides of her shoulders.

I aint joking, he said. Life's tough for Pakis.

Oh God I wish you wouldnt say that.

Say what? Pakis?

It's a horrible word.

The badge of shame. Heh heh heh. Mo was laughing, then shaking his head. He checked his wristwatch again.

Oh Mo, how can you laugh at that?

Because it's funny.

Helen pushed her arms round his neck. He made a choking sound. I'm not *letting* you go, she said.

A man's gotta go if a man's gotta go. Mo was peeling off her hands to free himself. There's a movie showing and we're going. Not this Thursday but the next.

What one? asked Helen, following him into the hallway where his boots were positioned on a sheet of newspaper. Mo crouched to pull them on.

Any one, he said. You're off I'm off it dont matter only it's got to be a comedy.

I hate comedies.

Exactly. You're amazing!

Helen pushed open the front room door to call to Sophie: Come and see Mo before he goes!

How could I *be* with somebody who hates comedies! he said. How is it even posseebleh mon dieu!

Helen had her hand on the front door handle. Now Sophie was there and Mo leaned to kiss her on the forehead. Sophie stepped back to avoid the contact but Mo moved quickly. You see that! he said.

I hate kisses, said Sophie.

Me too, said Mo and he kissed Helen on the lips. Helen had her arms round his waist and when they parted she muttered, Oh God.

Mo said, I know. He patted Sophie on the head and stepped outside.

Helen called, Take care. She and Sophie watched him walk downstairs. Sophie was holding Helen's hand; they entered the kitchen. Sophie said, Do you like Mo mummy?

Yes, said Helen.

All the time?

No. Helen grinned. No, she said, not all the time. Do you like me all the time?

Yes.

Oh no you dont.

Yes I do. You like me all the time.

Helen smiled.

You do.

I know.

Sophie laughed.

Houses creaked because they were old. Old everything. The washing machine was the worst. When it entered the spin it crashed across the floor and banged into the sink support. If that collapsed what would happen to the pipes and water supply? The whole thing, it was a nightmare and like the actual washing machine itself, if it dropped through the floor, imagine it, the family below at their breakfast. Mo had looked to see what was wrong but couldnt mend it, whatever it was, and they would have to call in a plumber or whoever to fix it. It was supposed to be 'feet' on the bottom. *Feet*, that was what he said, but they didnt work or something or was only three instead of four, it should have been four 'feet'. Mo was supposed to be getting the name of somebody to do the job but it was taking ages. You couldnt rush these things. Not when guys were doing a favour.

That was the trouble with 'favours'.

She shouldnt have been using the machine at all but the washing piled high, towels and sheets. She was doing a hand-wash at the same time. Three clothes-horses my God it was just crazy and couldnt be done. In the old days houses had pulleys on the ceiling.

No rain was scheduled: both washes could have been hung outside to dry, had she begun earlier in the day, first thing in the morning. But it never occurred to her first thing in the morning. Why should it have? First thing in the morning was last thing at night for nightshift workers.

There was a laundrette along the main road and she used their drying machines occasionally. It made a walk for her and Sophie. Nearby was a kebab shop; Sophie enjoyed their pizza and Helen enjoyed a break from having to cook.

Sophie's bed was to be made. It was awkward having to squeeze into the cupboard, sore on the back. But it was great how Mo and his mates had fitted it in. Men and DIY. Her ex was the epitome. He only did it to show off his biceps. Oh darleeng you are so strong. Helen yawned.

Sophie said, Why do you have to go to work?

To get our money.

But if Mo goes why do you?

The machine would be entering its final spin and she needed to listen to it. As soon as the spin-cycle started she would hold it down. Something was wrong with everything, so what? life was the usual, life was life. Sophie was watching her. She was engaged with a colouring-in book. She had an eye for colour. Helen said, That's nice colours!

Working at the sink she could see out the window. The kitchen looked across to the backside of the next street, and the row of houses there. Council apartment blocks were there too merging with the others. Women sat out the back together with small children and it was like how Helen had been brought up in Glasgow; the women did that there. It was nice seeing. Although here they had made wee gardens. If the weather had been warmer and time to spare Helen might have gone across to sit with them. Probably they would have been friendly. They grew herbs and things.

You could stay home, said Sophie. Why cant you? You could play with me and read stories.

That sounds good!

Sophie reached for other coloured pencils, bent her head over the book again. You could Mum.

Helen had expected to tell Mo about Brian but it didnt happen. She waited to say it but it didnt happen. It was her to have said it. It wouldnt if she didnt and she didnt. Why didnt she? Because she didnt, she didnt tell him because she didnt tell him. Anyway, it would have taken too long, him going to work.

She could have started with the folding bed, z-bed. If he knew what a z-bed was. She could have asked him that and then it would have led on to why, like why did she want a folding bed? Because it was useful to have one. If she kicked him out of their bed he would have some place to sleep!

But they were useful, just so practical, if somebody arrived out the blue, family or friends.

Silence. The washing machine was set to enter the final spin. Helen quickly rinsed the blouse and left it on the draining board, and placed both elbows on the right corner of the machine to steady it. Now it started, the spin building to its usual racket, an absolute crescendo, it was horrendous, actually shaking the floor; Helen could feel the trembling and she really had to fight to keep her elbows on the corner. Sophie was smiling. Helen said, I think it's going to fly up in the air. If it does we can hang on.

Sophie jumped to her feet and started bouncing on the spot. Stop that! said Helen.

She didnt, she was now hopping, actually hopping! Sophie!

Helen shouted: For goodness sake you'll go through the damn floor!

Sophie stared at her.

For God sake. Helen shook her head, her elbows pressing hard down on the corner of the machine to contain the movement.

I didnt mean it Mum sorry.

Look at me shaking, said Helen.

Sophie smiled but her upper lip was over her lower lip. Helen reached her left hand to her. Pizza?

Yes Mum please!

My teeth are chattering, said Helen.

Sophie had moved to the pantry cupboard, probably looking for the chocolate biscuits. Helen said, Take a banana if you're hungry or like plums, there's plums there too.

Plums?

Or a banana, yes.

I dont want a banana.

Well a plum?

No.

No *thanks*. Remember your manners.

Sophie returned to her dolls and the little chair. Helen watched her. Dont be sulky.

Sophie turned sharply: I'm not being sulky.

Yes you are.

I'm not.

Helen stuck out her tongue. Sophie smiled. The machine shuddered to a halt. Helen watched it. At this point the shaking seemed to increase in momentum: then the end.

There was time for a seat before emptying the machine. The remains of her last coffee. The cup was barely warm. It was amazing to consider but people drank coffee hot. They did! Even to sit a moment, so her mind, just being empty. Empty minds. Sophie was edging closer to her; she had a book in her hand and was offering it. Helen smiled but not to encourage her.

Sophie waited before saying, Will you read it to me?

I cant just now. I have to empty the machine.

Sophie's head lowered. Helen said quickly, But if you read it to me, for one wee minute, if you can, can you?

Sophie grinned and opened the book and began reading, stumbling and faltering but reading nevertheless. It was a story about a fish who swam off by herself. It was quite sad. It reminded Helen of a children's movie from years ago. Perhaps they had stolen the idea. People stole things all the time and you saw it in movies and television programmes and like news events too, they stole news events and made them into movies and drama. This wee fish was rescued from a fishermen's net off the coast of a Greek island. All the big fish were squashing her. That was so like life. Helen grinned. But even Sophie's reading, Helen had forgotten how well she was doing, my God, six years of age is all she was like at that age what was Helen doing? she wasnt reading, not as good as this. And with everything she had been through, even to survive! She was just like really, so good, she was, just so so good, she really was. Helen was so lucky, so very very lucky.

She had to empty the machine, once she had she could spin-dry the handwash. Thank goodness for microwaves. Or the pizza.

How long had she even been sitting? She opened the washing machine door.

Lost in her own wee world. Where was her head! Doolally, the old Glasgow one, Mrs Doolally, that was her, so absent-minded, in her mind and on her mind. All the time.

She hung the machine wash on the two clothes-horses by the radiator. It was still dry outside. Her mother would have hung out the clothes. Helen didnt. The shifts she worked made it more trouble than it was worth. Then if it looked like rain you had to bring them all in again. The truth is she preferred the clothes-horses.

Sophie was over by the little chair Mo found someplace. It was a proper child's chair like you saw on antique programmes. Of course Sophie didnt sit on it. But she did play with it. She had her dolls lined on the floor next to it, and ponies, she liked ponies, and she was talking in character, pushing them and the dolls about. She spoke in a wee shrill voice, but with a snobby English tone to it like on television, and addressed herself: Oh naow Sopheee you ovah theyah, Ell shell gao heah. And then answering in her own voice yet with a nasal American edge to it. Oh nohh Lindy, I dont waaant to. Oh boat yoh hev toh Sophee. Oh but I dont waaant to.

Helen stooped to lift a damp sock from the floor, it must have fallen when she removed the clothes from the washing machine.

The girl was used to being on her own. Perhaps she would become an actress. She *was* good at voices. As long as nobody watched. Then she stopped. It was best not to notice. She was just so *natural*. It was such a positive thing about her. She had a strength too. Even she could be tough. Like her Mum! Helen *had* been tough. She had. Tougher than Brian. She just *became* weak. She wasnt always. Far from it. Far from it indeed. Oh God.

But it was true. She didnt used to be weak. A tough little madam more like. Oh well, damn phone, it had been out of action the past eight days. What was he talking about fixing it? it didnt need fixing, it couldnt be fixed. She needed a new one. She would when she could, and get it herself. He knew some-body who got deals. He knew somebody who knew somebody who knew somebody. It was a running joke, him and his mates.

People always like *knew* somebody. The same in Glasgow. Her ex too, he was as bad. Helen wasnt keen on illegal stuff, if it went against the law like with DVDs and other rip-off things. Then if they didnt work properly, you couldnt even see the film. She hated that. Why bother? Then if you got caught, my God. Even if you didnt. If it was a rip-off thing and somebody had stolen it and you were to buy it cheap so then it was in your house, it was just there, and what if somebody came to the door? it was complete agony. Helen hated it, she just really – it was difficult to cope with, she found it so anyway; other people were different, and that was good, it was just how you were brought up. In her family everything was above board; that was Dad, the law was the law and if you had to put up with something you just did it and got on with your life.

But she needed her phone. All women did. The same at the casino, you saw it for the smokers. It was policy that staff had to use the lane round the rear of the building and not be seen by the entrance. It was understandable because this part of the city in the wee small hours, what did people think? If it was a female standing smoking with the clothes she wore. A phone was vital. People went in twos and threes.

But she needed it now and not the end of the month. A 'deal' was the last thing. She was hopeless at 'deals'. Her face gave it away, like if she was guilty, everybody knew, everybody, she was just so God silly, hopeless, in these situations. Proper name-brands is what she preferred. Okay you paid more but you knew what you were getting. Mo said they werent stolen. But if they werent, what were they? If they were so cheap, they had to be *something*. According to him they were made in the same country, even like the same factory, by the same people, only they stuck on different labels.

There was a hypocrisy there too that Helen didnt like. She

didnt understand it either. If it was south Asia and women workers, children too. Mo and other people gave money every week like charity, alms for people, it was good, it really was but then the next thing if it was rip-off deals, what about that? And if it was like young children involved as workers my God their wee fingers holding the needles, how did they manage it? these slave-owners, fourteen hours a day. It was heartbreaking and horrible and just slavery. Britain was so selfish, so so selfish, people didnt even care.

And they could change things if they wanted. Although could they? What if it was hospitals? What could be changed there? We dont know people's lives and assume everybody is okay, but what if they arent? People can be ill. If it was like Brian, what if he was ill? If that was why he was on the street. He was so wild-looking my God. What if he *was* ill? like disturbed, in the head – if he didnt know where he was, if he thought he was home and he wasnt. If he thought he was in Glasgow and he wasnt, if he just woke up and there he was in London, and didnt know how he got here.

People suffer memory loss. If he didnt know who he was. His own actual name. It was possible. So he was just wandering around. He didnt know where he was, or who he was, he was just like who am I? He didnt know. Until the guy with the limp helped him. People do help. It isnt all doom and gloom. Even ones who are down-and-out and living rough on the street, they help ones less fortunate than themselves. People have so so little and yet they share, even with strangers, if they are down-and-out and homeless. It is only rich ones who are selfish, poor people share. It is true, everybody knows it. Some say different but everybody knows the truth.

Helen didnt want to go to work. She didnt want Mo to go either. Mo had gone and so would she. She was in he was out he was out she was in. What a life but they coped, they coped,

Sophie too, Sophie most of all; thank God thank God, children survived and she was no different.

Azizah came at seven fifteen and had to be on time. Helen needed that hour and a half to get into the city; by train and tube, if the connection worked it was fine but if it didnt it wasnt. Taxis were out of the question except when three or four shared. Mo couldnt believe how much went on taxis but what choice was there? He never took a taxi anywhere. Either he walked or jumped a bus. So would she if she could, if she could she would, of course she would, only she couldnt.

The last childminder quit without proper notice. Helen found such behaviour difficult, even like bizarre it was so irresponsible. It wasnt so much being forced to miss a shift but the idea that your little girl had been left in the care of somebody like that. 'Care' was the wrong word. They were lucky with Azizah. She did the five nights and didnt mind if there was a sixth, and usually there was. She brought a backpack full of textbooks. She was going to be a lawyer. Mo knew her father from Mosque. She had a sister but no brother. Sophie liked her. Only she didnt look forward to her coming because it meant Helen was going to work. Somebody came and somebody went. Sophie came home from school and Mo left for the restaurant. Azizah arrived, and Mummy went to work. Mummy came home from work and Sophie went to school.

Once Sophie was in bed Azizah got on with her studies. That was the theory, but when did Sophie get to bed? Nine o'clock should have been the cut-off point but was it? Helen was never quite convinced. Sophie was devious. All children were. They enjoyed tricking adults, especially parents. They could be tough, they knew how to wound, they could be spiteful, hypocrites too my God, they said one thing and did another. And told lies to save their own skin. If they were a species of aliens, nobody would want to know them. That was the truth.

Even like treacherous, children could be treacherous. Helen too, when she was a girl

oh God, she could only sigh. Sighing was allowed. Yes she had been hypocritical. She had been, and a liar, and a cheat and treacherous, yes. These were not endearing qualities. Children *were* guilty. Helen was a child, so she too, yes, guilty! They did mischievous things, not very nice things. Although if these were 'traits'. Some had them and some didnt. Traits were traits and qualities were qualities. 'Qualities' belonged to everybody, 'traits' to some. Helen had traits. But that was childhood. Children do things, they dont mean it. Sell their parents for a packet of potato crisps. Sophie was as bad. When her father was there she acted up to him. It didnt matter about Mum then, Mum was forgotten! Mum was the mundane everyday and he was the wild exciting once in a blue moon, it was so unfair, really, and wounding, Sophie could *wound*. That was children, and unthinking, she didnt know she was doing it, apart from the need to hurt, and her own mother. Perhaps it was her father she meant to hurt but couldnt, so she hurt Mum. The easy option. They hurt the woman because the man, the man is the man. Helen was the same, she had been, as a child. But that was childhood and childhood was over, childhood was all finished.

There were times when Helen too felt strong, she did, almost *tough*.

Sophie's father was a bully. Not a real bully. Although perhaps he was. Men are bullies. Nice bullies or bad bullies, but one or the other. Mo was a nice bully, her ex wasnt. Mo looked after her; her ex didnt. Not that Helen had wanted him to. Nor did she expect it from Mo. But he did, and she looked after him. It was a partnership.

Life was gambling. You went with a man you didnt know. You even went home with him. You knew nothing about him, but what he told you. Usually it was lies to snare you into their trap. Mr Adams. But it wasnt lies with him, he just like disappeared. That was strange. She googled his name and there was nothing. She expected to see it someplace; the newspapers or television too because if he was going away, why wouldnt he have said? just disappearing, so if something had happened to him, something bad. She wanted to ask people. But who? The police. Just somebody. She didnt know. But some people would know because he was that kind of man. Ann Marie said not to be daft and to take it as a warning; like how things went on in the world it was best not to snoop and pry; people should leave things alone. But if something bad had happened.

It would not have been snooping. If she was trying to find out, that was all it was. Imagine she had. Sleuths. Of course she enjoyed detective stories, especially ones in the persona of young women and if they were Americans and not posh English so it was good-humoured and a laugh. It was only a story and they did things that were exciting, things that were dangerous and even could make you squirm because it was like everything was imaginable. Not with old women who were so self-contained and could give men 'knowing' looks like they knew them. Because they only knew them from the *outside*. Really it was like virginal, these older women. Because it was only *old men* they knew, from the older generations. So if they knew modern young men it was never having slept with them or like in touching contact, never, because if they hadnt slept with them how could it be? not *knowing*, they couldnt be so 'knowing'. Not with young men. It was like nuns always saying this and that about what girls werent to do and they hadnt seen a man's body. It was so stupid and just so presumptuous, it really was.

Old women didnt *know* young men. So they enjoyed life. They were always at ease and being witty. And young men were witty back to them, always charming and respectful. But it was only to them, the old women, because they werent like that with young women. Oh no. Young women were not witty, they were abashed and self-conscious, and like their bodies too because what could be concealed? even as a girl growing up, it couldnt be hidden; clothes didnt allow it so men always were looking, always their eyes looking at you and like seeing through, so it did make you squirm. Men enjoyed making you squirm, and nipples too, guys making comments. That was so outrageous, so unfair too because what could the dealer do? You couldnt do anything except not react, just like pretend not to know, you didnt hear the comment, and of course you did. She didnt tell Mo. Why tell your man about that kind of thing? it only would aggravate him.

It was scandalous he was a waiter. Jobs were ghettos, like how people got trapped.

But if she had told him about Brian.

After dinner Helen had taken out the old photographs again and spread a few on top of the cupboard. She settled Sophie down with a movie and while washing the dishes, crockery and pots she kept the photographs in sight. If Brian's health wasnt good he should have returned to Glasgow. That was almost like an obvious thing. Because Mum would have been so so pleased, she would have looked after him, and been glad to do it. Mum wasnt old but she was getting old. With Brian there, it would have been mutual, really, looking after each other. His presence alone, it would have been great for Mum. Really. And vice versa. They were close. They always had been. And Mum with the spare room; her flat was spacious, a castle in comparison to the place Helen had. Brian would have been comfortable there and just nestled in and made it his own. Did he have friends from the old days? Who were they? Helen couldnt remember. Did boys have friends? They did but not like girls, not like in the same way. The first time in London she met William Boyle in a pub along Charlotte Street. It was so weird. She was there with another girl from her work and just like ordering a drink and there was William just standing there at the bar. He had been in her class at Primary School and Secondary School so they knew each other quite well. Helen had been so like pleased to see him. But he had changed so much. He was always a talker and so very very cheery, always just cheery, but now he wasnt, he hardly spoke at all when she met him. Helen had to carry the conversation. And he wouldnt come to their table. Why didnt he? Oh he had to go, and that was him and away he went. Whatever it was he was doing, he didnt say but it made you wonder about him and his life because it was like not being comfortable, even if he was guilty, he didnt want to be seen. But it made you wonder, so he had something to hide.

Oh God, if it was Brian, why had he come to London? To disappear. People disappear. But Liverpool was a place, that was where he was, you disappeared there too, why would he come here?

There was no more to see in the photographs. A lanky boy, and quiet. What was she looking for? If he was unaggressive. That was like a criticism. Except he was. To the point of timidity. Quite meek really. Although that wasnt in the photographs. There wasnt much there at all, not if you searched and it was Brian you searched for. Quite a few of Mum and Dad and Helen herself, but Brian was like a shadowy figure, not hiding but not there either, like he hadnt connected properly with the camera or was keeping out the way. Trying not to be seen. But that was silliness. And wrong, that was so so wrong. Very very wrong. Like seeking ways *not* to help.

Helen was not doing that, she really wasnt. If she could help she would help. Of course she would if it was Brian; she wanted to help him and she would help him. If it was him she would. She just needed to know, if it was him.

And she didnt. It was so so – what? She couldnt even think. She had gone over and over and over it all, every last detail, again and again and again until her head was numb, and her brains, if she had any left. If there *was* something, she didnt know it. She didnt. It might have been him and it might not have been him. It was like watching a taped movie and you get interrupted by somebody and miss something important, so you have to rewind. Helen had to rewind. No she didnt. The whole day long my God rewinding, what else had she been doing? replaying and replaying, replaying or rewinding, doing both.

To find *it*. To find *it*.

The truth of it. She needed to. And she couldnt. Really, she couldnt. Even had she 'rewound' to the moment of recognition she could not do more than she had at the moment itself. A rewound moment is not the actual moment. That is a moment in time. She could only think about things and these things were in the past. The only way to find out if the man she had seen was her brother was to see him again, she had to see him, the same man. She had to, to be seeing him. That was the

Oh well.

Helen stopped what she was doing, although she smiled. Actually she felt quite – strange. It was like a – what? a decision. She had made a decision, she knew she had, a massive one, although that was silly, saying that, like it was a sort of

But it was a major thing like it was just so so – it was life-changing. She would have to see him, the tall skinny guy; she would.

Goodness, it was true. Oh well.

She glanced at the clock. Sophie was engrossed. She followed the stories now. Good. Children develop, their mind.

Goodness.

Helen felt quite weird really but okay too like she was just like – okay, really.

This was a moment she did not break and did not want to break. She sat by Sophie and gazed at the television. Soon Azizah had arrived and Helen was in the front room. When she opened the front door for the girl she was already pulling on her coat and ready to leave; she had been getting ready, so now she was, or nearly; everything she was doing she was still doing like still having to do. She didnt need to do anything more, only what she always did, same clothes same everything, same going to work. Not the *same* going to work. This was not the *same*. What was 'same'?

Relax and consider, take a moment. These thoughts were important, so not to rush them either. It was important not to. Helen felt this strongly: and not worry about time. She had plenty time, she allowed this for the journey to work. Helen could miss two trains and like manage in on the third; she could. It was completely fine.

Yes Azizah had arrived, she was in the front room with Sophie. Sophie didnt look at her. Poor Azizah. But it *was* hurtful. Helen would have felt it. Children are the tough ones. They learn not to be, not to be too tough. Helen had to and so do they all, including Sophie.

Bag, money, travel-cards; keys, wallet, no phone, brolly. That was her, ready to leave and set to leave, now in the hallway, crouching to pull on her boots. It was sad nevertheless, but true. What else to consider? Nothing really. Azizah was a great girl. Helen trusted her with Sophie. She was nothing like Helen. A completely different personality. Her books and her books and her books! She had a definite strength about her and Helen lacked that, she did. She was just a different kind of person. That was that. It didnt make her any the less. People *are* different.

Sophie relaxed with Azizah. She did. Wouldnt it have been nice if she relaxed with her own mother! Oh but of course she did. What a silly thing to say! Foolishness. Mrs Foolish, Mrs Fool. She *was* a fool; this is what she was. Mo said she was quirky but it was more than quirky.

She had her coat on, her boots on, bag, money, travel-cards; her hand on the outside door handle. That's me going! she called, then waited.

Mummy! Sophie came rushing to her. Mummy! she reached her arms round Helen.

A big cuddle, said Helen and winked to Azizah: She's to be in bed by nine o'clock at the very very very very latest.

Yes, said Azizah.

Helen smiled. Sophie stepped back staring at her, then the blink. Oh Sophie, you're not going to start crying?

Well you always go.

Yes but it's work, I have to go to work!

Why?

To earn money.

Yes but Mummy

So we can eat food and pay for things.

Sophie stared at her.

Oh honey! Helen leaned to kiss her. Azizah smiled in the background. A good girl, a nice girl. Helen wanted to say something, pass on to Mo, a message, because it was Mo, if she had told him about Brian. Why didnt she? She should have. She hadnt told Mo because she knew what he would say. I'll see you in the morning, she said to Sophie.

Oh Mum. Sophie smiled.

That's better. Helen saw that Azizah had taken Sophie's

hand and she winked to Azizah while opening the door. She waved: Byyeeee, and stepped outside, closing the door behind her, and she called: Love you.

Sophie answered: Love you Mummy.

Then Helen was downstairs and out onto the pavement. It was raining. When had it started? Helen had looked earlier and it was dry. Anyway, the brolly was in the bag.

The old settee was still lying on the pavement near her house. Caroline and Jill would have noticed it this morning. How could they miss the damn thing? It had been there for three days and was saturated and horrible. Her street was an embarrassment. The old fridge there too, with the door hanging off my God. People just dumped things. They said it was for poor people, asylum-seekers or like whoever, just leave your old furniture. People who need it will come and take it. But that was an excuse. Sometimes it was true but not always. Who would have taken that settee?

Except like a homeless person. But where would they take it to? if there was no place, if they had no place, not if they were homeless. That was homeless, you had no place, just like here there and everywhere, you just wandered.

Sophie was at the window, waving. She was up on a chair. Azizah wasnt to be seen but must have been behind her. She must have been, making sure Sophie didnt fall. But it was true, children got excited and if she fell it would have been through the window. She didnt need to stand on a chair. She just did it because – why did she do it? Because she did.

And old fridges either. Who would take them? Nobody. They were useless. You would have to be daft. People were not daft, they just were from other countries. They had nothing. That was life, it was so unfair, really. Not always but often. Some had millions others had nothing.

She passed the fast-food kebab shop towards the corner of

the street. It was busy. Evening trade. People did use it. Mo said the owners should have been arrested for serving gravy under false pretences but he was a food-snob. They served their 'specialty gravy' with chips. Children liked it. Why not? Once in a while. Nothing wrong with that.

Helen paused and half turned to wave once more. She couldnt see Sophie but she would still have been standing there, still waving until the last. Helen as a child. Who did Sophie take after! It was true but the wee soul, she so took after her mother. Never mind.

She enjoyed this part of the journey to work. She even looked forward to it! Walking. Yes! And she so hated it as a girl my God she did, really really, she did. And now, well, she quite liked it.

About fourteen minutes to the station. Twenty-three on the train, depending, a leisurely journey and really, a time to relax, it was, for her anyway it was, for other people perhaps not, not if whatever.

It was lazy. She liked that. The older stations too, she preferred them. There was something nice about them. You got on the train and that was that. Nothing you had to do. You just sat down and the window was there if you could get a seat and just stare out. She stared out. People worked on their laptops, or were on their phones, else texting, reading books or newspapers. Helen didnt, she was one of those who just whatever – stared, dreamed, who closed her eyes. She might have dozed. It was a private world, almost like a secret world, being in the middle of a city but not visible, in the back of the city, being *behind*. A peace descended. A 'peace descended' was her words for it.

So many railtracks and all the names, strange names, hundreds of wee towns and villages all filling the map, it was so unlike Scotland. How people lived! Their lives were so so different; quiet places and streets, little shops and beyond that too green pastures and bridges, canals and their boats. This was England. Helen didnt know England. South London wasnt 'England'. Caroline said that; her family came from 'the Cotswolds'. The Cotswolds. Where was that? Their trains must have been the fast ones. Trains to the back of beyond. Helen's was an old thing that took its time and had to sit at the side until the fast ones passed. Helen imagined them full of businessmen in their bowlers and thick coats all being rushed into the city and the houses where they lived like the ones you saw on television with bedrooms and lounges, kitchens and gardens, patios, a 'patio', imagine a patio and the sun is shining and the seat is there in the garden and just sitting there and a glass of lemonade, where the murder takes place, the Chief Inspector arrives to take down the details and the housekeeper is there too, Yes milady, and the servant girl back in the shadows, at the kitchen door, and the 'young master' – what? what would he be doing? It is all men anyway.

The train moved through one area Helen knew from weekend visits. This was an old factory and warehouse area where a couple of the less dilapidated buildings housed market stalls at the weekend. Each time they went somebody would tell them next week was the last because the council was closing it down. You could find so many bits and pieces, all bits and bobs, anything and everything. A dream for Mo. When they went they took turns rummaging while the other watched Sophie. You needed two hands at the clothes-stalls in the main market areas, especially if some of these women with big elbows were about and trying to reach something in front of you. Manners didnt exist. If you let a child out your hand for one second she would be off wandering, lost in the crush.

It was like from a bygone age. The Russian man Lenin, from the politics of that time, the Russian Revolution. He visited with his wife to give talks to people. Lenin and the Russian Revolution. It reminded Helen of the Barrows back in Glasgow; the ideal place to find a z-bed. One stall specialised in computer relics, old cables and gadgets. Mo knew the stall holder by name. Most of the junk he brought home came from here. No wonder the man was friendly. Mo was his best customer. One old place they called the 'warren'. If you disappeared in here you got 'lost forever'. Mo told her this with a glint in his eye but the very last time here they had a row because of it. He got 'lost'. It wasnt funny. Yes Helen was nervous. Of course she was nervous. Who wouldnt have been? He *knew* she didnt have her phone and yet he still disappeared, like for ages. He said he was only looking at things but my God. Eventually she and Sophie had to go inside to find him and men looking at her too. Even with a child beside you men 'looked'. He didnt think about that. No, because men dont, they dont have to. Then when he did come back my God like sauntering, just sauntering, hands in his pockets, and winking at her. He hadnt even bought anything. He called her a born worrier. Yes, and not ashamed to admit it. If she was a worrier; if she was then he was a dreamer. He so didnt think. Imagine her ex. If he had known about Mo and was stalking them, and just waiting his chance. Mo was defenceless. Against him he was. He would have beaten Mo up. He was just like – he was horrible.

Even if he had told her he would be gone a while. Her and Sophie could have gone to a café or into the place with the good toy-stall. There was one where the guy did demonstrations and it was like entertainment; a young guy too but thickset and with a baldy head and a wispy beard. His patter was hilarious and he made everybody laugh, picking out individual children and winking at the mothers. The last time he had big sort of space-truck things that he operated by remote control but they kept dropping off the stall, making everybody laugh. He had a bowl of boiled sweets and threw them to the children. He reminded Helen of somebody. Some conjuror on television. Now you see it now you dont. Then it came to selling them. I'm not going to ask for this and I'm not going to ask for that. He always had a crowd round his stall for the demonstrations.

A few people were poor. Really really poor. Immigrants and asylum-seekers, bags of old clothes and whatever. Men in small groups, and women with babies and toddlers. You had to be careful with your bag and purse. People said that, if it was true, probably it was but you had to watch your purse anywhere.

It was the kind of old place where she might have seen Brian. The people hereabouts wouldnt have looked twice at him or the one with the limp. Guys were standing about, leaning on rails and against the wall. Tough-looking men, drinkers and junkies, the younger ones arguing, laughing and horsing about, then looking when you passed. You would have had to be tough to survive, so so tough. Would Brian have managed? You heard these stories. Not just men but women too. Unimaginable. What sort of life was it? hell on earth. You would have to keep moving. You might be healthy at first but the more you were on the street the worse it would get. The worse *you* would get. And if you were mentally ill. It was the worst nightmare. Poor Brian. People looking at you all the time. When do you sleep? When do you get a seat? Are you allowed to sit down? Washing yourself. You heard stories about people using lavatory pans, men shaving themselves out the toilet bowl water, women washing themselves underneath. What diseases would they catch? Contaminated water and contaminated blood. It was like nightmarish zombie stories, just horrific. And the constant constant hassle. Not just the police but people shouting at you all the time and doing dirty tricks, even like beating you up, setting you on fire; there were stories about boys burning people alive, old tramps; it was horrific to think people would do that, and videoing it too, just brutalised, people were brutalised, children, they were, horrible. That was Brian having to cope with it. My God

It would be strange him and Mo. How he would react, if he was racist, probably he was. But perhaps not. But it happened anywhere. People looked twice. It didnt mean they were racist. Only she got so sick of it, having to think about it and always you did and if you didnt you soon had to because something happened. It put you off going places, even entire districts. Although she handled it better. It was true that most people were. Even without knowing it, the very words they used. They didnt like Muslims, even hated them. And without knowing any my God that made you smile, if you didnt cry, how bad that was, how just sick; really, it was; so prejudiced and shocking, so so shocking. His mates who came to the house, she saw them looking at her too; not in a sexualised way but like they were wondering about her and wondering about Mo; how come here they were together? But surely that was all couples and not just white and Asian? People get together. How on earth do they manage that my God it is just my God it is just like so amazing. And sleep together, just literally sleep together! The trust in that alone! Imagine! Lying beside another human being and asleep, and them beside you and you just lying, and you have that trust because just anything they could do and you are powerless, you are so so powerless, so like all you can do, only trust them, you have to, just so have to – and get beyond it if you can, you have to, because then if you do, if you manage it comes the peace, peace comes, you close your eyes, that is the trust, you can close your eyes and trust the person. Helen trusted Mo; she knew she did, and she had to, that was the other thing.

London was so old. She felt that looking out the window

189

too. The line passed through London Bridge station where they had the scary exhibition. Mo fancied seeing it. Helen did quite and would, but not with Sophie, definitely not with Sophie. That sense of 'plague', *plague* victims. It wasnt scary, it was sad, like zombies, zombies were sad, locked into their disease, the contamination, never satisfied until they infect everybody, if one has to die they all must die.

But it wouldnt be like that, people werent so evil, they were generous, they would want you to survive like with their bell too, people had a bell and rang it; that was like leprosy, they walked the street but kept to the shadows, and how their flesh was eaten away by it, just ravaged faces, and that was the old streets in London too like Jack the Ripper days, evil-smelling and foggy shadows, you would never leave the house, what a nightmare, the olden days, my God but then if it was like Asia or Africa, that was them right now; people were angry, no wonder; Mo was right when he said it.

Oh well, the tube or a walk? She enjoyed walking up from the station but tonight she was taking a tube; her railcard covered it anyway. It was her mind but her mind was *jumpy*. A funny expression, 'jumpy', but it was how she felt. If she could have relaxed she might have done it, she might have walked, because she did enjoy it, although she preferred walking down to walk-ing up. There were hills in London even if you didnt notice them.

But the night ahead, things to think about, she wanted to be clear and just have it worked out, work through things and what she would do, walking helped the process, it could.

Perhaps she would walk. She had a choice of tube stations too. Usually she travelled to the one nearest the casino but not necessarily. Really, it was six and half a dozen. What did it mat-ter? just save hassle, that was the important thing, making life easy, so so important, it was.

The train had arrived at Charing Cross and she still hadnt

worked it out but that was her and her indecisiveness; she was so hopeless when it came to decisions, she just seemed to do things, or else didnt do them. Why didnt you do it? You said you would and now you didnt.

I changed my mind.

She changed her mind. Was that 'allowed'?

But did she 'change her mind'? Did she even *have* a 'mind'? *Mind*. People were people. Helen didnt care about any of it, only Sophie, worries about Sophie like if the childminder, Azizah – Azizah was good and Helen was so lucky to get her, she was so nice, and responsible too, and clever, and would follow instructions. Sophie would be put in bed and would sleep. Azizah would leave the door open and sit in the corner with the reading lamp. Sophie would know she was there and be comforted, and that was that. Helen was walking across the station platform now, she was going to walk because she wanted to walk; it gave her time to think, to just think; clear her brain and think, and everybody rushing around too in the same way, everybody just like here there and everywhere, all roundabout, and bad-mannered too some of them it was like not even seeing people the way they barged past.

She paused by the exit then continued, glad to be outside – and the rain too, it was raining; she hadnt expected the rain, although why not? If it had been raining earlier, why not now? Quite heavy too, and heavier, getting heavier. She had the brolly, and kept walking while bringing it from her bag. People were even sheltering my God it *was* heavy. She returned the brolly into her bag, headed back to the station, and downstairs to the tube.

Even here the choice. Nothing came like in a straightforward way, decisions always; one tube or two? one with a walk and two with less of a walk. So so busy. People out for the night and going home, and here and there, others. Where they all were going. Hostels. Foreign people went to them, and students, downmarket hotels; DSS places with sheets of cardboard as pretend walls dividing the lodgers and these very heavy guys on the reception and grunting at you; broken locks and windows and dirt, and stains; and some lodgers were elderly people with nowhere else to go; their last resting place my God what kind of life? all their days, and working so hard just to survive and some not able to because not everybody is able, they cant all manage. People cant, they cant; they try and they cant. So where do they go? If that was Brian, that was the life, people are critical and they dont know the situation.

Even the busker, sounding so professional and so so accomplished, really, and yet here he was at the foot of the escalator, trapped, it was like slavery. Imagine his girlfriend, she would be so so angry, and no wonder my God such a fine musician condemned to this, is this all he would get from life?

It didnt matter about the *Big Issue* but she gave the woman the money, the same woman. Sometimes three nights in a week. She didnt look too grateful. Some do and some dont; different at different times. Everybody has a bad day, they cant always be cheery. 'Have a nice day,' and what is theirs? And if they were too grateful. For Helen it was like why? why should they have been? Did they think you were something? like if she was rich. Because people dress in a certain way doesnt mean they are rich, if they thought that. Helen might have had a job but that didnt make her rich either for God sake who would think that?

There was a wee old gypsy woman sold it too. She might not have been a gypsy. Just a wee woman and old. Where did she come from? Where did she go? What happens to people? It was like a dream or a figment. Was she ever there in the first place! A wee round woman and quite plump. How could she be plump if she had no food? sitting on the pavement; small and round and you thought about grandchildren and she would have been making a big pot of soup and kids would be home from school and having a laugh and she would make them all sit down and ladle them out the soup, that was her, near Leicester Square, her back to the wall. *Big Issue*. Nobody wanted it; nobody in the entire world. Helen had the image, her sitting there my goodness why was she smiling? she was always smiling and it was almost like *unpleasant*. Helen didnt like seeing her, and no wonder, going where she was going, gamblers gambling, and the winers and diners and money and jewellery flashing about. You saw the anger there too; sometimes you did. People just looked at you and just like oh you had money and they didnt. That was the attitude and they were so wrong, so so wrong.

Helen entered the casino via the main entrance lobby, downstairs to the cloakroom. Here the staff area was linked through a side door. The restroom was known as the 'green room' as though it was the theatre or television. It irritated one of the older women because she had been an actress. Helen could sympathise, but not too much. Casinos *were* part of the entertainment industry. And they had their own 'uniforms', the sexee ladee frocks, so they were actresses too. And the boys in their wee mauve waistcoats and black bowties, just silly, although they looked nice, quite manly, or else camp; both at once, appealing to the women and the men.

She was glad she had taken the tube for the extra twenty minutes; just being able to relax, my God. This evening was different, different but not different. She had no idea and no plan but something was going to happen. She knew it was. And she was going to do it, at the end of the shift. She was. She knew she was, and felt quite level-headed. If that is what it was, 'level-headed', just like relaxed, and her mind too, so so relaxed.

It wasnt true she had no idea or plan; only that she hadnt worked it out. She knew it was going to happen; something, whatever.

If she *had* walked from Charing Cross she would have got soaked. Not soaked, but wet. Only it wouldnt have been pleasant, not for a walk; walking was a pleasure and this evening it wouldnt have been. So it was a good decision. She could make them! good decisions. Not if you believed her ex, that was the last thing, any decision. You were seen and not heard, that was women. A dealer she knew so lost it with her husband she tried to stab him with a bread knife but his chest was like so so bony the knife bounced off. 'Bony bastard', that was what she called him. One of *these* 'Glasgow women'. That was how Helen thought of them.

Although she was one herself; and felt that she was. Oh well, if that meant a fighter, thank God. But was she? Sometimes she wasnt, like not a *real* Glasgow woman, she was just

what was she?

Oh God, she didnt know, she didnt know, just whoever, whoever she was.

So weird. But minds *are* weird. Mo would have laughed at her saying that but it was true. Men acted 'differently'. Men 'rationalised', women acted on 'impulse'. Men 'thought' it through whereas women didnt. So they said, if you believed *them* because it was *them* saying it; at the same time giving themselves a pat on the back. That was men, stealing compliments at the slightest opportunity.

But even 'it', what did 'it' mean, they thought 'it' through? it was just stupid, it was like thinking of the thing before it happened but how could they? they werent God, men werent God – they only thought they were.

The door opened. Michel came in; a Belgian man, he was older, he gave a little wave, cheery. Helen was finishing a cup of tea. Others had already arrived, including Jill. Nobody was talking. A listings magazine lay on a nearby chair opened at the classifieds. Helen began browsing. She needed new curtains.

They had to be thick, the ones she had werent thick enough. Old ones Mo got from somebody but so like thin a material the light came through, so how could you sleep? you could not sleep. Furniture too, if ever she got her own place and unfurnished so she could do it however she wanted, just however, her and Sophie, and real bedrooms, Sophie would have a real one, it would be wonderful, so wonderful.

An Inspector had moved in behind her chair. Helen was collecting the discards. She wished she could kick off her shoes. It was a silly rule that dealers werent allowed. Nobody would have noticed unless lying on their back beneath the table. Except the 'odour'. Management dont care for 'odours'. Of course the place already had one, according to a card tacked up on the 'green room' noticeboard: 'essence of greedy bastard' mixed with 'sweaty body'.

When gambling people are forced to wait. They have no choice. Occasionally somebody shivers. Two men once bet on how long it took her to shuffle and deal the next hand. It wasnt a criticism. Now a guy was looking straight at her. Why shouldnt he have been she was the dealer and it was allowed.

She finished shuffling the cards, handed the marker to the player whose turn it was to cut. If there was a smell she barely noticed it. Most places have a smell. Such is life. Think of dogs. Not only a smell: a look, a feel and a sound. That is what life is, if you dont like it.

Her right forefinger was tapping the baize where a bet was to be placed. She dealt:

a card a card a card, a card a card a card: and one for the bank, a ten.

A card a card a card, a card a card a card. Pause.

Card card stay, card bust, stay, card bust, stay, stay. Ten to the ten.

Helen raked in the chips and onwards:

a card a card a card, a card a card a card, and one for the bank, a seven.

A card a card a card, a card a card a card. Pause.

The same guy looking. She didnt care for the way he was doing it, that smile; no, she didnt care for it.

The Inspector had moved from behind Helen's chair but was watching her when she glanced in his direction. Inspectors have to 'watch', that is their job. Dealers as well as punters. If she fell asleep! Imagine, head lolling, that would be her. There *were* times she got tired, and she *could* have slept, certainly, just like dozed off in the middle of everything. Imagine the punters, their lucky day, reaching across for the chips. Would anybody waken her up in case she got fired? Yes, some generous soul. They werent all horrors; far from it. But when had the ogler sat down? she hadnt noticed till she saw him looking.

Whose word was that, 'ogler'? A dealer Helen worked beside who gave names to them all and was good at mimicking their mannerisms. Any oglers in tonight? Eyebrows up, down and sideways. He was another talented person. In every place she ever worked there was somebody. What was it about casinos? It was one of *these* jobs, like in Hollywood restaurants, who was serving the food? you never knew if it was a well-known actor 'between jobs'. So they said anyway, if it could be believed. Fantasy-land; people hoping to get 'discovered'. They expected it to happen. Everybody was somebody. They had their own talents or like things about them that were special or they thought were special.

The ogler was the opposite. He had nothing.

He was so not her type, my God. And if one person felt that

way then the other must also, they must know something, if there is not a single solitary spark, just the exact opposite, the opposite of a 'spark'. And surely if it is as strong as that my God!

Helen sighed. The Inspector would have noticed. Is there a problem? Yes, I am tired!

Split aces, doubling up. A player had halted proceedings and was waiting on her. His English was bad but he knew the game. She reached to sort out the bet. He nodded but not in approval; it was as if she had made a mistake and he had corrected it.

Between him and the ogler. And 'wealthy woman' had been at her table earlier. Helen called her that. It was her own name for the woman. Her man was the gambler, he played roulette and she kept out his way. She wasnt friendly. She didnt have to be.

Where did the money come from? What had her man ever done in the world? Unless it was her; she could have been something.

Then the ones who were there and werent there. That was how they acted, even like texting, and the cards were there and waiting; the game held up for them. So cool, just so cool. Money didnt matter, sitting at your table but like they were someplace else, gazing across to the other tables or over to the lounge or the bathroom or the exit, or a girl walking by with a tray of drinks or if a slot-machine was paying out. Anything at all, like they had no interest in the cards, fingering their cigarette packet. If they wanted to go out for a smoke why didnt they? Even when another player glanced at his watch, they looked at him doing it. Imagine looking at somebody looking at a watch. Was that not weird? What does that say about boredom? They wanted to be someplace else but here they were stuck in a casino, oh well, so they just had to sit at a table and gamble their money. Perhaps they were insomniacs. They only came because they couldnt sleep and were fed up with all-night television. Where else could they go? But did they have to go anywhere? Why didnt they stay at home and read a book? Or get on with the damn housework; they could do a wash or a pile of ironing. If people needed something to do Helen would give them the key to her door and they could go and do her ironing.

She didnt smile at the thought. But if she had. If she laughed aloud. They would all wonder about that. Some wouldnt like it. Dealers laughing. It wasnt encouraged. What were they laughing at? Weeks ago an elderly man caused a disturbance about this; he didnt like 'croupiers laughing'! You fucking smug bastards! He shouted it across the floor. All because they were laughing. And they were only laughing about something silly. It was nothing to do with him losing his money, or about anybody losing their money. Croupiers dont laugh when people lose their money, not even the ones they dislike. Anyway, not openly. And if it was an okay subject to laugh about then laugh, but quietly. Dont make a fuss. People dont want a fuss, not unless it is a jackpot, everybody crowding round, then it is okay.

The most smiling Helen did was to herself. Usually it went with what she was thinking. Or if she found something funny.

Then if other people didnt. It wasnt her fault.

Mainly it was silly things. Quirky things. Others didnt see the fun, so then if she had to explain it didnt seem funny at all. You just smiled to see it the first time. It wouldnt be funny if you were telling it because it wasnt happening, it was just you telling about it happening. Mo said she had a weird sense of humour. What was weird about that? Some things were funny and some things werent. Comedians on television were supposed to be funny but they werent. Most of them spoke nonsense. They had an easy life and brought other people down; that was how they got their laughs. They stood on the platform acting cool like in their smart outfits, clever clever and laughing at everything, laughing at people. Helen didnt like that. It was daft actions made her laugh, clowns from the circus. They were truly funny. Really, they were, and it was like *real* fun. Old black and white films too. They showed them in the morning so if you couldnt sleep you turned on the telly and that is what it was. Sophie at school and Mo out some-place. Helen could lie on the chair and enjoy them, like with the blanket over, just doze off, it was so so relaxing. She read through the coming movies for the week in the Sunday paper and drew a line round the ones that appealed. Mo said she was 'quirky'. Okay if she was. So that was another one, if she was 'quirky', she didnt care.

She stacked the deck, handed the marker to the next player in line: the ogler. Who else? Ogling her boobs. Oh well, yes, of course. Letting the gaze linger long enough for her to know what he was doing. Because he *wanted* her to know. It wasnt enough to ogle, they needed *you* to know.

They look at you and do what they want, if they want to smile and laugh at you they can. It is the easiest thing in the world because like you are trapped. Except you have your clothes on so let them look and just get on with it. Contempt is what Helen felt for them. And any women at the table because if they see it happening why do they not help? If one man gets you they all can.

She needed away. This is what she needed. She had too much going on in her life anyway, what did it matter, horrors like him, she had just so much, so so much, being stuck here, she didnt want to be and even thinking about home and sigh-ing at the table, apropros nothing, just sighing. Sophie was asleep long ago. Azizah too, home in her own house, long ago; she remembered things and was responsible, and a bright girl and just really responsible, she was, they were so so lucky to get her.

The bugger was pretending to be caught like with his hand to his chest, Who me? Infantile behaviour, yes, but more than that he was in control, and she was the one being controlled. Exactly, of course, so so obvious, so so obvious, she was a woman and she was the employee; so there it was twice; he was not only a man but a customer; he had bought the right to control. She would have been as well a prostitute. Bought and sold by Mr Ogle. Mr Ogle. He was whispering into his mate's ear. Guys like him usually had mates. Otherwise he wouldnt have been doing it. It was a show-off sham and that is all he was.

He whispered loudly enough to be heard by her and the other players. He used a stagey Scottish voice to make a fool of her and make a fool of Scotland. She ignored it. Once upon a time she smiled at that stuff. Not now. Others would have slapped his face and criticised Helen for letting him get away with it. Mum was one; oh yes, Mum. Although ignorant of the entire proceedings. Nothing about any of it. That is what she knew, nothing. Bloody damn all, except how to be critical, if it was Helen. Oh yes, if it was Helen, Mum would have given her the 'look' with that tut tut thing she did then the sigh. That was her like just so so – and she knew nothing at all about casinos, and about working in England, nothing, nothing at all. Had she even been in England? She didnt know a single solitary thing about any of it but when it came to being critical my God, if it was Helen, that was a bandwagon. Helen was sick of it. If that was 'family', what did it mean, blood and water, it was just nothing, only what you made it like if you made it important it was important, if you didnt you didnt. What kind of family did they ever have? Dad was Dad and oh God you could never escape

And her tummy. She just felt – horrible, why did she feel so horrible? and suddenly too. She hadnt been feeling it before. Because of him, it was him, dirty ogling thing that he was. He shifted on his chair, swivelling to speak directly into the ear of his mate who stood a little to the rear and was craning his head forwards to listen. They laughed quietly, heads bowed.

What else but her? Their little snidey comments. What did it matter? horrible comments, it didnt matter. Because she didnt care. She *so* didnt care, like if they were who they were and she was who she was, really she just did not care, she really didnt, she so so didnt, if she lost the damn job she would just lose it, putting up with this, she would slap his bloody face, in a minute she would, what did they think she couldnt fight? she was from bloody Glasgow, she would just bloody

dirty ogling thing.

So if the Inspector was watching, so what? she would still slap him. Helen knew exactly what he was up to because men like him made sure of that. She was only a poor wilting female under the power of these so truly dominating powerful men like they were so so very powerful, they just reduced her to a shrinking violet, my God, if it was not so pathetic; she would have, she would have laughed in their face, it made you so angry; sometimes it did. Because it was always there, that was girls, having to put up with it, having to cope with it, how do they cope with it? however do they cope with it?

She gathered in the discards from the last round, raising her head for a moment; the ogler was in her line of vision. Know thine enemy.

'Louts' was a good word. Thinking of this pair as opposed to somebody like the mad doctor, as a for-instance. He 'looked'. Of course he did. Jill was wrong about that. Perhaps he didnt look at her but he did look at Helen and it was not boasting to say it. What did she care if he looked or not? Not if it was like normal man and woman. He was a gentleman and it was only a natural thing. Men did look, of course they did. And that was nice, it was nice they did, if it was only that. Who is going to worry about that? Never. Men look. So do women. Women look too. So ha ha there. If men dont think they do, they do, women look at men.

Helen had shuffled the cards. The ogler grasped the marker. Helen had given him it. She had had to look at him directly. That was fine, that was easy. He tried to hold her gaze while inserting it into the deck of cards, thrusting it in. As unsubtle as a horse. He even resembled a horse. An ugly one, some are nice; horses.

She split the deck, returned it to the shoe, ruffling and smoothing down the cards; even individually cards could stick, they didnt always slide; why was that? dirt or grit, sweat; sweaty palms; or just bending the cards. Helen didnt like to see that. Although it was nervous, punters got nervous and *fiddled*. A dealer she knew in Glasgow gave them a row: Dont fiddle, you're bending the damn cards! Management gave the dealer into trouble. The money they lose they could buy the whole damn card factory.

The ogler was still watching her. Cool, he said.

So he was only admiring her expertise. Helen turned her head from him in a move, almost as though she hadnt heard him. His mate had the decency to look away. It would have been nice to laugh in his face. But it wouldnt stop him staring. 'Leering' was a good word. He had bought the right because he was at her table. He was a 'leerer'. No, 'ogler' was better.

He even had sweaty lips! Imagine! Helen couldnt, thank God. Why would she want to? Sweaty lips. It made her *groo*, the very idea. How ridiculous they were, some of them any-way, just so ridiculous; gross. Helen smiled. She would have called it a smile. She thought of it as one, like smiling without smiling, without moving a muscle. It was her own smile, it was only for herself she was doing it. Her actual face was expressionless. She wouldnt have allowed them the satisfaction, that was how little the oglers of this world meant to her. Although it could irritate. Of course it could. She concealed the irritation but not herself feeling it because she did feel it and she did think about it; so it did get to her

oh God, she was tired.

Although it was true, these people tried to hurt you. And they succeeded. They did. With her they did. Nowadays they did. All they had was money and they spent it gambling. Okay, a surgeon, he was different. But other ones? They werent scientists or faith healers or whoever, great actors, statesmen, they hadnt done anything, yet expected to act however they wanted, just like how they *felt*, like they had the right, going into a casino and treating everybody who worked there as though they were nothing. So so arrogant. They looked down on you. Some did. In their eyes you were funny; even they mimicked your voice. Oh it is just fun. Yes for them, nobody else. Mo didnt like her talking about it and he was right. It should have been water off a duck's back but it wasnt. It used to be. Not now. Now it was everything, she felt everything. That was the problem. Helen's problem. Too sensitive. She was. She should have been more of a tortoise. Was it the tortoise had the big shell? Something anyway, like with tough skins. That was what she needed, a leather skin, a hide. That was good, a 'hide', so you were hiding underneath it. It was an attitude people adopted in casinos. They thought they were something, and what were they really? Not anything. Only they acted like they were. The women were as bad, if not worse. Some of them. They had that hardness about them, they were tough. Helen had forgotten how tough. Perhaps it was worse in London.

They would eat you up then crunch your bones, just like whatever, they would crunch them. It was like

what?

What was it like?

Her brains were scattered. This happened dealing cards, you were in your own wee world till something dragged you back. It could be a simple matter like a man looking at his watch. Or the way he was looking at you – not ogling, looking – choo choo, where was your head and where your brains? scrambled, the train of thought. 'Real' gamblers are not supposed to 'look': not at dealers. All they see is the cards. Nothing else interests them. People say that. But it isnt true, not in Helen's experience. They sip at their drink and above the rim of the glass their eyes glint, watching. Not dirty old men either like if they happen to be old at all, and a lot arent. The ogler wasnt. He was early thirties, at the most.

Women watched too, and it wasnt freaky. They saw how you reacted to males. If it was a guy like the ogler, how did Helen handle him? There was a woman from Eastern Europe or someplace and she had that interest. Helen imagined her a spy or an undercover detective; she had quite a sharp demeanour and like her eyes too, seeing everything, they did, you felt that, and she never smiled. Even if Helen smiled she didnt smile back, and it wasnt a 'professional' smile like if she thought it was, perhaps she did think that. People have strange ideas. She acted as though she had never sat down at Helen's table before. Some were like that. They didnt want you thinking they were regular gamblers.

A young man came with her. He never smiled either. So their relationship, you wondered about that. Although they hadnt been in for a while. That was so like typical. People disappeared. Sometimes you didnt notice. They were regulars and then stopped coming. The only way you realised this is because there came a time you looked up and there they were, sitting right in front of you. Then you were surprised because it was the first you had seen them in ages. Weeks and weeks. You hadnt seen them. You didnt even know they were not there until now you saw them. Where had they been? You hadnt noticed they were gone till now they were back. Imagine not noticing. People's lives; they have them and dont have them. They live and die, we dont even notice. Had they gone to another casino or what? were they taking a rest? had they lost too much money? But this couldnt apply to the East European woman. She hardly gambled at all, too busy noting people's behaviour, and the young guy with her, like a male escort. You said hullo and they didnt even smile. Was that peculiar? Perhaps not. Perhaps it was Helen who was peculiar. Of course, yes, little Miss Peculiar. She sounded like a packet of sweeties, boiled ones, the kind old ladies like to sook.

Oh well, she dealt the cards, that was her, the dealer, the one who dealt, she 'crouped', croupiers crouping and dealers dealing. She should have been a smoker, smokers smoking, they had these wee breaks in the alley round the back of the casino. A rear passageway ran the length of the building. Steps led down to the rear exit. Staff smokers used this; they went in twos and threes. In the old days the 'girls' took their 'clients' here. Druggies used it too, tramps and rats, drunks; people went there to be sick. It was dark and secluded, shadowy and horrible; who would want to go there? except in emergency. Nowadays it was still secluded, but security had been increased; good lighting and CCTV. But still not a nice place, having to step over bodies, watching where they put their feet; needles and human waste. It wasnt the first time a croupier had returned across the carpet in the worst poo-covered shoes imaginable. People never knew what they might find. There were the comical aspects; couples interrupted in 'acts of gross indecency'. What the Smoker Saw, not the 'Butler'. Experiences from the back alley provided some of the 'green room' hilarity. Anyway, people quite envied the smokers. They said that, escaping to the fresh air, it was worth the bad lungs and whatever else. As long as they went in company, not just the one person.

The 'girls' werent supposed to use the casinos nowadays. Did they or didnt they? Ha ha.

But if they did they werent cheap. They would never have gone to back alleys. It would have been good-class hotels or someplace nice, fancy apartments with all good furniture and proper everything, space and whatnot, bedrooms. Not like out the back where it was full of risk and filth and dangers too. Women never went on their own.

Why did he laugh? The ogler laughed. He laughed because he had won. Helen paused a moment while paying out the money. Not only him, everybody. The bank had taken a card, and another, a picture card: bust. So Helen was paying out the money.

But for the third hand in a row. The bank had lost the two previous. Yes, so that made the difference. To them it did. So they had beat the bank three times in a row. And Helen was the bank. Okay, but why laugh like that? Not only the ogler but the rest of them, sharing it with him; beating her, they wanted to beat her. It was sad, so sad.

Such was her job.

Did they actually for one minute believe she cared one way or the other? like really cared?

'Wealthy woman' too – she had returned to the table – perhaps her jewellery would fall off, perhaps somebody would step on it and break it, just crunch it like a whatever, under the heel of your shoe. But then it wouldnt be the genuine article, if it could be so easily crunched, and hers was real. Her man was back at the roulette. She only came to keep him company. Not to let him out her sight. Or him her. Comical. Males and females. Rich or poor.

What did it matter?

Helen had passed out the chips. People confused her with the job, that was the problem like it was her personal money, if it was did they think she would be gambling it all away? Ha ha. It didnt matter one way or the other. Not to her it didnt; not if she lost every hand. Or if she won every hand, although she would have enjoyed taking his money; that would have been nice, and if he waited a little longer she would, because in the end the bank always wins. What a fool.

So things were getting to her.

No they werent.

The ogler was whispering to his friend. It wasnt annoying but

It was annoying. It shouldnt have been but it was. So she was letting him get to her. She should never have let him get to her. No emotion in this job. You werent paid for emotion.

Helen smiled to the ogler and his mate. Yes.

She was waiting for the bets to be placed. An elderly man had sat down at the corner of the table. He seemed familiar. She waited for him and another player to place their bets. The ogler had left his winning chips from the last hand, so that was his. At the same time impressing her with the size of his bet, trying to anyway. Always the size of something. Him and his money. So silly, so childish, but that was a trait in men. Helen, what is the outstanding trait in men? They are childish.

That would annoy him, smiling, why had she smiled?

What if she giggled? If she laughed aloud? That would annoy him even worse. Did his wife know how much he wasted in this place? He was obviously married. Even without the ring he was married. He had like arrogance, that certain arrogance.

He *knew* women. That is what it was. Did his wife even know where he was? Probably not. He would control everything. Even what she *knew*, what went on in her mind. That is what he would control, never mind the money. That was her ex my God oh yes, Mr Big Boss, he was the man, of course he was, arent penises wonderful? She could have carried one in her bag, dropped it on the table.

Goodness,

the card the card the card, the card the card the card, the card, seven players, and one for the bank.

the card the card the card, the card the card the card, the card

The ogler's mate was whispering to him. He wasnt so bad-looking; only the scar, the front of his ear down to his neck. That summed it up.

stay, stay

Card, asked the ogler. He was showing 12.

Helen turned a picture to bust him, raked in his chips and continued the hand. And to the banker's own she added an 8 to the face card showing, raked in the remainder of the chips, in a disinterested way. No comment from the ogler. She enjoyed taking his money. But did she? Perhaps she didnt, perhaps really it didnt matter, it didnt. She didnt care.

'Wealthy woman' passed money across and Helen exchanged it for chips. Usually with couples it was the other way about. The male played cards for pounds and the female roulette for pence. It was the competition. You could like beat somebody up at cards, but not roulette. At cards you showed who was boss. So they thought. But they thought wrong; blackjack and house-poker are the same, you bet against the 'house', not against people.

She rarely thought about money when dealing cards. If she did it would be all the time. She hardly saw it as money. She was an experienced worker. She listened to other croupiers but had her own opinions. She was a dealing machine and that was that. There would come a day when they wouldnt have any croupiers, it would all be machines. Already in the States they had entire casinos with machines. To each their own. The punters put in their money and hit a button. Money money money. Standing at the machines with that glazed expression, buckets of coins and buckets of popcorn; unable to hear or see, mindless. That was her ex, the proverbial.

All the people and all the money.

And up pops he. The bad penny.

Money money money. Mostly she didnt care. She had no control, like none, she had none. None! What did they think? In one casino where she worked an Inspector thought it was the dealer's fault. That was how he acted, just so so stupid. If he saw you losing too many hands he whispered sarcastic comments, the same as any punter, thinking individual dealers were lucky, or unlucky. Even some dealers believed it about themselves, they were lucky, or unlucky. Anyway, it was all mixed up. If your every hand was a losing hand it was lucky for the punters; to be lucky for them was to be unlucky at the cards. Lucky at the cards was lucky for the house. Back in Glasgow there was one guy only played at her table because she was 'far too good'. He said it to her when giving over his money: Helen, you are far too good, you are far too good.

So why come to her table? Was that not silly? just foolish. Helen, you are slick. Of course Helen was 'slick'; it was her job to be 'slick'. You take my money why do you take my money? Silly man.

Concentration concentration. She looked up from the baize. Her eyelids flickered. Waves in her tummy, slight little things, butterflies.

Nothing about the time forget the time, nothing nothing

nothing, the cards the people the money; what was the order? it didnt matter the order, people money cards, oglers.

Nerves, because Brian, what if he was there?

Oh God the time the time what was the time?

Oh well, if he was he was.

But it was true and she had to think because what was she going to do! It was nearly time and she was going home; she would be. Very soon; very very soon, that would be her, my God, if she shared Danny's taxi, like just as usual. Because with Caroline and Jill like if she *didnt* share with them, what would they think? They would think something. Better they didnt. Better she went home with them, same as usual, got off at her street same as usual, then when Danny's taxi was out of sight she would jump the next one back into the city. She had enough money, she had brought enough.

Helen knew what she was doing. She had thought about what she was doing. The whole damn day.

But she did know. Because there was a good chance they would be in the same area, roughly speaking, at roughly the same time. People are people, creatures of habit, him with the limp and the tall skinny one, and if it was, imagine it was. Although it was unlikely. But you never know, because with Brian, Brian was Brian.

Taxis were so so expensive; going home then back was like a return so twice the money my God it was like half a night's work to pay for it, a third. It was just so much. She would have to tell Mo. There was no choice because it wasnt fair if it was house-money, extra for this and extra for that on top of the debt my God two taxis was like a day out for the three of them it was so – indulgent.

Although if she *had* to do it. So it was not 'indulgent', not if she had to. If it was Brian. She would never forgive herself and like Mo too, if she told him. And she would tell him, whether she found Brian or not, he would have to know because if he didnt oh God that would be so bad of her. It would be. Because not taking him into her confidence like not trusting him and she did trust him, above all, she trusted him.

It was true! She trusted Mo, she really really did. He was her family, so if it was Brian. If it was Brian it was Brian.

She closed her eyes, rubbed at the side of her face. Why did people not go home? And Helen too, if only

only only, only the lonely,

a card a card a card,

So if he *was* ill. Perhaps he was. He had been a good big brother to her. If it *was* him. *If* it was. Only she had to know. She at least would say hullo. So if he was homeless. Poor Brian. None of it mattered, bloody oglers and nonsense.

What time was it?

Hi . . . came the whisper. The relief Inspector had moved in behind Helen's chair as she dealt. Felix, quite a tough-looking guy. Her knight in shining armour! She knew he liked her. At least he wasnt creepy. And his lips. Some lips she didnt like. He leaned closer: Okay?

Yes. Helen smiled.

The ogler and his mate had gone. When had they gone? If management wanted to stop the ogling they would give the girls different-style dresses, higher necklines to begin with. Roll-neck collars. Scarves and overcoats.

Perhaps Felix had a word in his ear; whatever. She hadnt noticed him leave. Things happen. People come people go. A young man was in his seat. Helen smiled and he smiled back. A hand later she bought two 10s to bust so now everybody was smiling. What a wonderful world. It put people off if you always won.

She paid out the winning bets. 'Wealthy woman' reached for hers then gathered in all of her chips. Her man had beckoned!

He had, he had finished with the roulette and was signalling her. Dance to your daddy. 'Wealthy woman' rose from the table.

Helen smothered a yawn. The relief Inspector had moved to another table. Across the floor she saw Caroline walking. Thank God.

On the next round the marker appeared; she collected the discards to begin the shuffling process. But Rob was there, her relief croupier. He winked. He was only young. She felt like hugging him. She really did. Not because he was nice, although he was, but too young, it was just that she

she was glad. What about? She didnt know, like a break, that was all, she needed a break, like from everything, just everything. She had no illusions. What about?

Anything; anything and nothing.

She smiled and was tired.

Jill had gone on ahead to pacify the grumpy male. Although what difference did it make to Danny the driver? If it was a contract hire. They were waiting on Caroline who was still in front of the mirror, still fixing her hair, having her 'last sip' of tea and yapping about her two sons. Nothing changes. Actually it was relaxing. Even the gossipy nosiness, Helen quite liked it. Except she went on and on and people were waiting. Helen glanced at her watch again, checking the time by the clock on the wall.

Caroline noticed: Sorry sorry, she said.

Helen was about to speak, she smiled instead. One 'sorry' would have been 'sorry', two meant she wasnt really.

That's me now, said Caroline, making to get up from the chair, but instead she peered at her telephone; was she going to text somebody? and another 'last sip' of tea. Why, why did she do that? She knew people were waiting on her but still she did it.

Why have a last cup of tea at all? Although Helen could have done with one herself, except there was no time. Plenty time but no time. Was that life? That was life. Hers anyway. Caroline could but Helen couldnt, or wouldnt. Workmates are friends too. If a friend doesnt want you doing something then you shouldnt do it, not if they dont want you to, if it is a friend. What else is a friend? You watch out for friends, you make allowances.

The door had opened and Jill appeared, and Jill was a friend. She didnt have to speak.

Caroline poked her tongue out at her, making fun of the situation. Jill smiled slightly and retreated. Caroline said, Denny's been waiting for ten minyoots – in a vague imitation of Jill's voice – then added, I think she's annoyed at me.

Caroline had returned her attention to the mirror but now she had the telephone in her hand again. Comical and sad. Helen didnt feel anything, annoyed or what, nothing. She lifted her bag from the table, buttoning her coat.

Outside she walked to the cab. She gave Jill a wave. Danny was standing chatting to the driver of another cab. He saw Helen but didnt acknowledge her. Too cool. That was a thing with guys like him, how they were so cool, they were just like so cool.

The other driver was Nicky. He was okay. There were times his gaze lingered. Not only was he fifty years of age he had a bald head and a stupid moustache; father of four, still wanting to look. Look but dont touch. It would have been funny if it wasnt so

what?

God, what did it matter? Cheery . . . Sometimes anyway, that sort of male stupidity, it cheered her up. It was like the *real* world, coming after the casino, that coldness, there was a *coldness*. She wasnt always so sensitive to it but tonight she had been. She didnt blame people, it was just something, an overall – some feeling she had, she couldnt describe it, you cant always, Helen couldnt. Sophie once complained about her skin being *too tight*. Oh Mum, and stroking her arms when she spoke, she said her body was bursting, the skin was too tight for it and it needed more, more *skin*. What did that mean? It was a while ago she said it. But what did it mean? These things children say, they mean something and you cant work it out. A pure physical thing. Uncomfortable in your skin.

Then stories. Azizah read to Sophie the last thing at night, and some went on and on forever the way Sophie spoke about them, and they were like scary too; some were; people getting their heads chopped up into little pieces, chased into deep valleys by elephants and boa-constrictors; they were more like boys' stories, but Sophie liked them. Children were an alien species. Of course the stories were exciting but they had to get to sleep. So if Azizah started the story too late. No wonder she was tired in the morning. It explained things too about her concentration, how she got so involved in things, and didnt hear you talking; she just seemed to switch off from listening. People did that. When things got tough how else could you cope?

Oh God.

But it was true. You had to survive. So you had to switch off. You did. It was sophisticated too, behaviour, sophisticated behaviour, for her age, really, quite mature

Helen was shivering, rocking from one foot to the other, so that was skin, that was flesh, flesh and bones and everything. It wasnt that cold either, not temperature-wise, but she really was shivering, she was, like nerves, nervy she was nervy, she was, very very nervy; this shivering, she couldnt stop, so so just oh God, she felt so folding her arms; no wonder just no wonder.

Oh well, she had to. Had to what? Relax, if she could. She could, she had to, she had to just like *be ready*. Because things

Across the road a queue formed at the taxi-rank. This time of the morning people were still going and coming, mostly from clubbing, sitting in all-night restaurants or wherever else people went – casinos. Why did they go out in the first place? Some would have had nice houses, gardens and kitchens, and a proper bathroom where you had an actual bath, imagine a bath, like being able to relax and just *lie*. Imagine being in the bath and a magazine and hot chocolate, that was you and your day-off, last thing at night and Sophie asleep and you were there in the house and able to just – if you ran the bath, relaxing and nothing at all, not even anything to think about

Oh God stupidity.

There were others just hanging around the way people did up west; guys you didnt want to know, looking at you in that way they did.

Three girls passed, wearing hardly a stitch and talking in loud voices; teens. They must have been freezing. Just looking at them made Helen feel old. How long since she had been one of them? Never.

Not true. But why were they so loud!

Helen enjoyed clubbing. She used to anyway. Not nowadays, not so much, all the bodies, all close up and breathing over you, people out their mind, beer-soaked breath and cigarette smells, and these big guys, just like *big guys*; forget zombies, although some of them my God that is what they were, zombies, then if they slipped you something.

Nicky's taxi had gone. Danny was standing by the door of his, hands in pockets and whistling a wee tune, acting like he didnt care. Helen whispered to Jill, I know where she'll be, she'll be having a smoke.

Jill didnt respond.

She'll have come by the back door exit and round the alley.

Yes.

I dont know why she does it; we're always last.

Jill shrugged. She doesnt want to go home.

Perhaps she's having an affair. Sorry, said Helen. Only it explains things. The thought just struck me; sorry. Helen got into the back of the cab. She closed her eyes a moment.

Jill followed her into the middle of the back seat. Now Caroline appeared from the rear of the building. Jill whispered, You were right about smoking.

Helen whispered, I didnt mean anything about what I said there, about the other thing, it just came out.

Caroline had the cigarette in one hand, telephone in the other, snatching a last puff before flinging the butt into the gutter, and moving to enter the passenger side. She pulled shut the door, mouthing an apology while affixing the seatbelt.

Danny waited a few moments before entering the driver's seat. He shut the door firmly, stared into the rear-view mirror a moment longer. Helen saw his eyes. Eventually he said, That us now girls? Our little noses all powdered?

I dont know about yours, muttered Caroline.

Now dont be like that, he said.

Sarcastic bugger.

Yeh dear yeh, but with a home to go to.

Home for the disturbed, she muttered.

Helen smiled. She muttered something else and Helen smiled at that too, whatever it was, the same old stuff, repartee. Jill wasnt listening but gazing out the other side window, in her own wee world, wherever that was, dreams, nice things, perhaps not; she also had her troubles, poor Jill. Poor everybody. Having to bother about everybody. Nobody was there for her but she was to be there for them. True. That was how it felt.

Brian was lovely and a good big brother, he had been. But he wasnt there. She would have liked him to be but he wasnt. But she was to do it for him, whatever, she had to do it, and be there, she had to *be* there. The whole thing, it was just like

escaping

Imagine your own car. She wouldnt have had to wait for anybody. She could drive it to work. Central London was a nightmare, but people did find parking places. It could even be south of the river. Some did that, then took a tube or a bus. Not worrying about other people, they could do what they wanted. That would be good in itself, that would just be like so so good, worth any hassle for the independence. And they could go places. Sophie would love it. Helen would have to drive because Mo didnt.

Except London traffic, but she would get used to that too. The coast wasnt far either. Oh my God seeing the sea, she so missed the sea. All these wee towns and the country roads, exploring them. Mo would learn. He would. She would teach him. Imagine not having a licence. What you need a car for? That was Mo. Nobody needs a car in London. Yes but to get *out* of London, that was the point. Everybody would if they could, summer especially.

My God the junction already, that was her head.

Danny was not stopping. The lights were green. They were green and not for changing. So no need to stop. If there was none, no need.

She looked out both side windows, nobody, nothing. She had assumed they would stop and they didnt. Oh well.

Goodness but it was a surprise. She hadnt expected this to happen. She did but she didnt.

Unanswerable questions. If the pair had appeared. She would have asked Danny to stop the taxi, and got out. She wouldnt have said why. Or drove on to the next set of traffic lights, got off there and walked back, even from across the river, or else – whatever, just whatever. But she couldnt have done that because what people would have said, if she was getting off there, why would she have been? It was just like – she couldnt have done.

Caroline was speaking to Jill. What about? They would have assumed Helen was listening. Whatever they were talking about. But Helen wasnt listening. She couldnt have anyway because they were leaning forward with their heads turned to each other. Helen would have had to sit forwards on the edge of the seat and just like whatever because the way they were speaking, it was very hard to hear.

But if the two men had been there! Stop stop! Let me out let me out! Imagine they had been and she did. What would they think? The worst. Whatever it was. People always think the worst. But who could have guessed the truth? Nobody. So it was hardly their fault. Helen couldnt have blamed them. She wouldnt anyway, they were decent friends. Workmates. She didnt meet them outside. She didnt meet anybody outside. She didnt want to. She had Sophie and that was enough, her and Mo.

Oh dear! Her life anyway. She glanced out the window, she glanced at her watch. Oh God, what was she thinking? nothing, everything, nonsense, just nonsense

But she knew what she was doing. She did. Whatever time it was. Not long anyway, just whatever, and home before five thirty, easily. They would still be asleep. She had time, *time*.

Jill and Caroline were looking at her. Helen frowned. Caroline said, You were talking to yourself.

No I wasnt.

Jill said, You were.

Sorry. I hope it was sensible.

No.

Oh well . . . Helen smiled, and tried to yawn. Are you two not tired? she said. I'm exhausted.

The taxi approached her area. She settled back in the seat. Whatever she was deciding. Although she had decided. She didnt know when, but that she had. So just like how to do the next stage, that was her; how to go forwards because like her mind was haywire, all night long, with useless stuff, nonsensical stupidity and nonsense, such stupidity and so so nonsensical. She thought about things and then she didnt. The last thing ever was what she would do. Yet she knew she would do something. Even changing her clothes to go home; back in the 'green room'. She knew it then. Her mind had, without her knowing. Decisions decisions. She had decided. Her mind had done it for her.

The taxi turned into her street.

Danny watched her in the rear-view mirror. She unlocked the seatbelt. Caroline opened the door and shifted to allow her out. Not tonight but tomorrow, said Jill.

Helen smiled. Not tonight but tomorrow, whatever that might mean. She waved while heading towards the steps up to the house. Once the taxi was out of sight she returned along the street.

There was little traffic. She walked for nearly ten minutes before the next available taxi. It must have been the changeover period from night to dayshift. Ten minutes was a while. That was the trouble her phone not working, she could have called the local minicab office. The people there were okay.

Anyway, the hackney was good for anonymity. Although the guy was so slow, so very slow. Some drivers do that, why do they do that? Nobody knows. Life has its secrets!

She could have gone to sleep there in the back seat. It was still dark, although only just, and a strong bleeze blowing. She didnt have a plan, not a proper one, only to arrive at the junction, at the traffic lights, and follow in the direction they were headed yesterday morning. It wasnt too forlorn. London was an impossible place anyway. She needed a point to begin. This was the best, the obvious. Where else? There wasnt any else.

If others saw it differently. How could they? That was them if they did. Helen was Helen; she could only do her best. She paid the driver and set off walking. At least it was dry.

The driver didnt drive off immediately, he was watching to see where she went. Strange how they did that.

She crossed the road, glancing over her shoulder, walking steadily towards the corner under the streetlights. The street off from the main road. She walked towards here, and along. It was quiet. And risky; of course it was. Women should be able to walk the street at night but there is a difference between should and could. If she had been giving advice to Sophie or any young girl it would have been never to do what now she was doing. But people do things and they have to; it is wrong to see choices, not if there arent any.

It was almost like claustrophobic. Or no, what was it? Some other phobic. A phobia. She had experienced a thing similar in the past to do with confidence, and her ex, it was him and whatever, she didnt know what to do just like standing still, that was all, like a panic but just so quietly and that cold sweat, just so – not able to move.

She was not cold. She didnt feel cold, she wasnt, except shivering, if she did, if she was.

She *was* cold.

On the other side of the street, what was that? a walkway? There was a grass verge then a walkway, concealed partly by bushes. This skirted down a little slope. How close was the river? One of the main city bridges was less than what away? A good walk. In this vicinity homeless people were rumoured to live underground. Caroline believed it: Jill didnt. Neither did

Helen because where? It seemed impossible. Although there were places farther along where the bank of the river rose quite high and you could imagine underground chambers and passages. Old London, it was a creepy place with these old underground streets and stuff from ages back. It was so *not* far-fetched. Really. And these old mine-workings. Nobody even knew where they were, except they were everywhere, old mines and dead bodies, trapped workmen in their vaults, collapsed beams and landslides, all the coal breaking through and smothering you, like the worst dream imaginable, being a miner. These underground places could connect via the sewers, like in movies about New York, opening a cover in the street and hearing voices, seeing lights and down you go and people all are living there, flotsam and jetsam, the dregs, they called them the dregs but they were just people. But how ever could they enter without being seen? The police stood by and watched, or else had their camcorders in position, recording everybody, escaped murderers and serial killers. You couldnt believe what you heard or read. People blabbed and told lies in the newspapers and television, reporters and politicians, men of the church, you saw their faces when they were telling you, child abusers, and they were just like blabbing and it was all lies, people hanging themselves and apples in their mouths, to do with perversions and all the sordid details, dressing up like chickens or babies wearing nappies. Laughable if it wasnt so dreadful, and they didnt care if it was babies anyway, they didnt care, just like their own needs and desires.

She was not going along the walkway. There was lighting. She was not going. If it was a place the two homeless guys would have gone. Probably it was, if there were benches; probably there were benches. So a place to sit, to rest, if you were homeless. God. But Helen was not going along it. These places were creepy, very very. Okay she was brave but not foolish.

She *was* brave.

But she was.

One thing about working in casinos, like creepy guys, it prepared you for them. Every night of the week there was something, including 'propositions'. She told Mo about them, she shouldnt have. It was to see the funny side. Although it was true, men did ask her out on a regular basis, and they werent all drunk! And they werent all creepy. Some were nice, not bad and not horrible. Mind you it was better he *didnt* know about them. That was a mistake she made with her ex. She thought he wanted to hear. He said he did but he didnt. Some did: they liked hearing about other men fancying their women or whatever, even sleeping with them, him and his nude sunbathing, why didnt he do it? Helen nearly told him about Mr Adams. He was the very one she wanted to tell. That was so so strange. He was the very one never to tell but she was wanting to, so so wanting to and like having to stop herself doing it, put a scarf in your mouth my God what would he have done he would have killed her.

A car coming. She turned her head to avoid the appearance of looking, in case the driver thought something he shouldnt. The car continued on but quite slowly like she was 'on the game', if they thought that, the driver. God, if she *had* been. She wouldnt have been walking the street. Never, never never.

What would she have been doing?

Not in the street anyway! My God it was so so uncomfortable!

But it wasnt funny why was she smiling? she was smiling, why was she?

It was cold and damp, at least not raining, very quiet, lonely. The car had gone thank heaven.

She would have had a proper flat, not taking terrible chances down alleyways and car-park spaces; behind bushes in grass squares and even the back closes of office buildings, it was appalling, there was always news of prostitutes found dead, and tortured; tortured. Men tortured them, they tortured the women, the worst most horrible things. How could people torture people? Other human beings? What happened in their life? Something must have happened. They couldnt just be evil. Mo said they were like if they had lost God, if they had turned from Him, so they had to find Him again, because it was Hell if they didnt. Mo believed in Hell. He didnt say he did. But he didnt say he didnt. He was supposed to. Hell was there and so were angels like for Catholics and Protestants. If he believed in them. Perhaps he did. Although not Hell, surely not Hell? Not with children. How could you with children? It was horrible if he did. Because just like that was his *belief*, and he was clever, he was, and just common sense, that was Mo, common sense, so if *he* believed in Hell. He didnt say he did but he didnt say he didnt.

Although Helen did believe in God. Truly, she did. What else could explain things? She hadnt been sure before but she did now, she really did, she did believe. But not Hell. Imagine children, that was so so *unimaginable*, just like – unimaginable.

But she would have had a proper flat. She wouldnt have taken such risks. These women took terrible risks. Why do people take such risks? Helen would never have walked the streets.

She smiled at the thought, even she could have laughed; almost she could have. It was so ridiculous. The conversations she had with herself were fantastic. Now she was a prostitute and being choosy about her clientele! What next? Even as a child. Honestly, she hadnt changed. In school she was known for it. She once told her schoolmates that her mother was a famous dancer and her legs were the longest of anybody and had to be insured for lots of money in case they got broken and she couldnt dance. Her pals believed her! What is wrong with an imagination? Children have them, like it or not. They need them too. They take you out yourself, and you need that, coorying down with the blankets over your head, into your own wee world and just safe and away from everything, away, that was all, she wanted that and needed it, like a lot of children, that was her; she was not unique, she was *so* not unique. She didnt care about any of it, only having to find things out. Children do, they have to. Because if the adults dont tell them. Why dont they tell them? Why dont adults? They dont tell them. Tell the children. So so horrible and unfair. So they have to find out for themselves, if the adults dont tell them. So they make mistakes. Helen made mistakes. Girls do. All children. Sometimes it was funny, like so funny, just how the misunderstandings. Sophie got all mixed up with what she was to do and not to do. Strangers were bad because they said naughty words. No Sophie. Perhaps they did but that wasnt why children had to avoid them. Like taking sweets from strangers; if you didnt take them the strangers would take them away and give them to somebody else; take what away? the sweets or the children? It was comical.

Helen would have gone with anybody when she was a child. It was only natural. Sophie was the same. Only never hit her. Never hit a child. Why hit a child? And if it is not her fault? It is so horrible.

She could have gone to the police about Brian. Only what would she have said? It wasnt the case of a missing person. The person was there. He might not even have been missing like only if he was missing to her and Mum. Because he didnt want them to know where he was. And if he was on the street. Of course he wouldnt want them to know. He would have been ashamed, especially in front of his little sister, even more than Mum.

So if it was him. Either it was or it wasnt. She had to know. She had to.

Only not dwelling on it, one way or the other. If she found him she found him. And if she didnt, better letting it rest, if she could. The past was the past. Why rake everything up? She had no intention of raking everything up. Only like if it was Brian she wanted to see him; she truly truly did. Even to know it was him. Not having to do anything *more*. She didnt feel she had to. She didnt feel *forced*. Only *if* it was him. Why else was she here? If she didnt want to find him. Of course she did. Because if he was ill. Else why was he walking the street? He should have been in hospital. That was it with people, they had no place to go, so they walked about, with that look on their face, my God! The way he stared at them! He frightened everybody.

It was almost like he was mad or something. Perhaps he was, just mentally like how people are ill and should be in hospital. Not mad so much as angry, so so angry; he was, and it changes your brain. How could Helen take him home? Not with a child in the house.

She wasnt going to feel guilty about it, if he *was* sleeping rough. She had enough problems. If it wasnt one thing it was another. What was she going to do? There was hardly room to swing a cat in their place my God.

Even thinking about it, she hated thinking about it. Thank goodness it was quiet. Although she knew what she was doing: home. Straight home. She had decided. If it was to be it was to be and if it wasnt it wasnt. Then the car from behind. She heard it and glanced back over her shoulder as it passed her by so slowly. Several yards on the driver braked sharply. Helen stopped walking. Two figures were inside. Three. She continued walking, steadily, staring to the front. But as she passed the car began moving and the passenger door swung open suddenly but also like *calmly*.

How could it be *calmly*? But it was; and that was the effect it had as if nothing else for it, only just get in, get in, like a trance, the guy calling to her, so getting into the car, if she was to get into the car. Keeping pace with her as she walked. She stared straight ahead.

A guy called to her: Hey, darling . . . You fancy a little run? You want to come with us? What d'you say? Hey, hey darling, fancy a little run?

She kept walking. The car kept moving. The men were laughing, but the *urgency*, she knew the urgency, she knew it; men, she knew it, in this man's voice, almost like a tremble. Hey darling, you are beautiful, yeh, total pleasure guaranteed, you want to come with us?

She kept walking.

You hear what I'm saying, mature man knows the ropes yeh, check the adverts, like your pleasure, yeh, is our guarantee.

The car jerked ahead now and halted. Helen paused then stepped up to the car door and grabbed at it shouting: Fuck off will you! Just fuck off!

She shoved the door shut and strode on. Was it laughter she heard? She didnt know, couldnt make it out, if it was or just like in her head, whatever. Then another car engine and she quickened on faster till she saw it was a taxi thank God and was running and calling, Taxi! Taxi!

It stopped for her. The other car had gone. Cowards, such cowards. She fumbled the passenger door open, but didnt climb inside. She held onto the door handle.

You alright sweetheart? The driver had a concerned look, and genuine.

Helen attempted a smile. It didnt work. She released the handle and backed off, and waved him away.

The driver's irritation was obvious. Oh well. If he hadnt called her 'sweetheart'. 'Dear' was bad enough, she didnt like 'dear', but 'sweetheart', that was like 'pet' or 'flower', bloody dandelion. The taxi had disappeared.

At least she knew what she was doing. Home! Right now. So why let the taxi go for God sake Helen Helen Helen? because she was going mad, simple and straightforward. Mrs Simple. Tomorrow was her day-off.

Today. Tomorrow was today for nightshift workers. Her and Mo would go someplace with Sophie. The whole day was theirs. He would make the food. Or her. Or together, and Sophie helping. A movie. She so looked forward to it.

That was so typical of her letting the taxi go. So so – just foolish. She was. Then they were on the other side of the street my God the familiarity like she had been dreaming about and here they were the two of them, coming out of the shadows along from the walkway, the one with the limp and him with the beard and the woollen cap.

They were quite a distance away but the shape, the resemblance, it was so so Brian, really and truly my God! the height and the skinniness! coat-hanger shoulders, that was Dad, Mr Malinky and that walk of his, that walk, who else? Helen laughed to see it, she did, it was just so Brian my God it was her big brother, just so amazing; how strange was that, just so amazing. What a strange strange moment. If he turned to look back. He didnt, he just was walking and pausing, going that slow way to keep pace with his mate.

A white van approached in the opposite direction towards the traffic lights, then through on the green and out of sight.

Helen was clutching her bag, and aware that she was, staying on the other side of the road and that distance back from them. If they didnt turn round. They didnt, so didnt see her. It was like *her entire existence*.

They were heading toward the bridge.

She wanted to run but to keep a safe gap between them too, needing to be sure. She was sure but needed to be even more sure, just like for certain, so she knew for certain.

The two guys walked so slowly she would catch up and she didnt want to. She kept to the side of the pavement, the shadows, and paused by a wall. The smell of urine. Oh well.

You know something. There was no reason to do anything. Helen felt that so so strongly, so like just strongly. If she didnt want to do anything then nothing, so be it, just like nothing.

But it was true.

She smiled. Because really there was no going back on the decision. That was cheery. Although what was it she was to do?

The two homeless guys

She started running immediately, running after them. It was just to get to them, to Brian, also like explaining, wanting to explain it to him, just about everything, everything, everything she thought and felt, that had happened, everything. If she missed him now she would never find him again. She knew that clearly.

She knew everything clearly, really like she knew, she just *knew*. Her entire life, the strangest strangest feeling like never ever, destined never, how her life never, would *never begin*. That was so so strange, never to begin and here she was with a six-year-old daughter my God and it was her life, her life to begin, and it had begun. And Brian didnt know. He didnt. She would tell him. Everything would be out in the open.

About Mum and Dad too, how it was their life, and just so unlucky, that was how it was for so so many people and if the cards turned that way it was like bust, you were. Brian too, it was just unlucky, he had had an unlucky life and that was so so unfair, just so unfair. But Helen was the same. Most people are. She couldnt have done anything. She didnt have that control. Girls dont. If Brian thought otherwise he was mistaken, very very mistaken.

She needed to tell him that too and everything that had happened, how things had been for her in her life and her marriage; he didnt know any of that, and about her ex, if he had been there for her but he never was. If he thought it had been easy for her my God how wrong he was like so completely completely wrong, completely wrong. It was all such a fight. She could have wept. Such a horrible bloody fight, if he thought she was lucky, how wrong was he just so so wrong. What had he done in his life? He didnt think about her, just a wee girl, if she needed a brother. Of course she did. What girl didnt? She would have loved that brother. Only it was him.

There was a man in a dark suit coming towards her and he moved sideways or she might have crashed into him. She had started running, clopping along in those heels

Up ahead the one with the limp lagged a little, then the two stopped a moment, perhaps hearing the sharp clop clop clop of her shoes, and they glanced back. The tall skinny guy frowned and turned away, but edged to the kerb, expecting her to charge past. Instead she clapped her hand to his shoulder, as though grabbing him. He was taken by surprise and tried to shrug her off, shouting at her, something. She grabbed at his left arm, grasped it tightly, clinging onto him, not even hearing his voice just like what he was saying, what was he saying? she didnt know and he muttered something and swung round, locked his right hand on her throat for her so to let go, to make her let go his arm, and her trying to gulp, she was choking and clawing scratching at his hand. His grip was locking off her breath and she was forced backwards how he was forcing her backwards, till she staggered and crumpled to the ground, the other one shouting, whatever he was shouting. Then she was lying on her side but seeing to the sky. The tall skinny one was bending over her but it was all just shadows and spots, and she stayed lying there, and when her eyes were open properly the two of them had vanished.